Richard Underwood

FAKE WITNESS

FENECHTY PUBLISHING

First published in UK 2021 by Fenechty
Publishing
https://fenechty.com

Copyright © Richard Underwood 2020

The right of Richard Underwood to be identified as the author of this work has been asserted by him in accordance with
the Copyright, Designs and Patents Act 1988.

ISBN 978-1-7399490-0-6

A CIP catalogue record for this book is available in the British Library

This novel is entirely a work of fiction.
The names, characters and incidents portrayed in it are the work of the author's imagination. Any resemblance to actual persons, living or dead, events or localities is entirely coincidental.

Printed and bound in Great Britain by Clays Ltd, Elcograf S.p.A

All rights reserved. No part of this publication may be reproduced, stored in a retrieval system, or transmitted, in any form, or by any means (electronic, mechanical, photocopying, recording or otherwise) without the prior written permission of the publisher

Book One in the Ann Perkins Detective Agency series

Chapter One

Ernie Wright had never robbed a bank or walked the streets of Manchester in a dress and high heels, but the death of his wife and current redundancy had changed him beyond all recognition and propelled him to action.

From the disabled toilet, he made his way down the escalator taking the opportunity of looking over the heads of those on the ground floor and scanning the store for danger. The bottom step arrived whilst he was still looking around, and he almost fell as he staggered off. Walking in heels still required a concentration he momentarily lacked, but nobody seemed to have noticed and he made it to the door without further mishap.

The spring morning sun had little warmth, and shoppers between him and the bank all wore coats. He stepped back into the shadow of the doorway and wrapped his arms around his body to fend off the breeze. Today, he told himself, was not the best day for a robbery. Pushing the thought aside, he checked the carrier bag to ensure the layer of clothing still covered the gun.

He turned his attention to the bank. Nobody looked into it as they walked past, but they wouldn't have seen anything because of the posters covering the windows. They were the reason he chose the branch, but he hadn't expected them to cause him problems too. He couldn't see how many people were in the bank, or whether there were any security guards.

Ernie wobbled slightly as he crossed the pedestrianised area toward the bank. He had never worn heels until last week, but he'd worn them at home over the past few days and thought he had got used to them. This was the first time he'd worn them in the street and the pavement had a different feel to the carpet he'd practised on.

Standing back from the door he saw a small queue with the solitary cashier serving a woman at the counter. A woman at the front of the queue had a crying toddler with her, and behind them were two pensioners talking to one another followed by a man in his late fifties wearing an orange boiler-suit. Two younger men walked in whilst he was watching, each taking their place at the end of the queue. Everything else blurred as Ernie focussed on the woman being served and he told himself he could do this. As she turned away from the counter he stepped towards the door.

"Out of the way." He hadn't even seen the man who barged past him and almost knocked him over. Ernie followed him in and expected him to join the back of the queue. He was about fifty years old, dressed in jeans and a scruffy-looking jacket. Ernie looked past him to the now empty counter. He could see the woman at the front of the queue gathering her toddler and getting ready to move forward, but Ernie knew he would beat her to the counter. The man who had pushed in front of him at the door still hadn't joined the queue, and Ernie's fingers clenched into a fist at the arrogance of someone who thought they could push their way past him to get to the front. Ernie gritted his teeth and reached into his carrier bag for the gun, determined not only to rob the bank but also to teach the man a lesson. Once the gun was in his hand, he would force the man aside and teach him some manners.

"This is a robbery. Give me the money."

Ernie had been going over the words in his head as he strode towards the counter, and for a moment he thought they were his own before realising he hadn't spoken. The man in front of him was waving a gun, and the bank clerk was staring at it wide-eyed as everyone else looked on stunned. Ernie's angry determination had kept propelling him forwards at a pace he couldn't stop. He was already unsteady on his feet, and as he reached the robber the momentum as he fell took both of them to the floor.

The only person more surprised than Ernie was the robber. One minute he was committing a robbery. The next minute he was lying on the floor with a strange-looking woman on top of him.

Ernie's action broke the spell. The woman at the front of the queue screamed and grabbed her toddler. The man in the boiler-suit tried to move forward to help but the two pensioners backed into him. Both younger men at the back of the queue sidestepped the other customers and piled into the melee in front of the counter. Ernie tried to stand up but had to hold on as the tangled mass of bodies writhed on the floor.

Ernie had been holding his gun as he approached the counter and dropped it as he fell, but during the struggle he saw it under one of the robber's thighs and quickly put it back into his bag before anyone else saw it.

One man eventually got the gunman in an arm-lock and forced him to his feet, enabling Ernie and the other man to extricate themselves and stand. Ernie was unsure what to do next, but the man who stood with him picked up the robber's gun, took out a police warrant card and waved it in front of the man's face as he cautioned him and told him he was under arrest.

The robber struggled unsuccessfully to get out of the arm-lock. "You bastard. Get him off me. He'll break my arm."

"I'll not do that," said the man holding him, "but you'll break it yourself if you don't stop struggling. You're not going anywhere."

After making sure the robber was being firmly held, the police officer turned toward Ernie and smiled. "You are one brave lady, tackling a man with a gun."

Ernie was shaking his head in disbelief, stunned by what had happened. It had all taken place so fast and it was only now sinking in. He wasn't brave, and he wouldn't have tackled the gunman if he'd had time to think about it. He had been so angry, and his determination to push the man away and reach the counter had made him blind to the danger.

"It was nothing," he said.

"But it was," said the officer. "It was a very brave thing to do. You knocked his gun away as you tackled him to the floor, and that prevented him using it." The police officer looked at the gun he was holding. "It's only an air pistol, but you couldn't have known that at the time because it all happened so fast. It looks like a real pistol, and it would still take an eye out and do some real damage. You were very brave."

Ernie was still processing what had occurred and trying to work out what should happen next. Should he just walk away? Would they stop him? What should he say? What should he do? His mind became a maze of unconnected thoughts and half-formed sentences.

The cashier had moved her foot to activate the floor alarm as soon as the robbery had begun, and Ernie could now hear sirens from the approaching vehicles. He was desperate to escape. His mouth was dry, he was conscious of every time he swallowed, but he could see no way out. The man in the boiler-suit had appointed himself the guardian of the bank's door and was preventing anyone from entering or leaving. The police officer was standing within arm's length and saying something about bravery.

A screech of tires announced he was too late. A dark-coloured range-rover stopped outside the bank and four armed uniformed police officers leapt out of the vehicle together, each from their own door. The automated alarm only informed them an armed raid was taking place. They didn't know if it was real or a false alarm but were taking no chances. The first two entered together, fanning out left and right and pushing the man in the orange boiler-suit away. They remained close to the door, from where they could secure their own exit whilst threatening those trying to leave. The remaining two members of the rapid response team followed, going deeper into the bank.

"Armed police. Do not move."

The team's sergeant recognised the detective inspector straight away.

"What's going on, sir?"

"It's all over. Your men can relax." He pointed to the robber who was still being held in an armlock. "I've arrested this man for attempting an armed robbery." He held up the gun, "He tried to rob the bank using this, but unluckily for him I was in the queue." He then waved towards Ernie. "Even more unluckily, this lady attacked him, knocked him to the floor and disarmed him before the rest of us had even moved. I've seen nothing like it. She was really brave and deserves a medal."

Ernie still didn't know what to do, but he knew he couldn't escape with two armed police officers guarding the door and another two beside him. The Firearms Unit sergeant was smiling at Ernie as the detective inspector described his heroics. To Ernie, the smile and gun seemed at odds, as though the same person should not be displaying both.

Ernie's adrenalin level had decreased and his brain began making sense of what had happened. He realised the robber could have shot him, or if the robber had not been there and Ernie had robbed the bank, the armed police could have shot him. He wondered if the sergeant would have smiled as he pulled the trigger.

Other police cars were arriving by the second, and more uniformed police officers entered the bank. The detective spoke to one of them. "If you take the prisoner back to the station, I'll catch up with him later. We need to take statements from the cashier, from the guy who helped me, and from this lady. With my statement that should be enough. He'll hardly plead not guilty when I've seen him do it, but take everyone else's name and address just in case."

Whilst the detective was speaking, Ernie had been pondering how things may have turned out if they'd shot and killed him. He imagined what his wife would say about him turning up in heaven dressed as a woman and imagined her telling him off. Her stern voice would have cracked into the laugh she usually gave when he acted ridiculously and they would both have giggled like children. For the first time that morning the thought almost brought a smile to his lips.

"Perhaps I can start by taking your statement, madam?" The detective's words brought him back to the present and also brought a moment of clarity.

He needed to leave, and the sooner the better. He did not want to make a statement. He did not want to give his name. He did not want to give his address.

Dressed as a woman he would have to give a false name, but that had never been part of his plan. His address would be a problem too. If he gave a false address, and they checked it whilst he was still there, he would be in deep trouble. Not as deep as if he'd robbed the bank, but deep enough. They would ask him questions he couldn't easily answer.

"I'm dying to go to the toilet. Is it okay if I pop over to Debenhams to use their customer toilet before I make a statement?" He hopped about to emphasise his desperation but half expected to be told he could use the staff toilet at the bank.

"You go," said the detective. "I'll start with one

of the others and I'll take your statement when you get back."

Ernie didn't need telling twice. "Right," he said. "I'll only be a few minutes."

Another police car arrived as he was leaving the bank, and he pushed his way through a growing crowd, all eager to see the prisoner being escorted out of the building and into the rear of the vehicle. The crowd were jeering, hurling abuse, and pushing forwards as Ernie made his way through in the opposite direction.

Once having escaped the throng, he made his way across the pedestrianised area and entered Debenhams for a second time. He'd planned for a scenario similar to this, and Debenhams had always been his intended escape route. He was still carrying his carrier bag containing the gun, his change of clothing, and makeup. The only missing ingredient from his original plan was the money he had intended stealing from the bank.

He rode the escalator to the top floor from where it was only a few strides to the disabled toilet. It was still empty, and he entered straight away, locked the door behind him, leaned against the door, and allowed himself to slide to the floor. He shook uncontrollably as he sat there sobbing for several minutes with his head in his hands.

After a while, leaving his bag on the floor, he struggled to his feet and looked in the mirror. He expected the morning's events to have changed him and it surprised him when he looked the same. Smudged makeup and an off-centred wig, but the same.

He took the wig off, combed his thinning dark brown hair, and washed the makeup off before changing into his own clothes. He was unsure what to do about the gun. He didn't know if he would have the nerve to try again and debated whether to keep it or throw it away. As he took the gun out, he realised it was not his. The small hole in the barrel that had only been large enough for an air gun pellet, was now big enough for a full-sized bullet.

Pushing the gun deep into the bag of clothes to be sure they covered it, he decided to think about the gun later. His current concern was to get home as soon as possible.

He opened the door of the disabled toilet and walked out into the glare of a man in a wheelchair. The man never spoke to him, but the way he was squirming, and the speed at which he pushed himself in, showed he had waited too long. Ernie last looked at his watch after getting changed before going to the bank. He looked at it again and saw less than thirty minutes had elapsed.

The bank was almost opposite the main doors of Debenhams on Market Street, but there were other doors and he left by the High Street entrance and made his way to Saint Peter's Square from where he could get a tram home.

He and Doreen had shared a two bedroomed semi. The extra bedroom prepared for the baby destined never to arrive home. He could do nothing to prevent the stroke which snatched Doreen and her unborn child from him, but that did not stop him feeling guilty he should have done more. Almost everything in the house reinforced his guilt, and although it felt wrong to give up on the home they shared, the pain of remaining became overwhelming.

As a single man, he was not high on the council's list of priorities but they were short of two-bedroom houses and gave him a one-bedroom flat in a low-rise block in Droylsden, half-way between the city centre and Ashton-under-Lyne.

He had hardly ever earned more than the minimum wage, but did eventually get a job with better prospects. Still grieving, he had only just learnt to cope with his loss when they made him redundant. No wife, no child, no job. Ernie considered suicide, but didn't have the nerve to go through with it.

Time didn't heal him but it changed him. His grief induced depression turned into an anger directed at the entire world.

Nothing would bring Doreen back, but one way or another Ernie became determined society would compensate him for his heartache and pain. Resolved to improve the hand life had dealt him, he eventually settled on robbing a bank. Doreen always had high moral principles, so he knew she would not have approved but he was past caring. If she'd wanted him to stick to her moral principles, she shouldn't have died and left him to cope alone. His depression left him angry with himself, and to prevent his suicide his body deflected that anger on everyone else. He was angry at the world, angry with God, angry with his wife, and even angry with his unborn child. He was utterly bereft and alone,

Ernie could see no downside to robbing a bank and convinced himself nobody would catch him provided he planned things properly. The disguise, the gun, the getaway. Weeks of planning had culminated in today's fiasco. He had changed into his disguise before entering the bank, and he'd changed out of his disguise and escape the same way afterwards. It was just the part in the bank that hadn't gone according to plan, but that was not his fault.

His situation was unchanged. Still grieving, still unemployed, still living in his crabby flat, still broke, and still bloody angry. On the plus side, he now had a real gun, still owned his disguise, and could try again. Ernie, not knowing how wrong he was, consoled himself with the belief that at least he would have no further dealings with the bank robber.

Chapter Two

Detective Inspector Arthur Jones had let his star witness leave the scene and when she hadn't returned, he sent some of his uniformed colleagues to find her, but they returned empty-handed despite having searched every floor of Debenhams with the store security staff. There was video footage of her entering, but none of her leaving, and it annoyed him he hadn't taken her name and address before allowing her to leave.

Despite his annoyance, Jones didn't expect her disappearance to cause problems. He had often come across reluctant witnesses before, but in this case it shouldn't make any difference. He'd had no previous dealings with Hinchcliffe and hadn't recognised him when he saw him, but he had recognised the name and knew the man had lots of previous convictions. The woman's disappearance was unimportant. He had seen the robbery himself and arrested Hinchcliffe at the bank, so he was sure Hinchcliffe would plead guilty.

It was mid-afternoon by the time the detective inspector returned to his office at Manchester's Central Park Police Station. They brought Hinchcliffe into the interview room, and the inspector and Detective Sergeant Sarah Carter sat opposite him.

He reached over and turned on the recorder. The few seconds it took before it was ready to record gave him the opportunity of having a look at Hinchcliffe. He was wearing jeans and trainers, and a short navy jacket open to display the Manchester United top he wore underneath.

"Interview between Robert Hinchcliffe and Detective Inspector Jones of Manchester C.I.D. commenced 4:07 pm Thursday 21 March 2019. Also present is Detective Sergeant Carter. I need to remind you, you are still under caution and you still do not have to say anything, but it may harm your defence if you do not mention when questioned something which you later rely on in court. Anything you do say may be given in evidence. Do you understand?"

"No comment." Hinchcliffe may not have been a very successful robber, but he was experience enough to know not to answer questions.

"I arrested you in the Santander Bank on Market Street, Manchester, earlier today. What were you doing in the bank?"

"No comment."

"I found you in possession of a firearm," he said. "Could you tell me where you got the firearm from, and what you were doing with it at the bank?"

"No comment."

"I was in the bank myself Bob, so let's not play silly buggers. I saw you robbing the bank and there were loads of other witnesses too. Why don't you just admit you were robbing the bloody bank?" Jones usually avoided swearing on tape, but he couldn't help himself. He'd seen him commit the offence. He expected Hinchcliffe to at least acknowledge he'd caught him in the act.

Hinchcliffe sat there with a smirk on his face whilst looking directly into the detective's face for a few moments before answering. "No comment."

Jones also took his time, he stared back into the eyes of Hinchcliffe determined not to show his anger again. "Please yourself. You have every right to stay silent, but we both know you're guilty."

"No comment."

Jones was used to prisoners not speaking, and it was only because he had been at the bank when the robbery took place that he became angry this time. The interview was no different to many others, but he was still disappointed Hinchcliffe had not immediately confessed. "Is there anything you do want to say?"

"I want to make a phone call to my solicitor."

"I'll arrange that. Anything else?"

"No comment. Not till I've spoken to my solicitor."

"Please yourself." Jones stood up and reached towards the recorder. "Interview suspended 4:09 pm."

He turned the tape off and looked towards Detective Sergeant Carter. He had got nowhere, but perhaps a fresh approach would work.

"They'll throw the book at you if you plead not guilty, Bob," she said. "You'll get a shorter sentence pleading guilty. Think of your wife and kids."

"No comment."

"Plead guilty to the bank job and we'll ignore the more serious offence."

"What more serious offence?" Curiosity had at least changed his instinctive no comment.

"Wearing a United shirt in front of two City supporters," she said

Hinchcliffe couldn't help but smile. "Bloody City supporters. Definitely no comment."

"Listen, Bob." She thought using his first name may help. "I'm not joking. The detective inspector saw you robbing the bank and they'll throw the book at you if you plead not guilty. Plead guilty, and you'll get a shorter sentence. How about it?"

"No comment."

Jones stood up, opened the interview room door, and beckoned to the uniformed police officer who had been waiting outside. "Back to the cell with him then." As Hinchcliffe was being escorted out, the detective inspector tried for a last time. "You'll be going to the magistrate's court in the morning. We'll be asking for a remand in custody pending trial at crown court. Do you have anything to say off the record?"

"No comment. Not till I've seen my brief."

"Okay. Take him away." Hinchcliffe's lack of answers wouldn't change the result. The Crown Prosecution Service thought it was an open and shut case and had already authorised his prosecution. They had to decide whether there was enough evidence for a jury to convict and whether it was in the public interest to prosecute, and they had already decided the answer was yes on both counts. Hinchcliffe having a word with his solicitor would change nothing.

A further interview took place once the solicitor had arrived, but it was shorter than the initial interview as the solicitor's presence prevented any unofficial follow-up questions. Detective Inspector Jones asked the same questions, and on the advice this time of his solicitor, Hinchliffe answered, "No comment" to every question asked.

After the interview, they charged Hinchcliffe with attempted robbery, with the unlawful possession of a firearm, and with possession of a firearm with intent to commit an indictable offence.

His wife visited him in the police cell with a change of clothing, so by the time he appeared at the magistrate's court the following morning he was wearing a smart suit and a collar and tie. The change had no effect on the proceedings, and the committal hearing lasted less time than either of the two police station interviews. The magistrate asked him to confirm his name before reading out the charges and remanding him in custody to appear at a later date at Manchester Crown Court. His solicitor could have asked for bail, but given the seriousness of the charges, he didn't waste his time.

MANCHESTER EVENING NEWS
Thursday
21 March 2019
Mystery Woman Foils Bank Robbery

Police are appealing for information to help them identify the heroine of yesterday's bank robbery at the Market Street branch of Santander Bank in Manchester. The woman tackled the gunman to the ground, enabling off duty Detective Inspector Arthur Jones of Manchester C.I.D., and Private Sam Ethelwhite of the Parachute Regiment based at Colchester who was in Manchester to visit his elderly mother, detain the man until additional police officers arrived and took him into custody. The plucky customer (pictured) who tackled the armed robber left without leaving details. Detective Inspector Jones said, "This lady deserves our gratitude. If anyone recognises her from the description or CCTV image, we would like to thank her." The alleged gunman, Robert Hinchcliffe of Beeston Street, Harpurhey, Manchester, appeared at Manchester Magistrate's Court this morning and was remanded in custody to appear at a later date at Manchester Crown Court.

The article described the heroine in some detail and provided a phone number by which anyone with further information could contact Detective Inspector Jones.

"It's a mystery," Jones said as he entered the police station with his detective sergeant. "I've never had a witness disappear before, not unless friends of the defendant have threatened them."

"You don't think someone could have threatened her in this case?" Detective Sergeant Sarah Carter asked.

"I suppose it's possible. There could have been an accomplice outside the bank who saw the entire thing and threatened her as she left, but I don't think so. I'd have thought someone would have noticed, but it may be worth following up just in case. I'll leave that to you. You could check the local CCTV cameras."

Sarah Carter sighed inwardly and tried to hide the displeasure from showing on her face. She should be used to her boss by now. Most cases involved her doing the work and her boss getting the glory. Despite Hinchcliffe being caught bang to rights, she was still being asked to trawl through all the CCTV images from cameras in and around Piccadilly Gardens. It would take her hours. "Right, boss. I'll get right on it," she said.

As they finished their conversation, one of the uniformed inspectors walked past, chuckling as he did so. "Lost any little old ladies lately Arthur?"

"It's not funny. And she wasn't little and wasn't old." He knew there was plenty of gossip around the station about how he had lost a vital witness, but he grinned despite himself. "OK, it was funny. You should have seen Hinchcliffe's face. One minute he's waving his gun about and threatening everyone. The next minute he's flat on the floor with the woman on top of him. She poleaxed him. I'd love to know who she was. Probably find she's a female wrestler. Whoever she was, she was one gutsy lady. Can I have a quick word with your squad before they go out?"

"Yes, sure, give me a few minutes to deal with routine stuff, then they're all yours."

"And just for the record, I didn't lose her. I've just temporarily misplaced her."

"If you say so. Lost and misplaced seem the same from where I'm standing."

Detective Sergeant Sarah Carter had kept out of the conversation by wandering a discrete five yards away along the corridor. They had been making their way to the C.I.D. squad room when the uniformed inspector walked past, and she thought it prudent to continue further down the corridor as the banter progressed between the two inspectors.

"And you can wipe that silly grin off your face." The detective inspector had caught up with her.

"Sorry Boss. I was smiling because you got that scumbag Hinchcliffe bang to rights. He got seven years last time and he'll get even longer this time." It did no harm to butter her boss's ego. "Bit of luck you being in the queue. You're always in the right place at the right time."

"That's as maybe, but the papers are full of the woman so we need to find her as soon as possible.

It makes us look stupid if all anyone is talking about is how we allowed a witness to walk away. Even the superintendent has asked how we allowed her to disappear and how long till we find her again. The sooner we track her down, the better."

As they entered the squad room, the detective sergeant took her usual seat at the desk nearest her boss's office. She hoped it would be hers one day and looked forward to having her own team to do the legwork. For now, the legwork was down to her, and Sarah reluctantly began going through the CCTV images looking for the woman from the bank. She was unaware of the profound affect the woman would have on her future prospects or she would have embraced the task with more enthusiasm.

The detective inspector picked up a file from his desk and walked out again. "I'll be in the uniformed squad room if anyone wants me. Back in a few minutes."

The uniformed inspector was just finishing his briefing when Jones walked in.

"... and keep a lookout for both vehicles. I don't want you approaching them. No heroics. Just radio in and we'll take it from there. Now then, Detective Inspector Jones wants a word."

"Thank you. You'll have heard about the attempted bank robbery yesterday. The man arrested was forty-nine-year-old Robert Hinchcliffe from Harpurhey. The magistrate's court remanded him in custody this morning. Some of you will know him. He's got lots of form. Whilst you're doing your other jobs today, if you get any information to help identify the woman who floored him, please let me know. We still need a statement from her."

"You heard the Inspector. Report to him if you hear anything. Don't do anything I wouldn't do. Keep alert. Keep safe. Dismissed." The uniformed inspector knew it was unlikely any of his squad would think about the woman once they left the station. A few were on foot patrol in the city centre. They would have their hands full giving directions to tourists or going from store to store dealing with shoplifters. They would call car drivers to take arrested shoplifters into custody, but most of the time the car drivers would attend domestics, deal with public order offences, serve summonses and execute warrants.

For the ordinary copper, on foot or in a car, finding the woman from the bank was not high on their list of priorities, but unknown to the police they were not the only ones searching.

Chapter Three

"That bloody woman. The papers have turned her into a bloody hero."

Alf Sidebotham was angry about what had happened at the bank. He believed in discouraging bystanders from having a go when a crime was being committed, and the best way of doing that had always been to make them afraid to intervene. Fear stopped other criminals muscling in on his business and stopped members of the public disrupting a crime in progress. Instilling fear into as many people as possible was an essential part of his job.

He believed Bob Hinchcliffe's gun should have been enough to stop bystanders interfering during the robbery. Bob should have been able to rob the bank with no difficulty, but now they'd arrested him they would send him to prison for a long time. It was that bloody woman's fault. He needed to find her and teach her a lesson to prevent others following her example.

Alf had begun as a small-time crook, but a near disastrous house burglary had propelled him into the big time. He had broken into a house through the rear conservatory door whilst the occupiers were still asleep upstairs. Everything had gone well until someone broke into the car parked on the drive of the same house and set off the car alarm. Alf made his escape out the back as the householder stormed downstairs to apprehend the car thief at the front.

That incident was the catalyst, but his life changing idea came to Alf a few days later when he was watching 'The Great Escape' on television. In the film, those planning to escape from the Second World War prison camp in Germany had to have their plan accepted by an escape committee to ensure one person's escape didn't have a detrimental effect on anyone else's.

He thought something similar would work in Manchester, so he set up a one-man committee to approve crimes in advance and ensure one person's crimes would have no detrimental effect on anyone else. As the sole member of the committee, he also decided other criminals should pay him a twenty percent fee from proceeds of any job he approved.

Not everyone approved of Alf's plan and initially it had been difficult to implement, but he gathered a team of equally ruthless men around him and paid them well to ensure their loyalty. If anyone stepped out of line, he dealt with them extremely violently and quickly earned a reputation as someone it was better not to cross. His reputation for violence soon made him Manchester's undisputed gangland boss.

He began by asserting his leadership over criminals engaged in high profile crimes like burglary and bank robbery, but gradually included drug dealing, people trafficking, and online fraud. Other villains may not have liked it, but they all complied eventually because the consequences of none compliance could be detrimental to their health.

After establishing his reputation, things became easier for him. The threat of violence was usually enough to prevent Manchester criminals committing crimes without giving him a share of the proceeds. Criminals sometimes drove from other parts of the country to commit a crime in Manchester, but a message to his counterparts in those other areas usually had the desired effect.

Alf had been in business for many years now and was in his early fifties. He should have been enjoying a stress-free life, but there had been two recent occasions when up-and-coming criminals in their mid-twenties had challenged his authority. On the last occasion, the youngster gathered a few of his mates together and tried to take on Alf's heavies. It had been a troublesome time, but hardened experience had eventually beaten youthful enthusiasm. One youngster ended up dead and several others ended up in hospital.

A few more years and he could relax. His money had taken his kids through school and university and both had married well. They were off his hands now, and neither had any idea about his criminal activities. With sons, he would probably have disclosed his real occupation and groomed them to take over when he retired, but his daughters had grown up ignorant of the fact their father was not the property investor he claimed to be. He did own some property, a small portfolio from which he received a steady rental income, but his girls were unaware his income as a landlord was nowhere near what he had spent over the years indulging their every whim.

He was planning to buy something on the Costa del Sol and retire, and his only regret was that his wife who had died a few years ago would not be around to see it.

His business had no accepted successor. Whenever anyone had threatened his leadership he had got rid of them, sometimes permanently. It had never ceased to amaze him how easily he could sail out to sea with a dead body, weight it down, throw it over the side, and then return his yacht to the Fleetwood marina with no one being any the wiser. No customs, no police, no problem. He no longer enjoyed having to kill someone himself, but on some occasions it was still necessary to reinforce his authority.

He had no concern about what would happen to his business once he retired. He intended being in charge one day and gone the next, and by the time anyone missed him he would be in Spain relaxing in his outdoor pool. Most of his money was already in a Spanish bank account and he only intended working for another couple of years before disappearing and leaving all his problems behind. What happened to his criminal empire once he had finished with it would be someone else's problem.

The last couple of years had caused him a few sleepless nights. There were increasing numbers of youngsters with little respect, villains coming in from other cities, and criminals from immigrant families who had never heard of him. All those things were getting on top of him.

Other people had noticed too. He had always been tough, but rarely lost his temper even when instilling discipline. If he had to do something unpleasant, he did so resolutely but calmly and had always been proud of his ability to discipline others whilst keeping his temper. Lately though, he'd been prone to raise his voice at the slightest thing.

He'd noticed the change, and others noticed too. The lack of sleep and the constant stress was making it harder for him to hold things together and had brought a growing anger. The latest bank robbery turning into a fiasco was the final straw. He was seething with an intensity arising out of his growing insecurity, and he felt compelled to make an example of someone to deflect attention from his declining authority.

Alf had approved Hinchcliffe's plan to rob the bank despite his misgivings. He knew the real money was in online fraud and not hard currency. There was little money to make robbing banks these days, and Alf had tried to explain the gains were not worth the risk. Hinchcliffe wouldn't listen, and when Alf eventually approved the job, it was inevitable he would get some of the blame when it went wrong. Members of his gang were already whispering that he shouldn't have approved the job and was losing his touch.

Alf was aware of the whispers, and if he'd been his usual self, he'd have felt no guilt and would have brushed things aside. Instead, his stress magnified the comments, and his guilt gnawed away at him. He needed to stop the whispers and assuage the guilt in the only way he knew how, and that involved blaming someone else. The woman, he decided, filled the bill nicely.

He needed a release for his guilt. He needed to assert his authority. He needed an act of vengeance to keep everyone in line between now and his retirement. The papers had given that bloody woman lots of publicity and made her a hero. He decided the publicity surrounding her death would send a much-needed tremor through Manchester and keep everyone in line until his retirement.

Chapter Four

Ernie did not know what to do. The morning at the bank had been exciting, but the adrenalin fuelled high had morphed into an equally deep low which propelled him back into his old depressing routine. Standing at the window of his flat, he watched the traffic and imagined everyone driving past had somewhere to go. Work, shopping, visiting friends or relatives. All had some reason to be travelling, and some purpose to their lives.

His situation was unchanged. He still grieved for Doreen. Still missed the laughter which had pulled him from the brink of despair so often in the past. The loss was physical. His mind, his heart, his gut. Losing Doreen had affected every part of him. Their child was the confirmation they would leave their mark on the world, but it had all gone, snatched away from him in a moment he could never forget. He ached for a return to the past, but remained alone, unemployed, with little money, and still angry.

The image from the CCTV at the bank had been poor, and when printed in the newspaper it became worse. He was sure nobody would recognise him from it. He had been in disguise, and only spoke to the detective for a few minutes, so he didn't think the detective would recognise him either.

Ernie's attempt to rob the bank had gone wrong, but he had come out of things unharmed and unrecognised. Still in possession of his disguise and gun, he considered trying a different bank.

He imagined himself entering a bank, pulling out his gun, and walking out with a bag full of notes, but even in his own imagination things never ended well. He couldn't get the image of what happened to Hinchcliffe out of his mind, and in his imagination a customer would tackle him in the same way. Sometimes he imagined himself shrugging off the attack and completing the robbery, but it still ended with members of the armed response team arriving to shoot him as he left the bank. If his past had taught him anything, it had taught him to be a pessimist, and the more he tried to imagine a happy ending, the more unsuccessful the ending became.

He believed there must be somewhere safer, where nobody would interfere with the robbery as it took place, but couldn't think of anywhere.

His life took on a routine in which he half-heartedly looked for a new job, and half-heartedly looked for somewhere safe to rob. He would lie in till late morning, have a quick look at the job pages on his phone, check his social media and emails, and then walk into the centre of Manchester.

He had read that exercise was good for depression, so he got into the habit of walking through Saint Anne's Square before turning right onto Deansgate. His daily walks helped manage his anger and ease his mood. Looking in the shop windows, watching other people as they went about their daily lives, and even saying hello to the same homeless person every day took his mind off his problems. Eventually though, his walks had the opposite effect. He became bored with the same streets and shops, and he felt his depression getting worse. Ernie still saw the same things, but increasingly thought about his problems rather than anything displayed in front of him.

To stop himself thinking about his problems he changed his route, and instead of turning right at the end of Saint Anne's Square he continued straight on towards King Street. He had almost walked past the jeweller's before realising what he was looking at.

He had given a cursory glance through the window as he passed and the ring with a price tag of twenty-nine thousand pounds had almost not registered. He stopped, went back, and took a longer look. All the other items in the window were just as expensive. A quick calculation told him the jewellery in the tray nearest him was worth almost a million pounds and there were at least a dozen trays on display. He realised there was only one pane of glass separating him from a million pounds worth of jewellery, and imagined putting a brick through the glass, grabbing a tray, and running away. He knew it would not be that easy. Probably shatterproof glass. The metal strip around the edges probably an alarm.

When he focussed his eyes past the display and into the shop itself, he saw it was empty. There was no queue and no customers, only a solitary member of staff behind the counter.

The last thing making the jeweller's stand out was the smartly dressed doorman standing outside. The shop had two bow windows creating a long entrance porch between them with the door at the far end, and the doorman was in the porch immediately in front of the door. Ernie looked at the man out of the corner of his eye as he looked in the window. He was tall and smartly dressed in a light grey suit. His broad shoulders almost filled the width of the entrance and it was impossible to get to the door unless he moved out of the way. He was obviously a guard, and Ernie assumed the man had locked the door behind him and would only open it once he satisfied himself the person approaching was a bona fide customer.

Ernie browsed the shop window for a while trying to look like a potential customer rather than a potential robber. Everything remained the same. There were no customers, the jeweller stayed behind the counter in the shop, and the doorman remained inside the entrance porch apparently paying him no attention.

A short distance further on there was a coffee shop, so Ernie bought himself a coffee and sat near the window. He kept his eye on the jeweller's whilst apparently reading the newspaper provided by the cafe proprietor. Two coffees later and nobody had entered. At those prices, the jeweller would not expect many customers, but they wouldn't need many. One or two customers a day, each spending tens of thousands of pounds, would be more than enough. It looked to Ernie as though the jeweller's would be empty most of the time, and there may even be complete days with no customers at all.

His earlier despondency had quickly changed to excitement and his mind was working overtime. For once, he was not thinking about his problems in isolation, but was thinking about how he could ease them. Only the two members of staff stood between him and millions of pounds.

Ernie had stopped looking forward to his walks and had only continued out of habit, but passing the jeweller's reinvigorated him. Over the course of the following week, Ernie regularly stopped off at the same café at various times of the day. He also found another cafe further along the street where the view was not as good, but from where he could still see if anyone entered or left.

During the six days he spent observing the jeweller's he only saw three people enter. Ernie reckoned the chances would be high the jeweller's would be empty whenever he robbed it, and given the price of the jewellery, and their size, a single bag of jewellery would easily exceed several million pounds.

He had gone through the entire thing in his mind several times whilst watching the shop, and each time the robbery had gone smoothly and with no hitch. There was still an element of risk, but nowhere near the risk he had faced in the bank. This time he had a real gun instead of an air pistol. It was loaded too, and a shot into the ceiling of the shop would prevent either of the men from tackling him.

His imagination of how the robbery would go left him in no doubt things would be okay. No customers, scared staff, a bag of small jewellery. It would all be fine, and it was only when projecting the robbery forwards that he envisaged a problem. Robbing the jeweller's would leave him holding millions of pounds worth of jewels, and he would need some way of converting them into cash. In his mind, the robbery itself would be no problem. The difficulty would be finding someone who would pay hard cash for goods they knew he had stolen. He would need a fence. Ernie had never stolen anything before, so had never needed a fence. He only knew the word because he watched so many detective stories on television, but he didn't know how to find one.

He tried to think through all the various possibilities. Going by the amount of crime in Manchester there must be a fence in the city, and probably several. In television detective stories the fences all seemed to run antique shops or second-hand shops, but he could hardly go into an antique shop and ask them to fence something for him. The old second-hand shops were long gone, transformed into charity shops. From previous experience when he had sold an old phone, he knew modern day second-hand shops always asked for identification and took pictures before buying anything.

Like he often did when at a loss about what to do, he went to his window and daydreamed as he looked at the traffic. He wondered if anyone driving past was a fence, but he couldn't see how anyone could tell simply by just looking at them. If a fence looked like everyone else, he thought it would be impossible to find one without knowing who they were in advance. He was going around in circles and getting nowhere.

He gave up, turned away from the window, and went into the kitchen to make himself a drink. As so often occurred when he stopped searching for answers, Ernie had his eureka moment as soon as he sat down. The two places he was most likely to find a criminal were at court and in prison.

He had no intention of going to prison. He would not know who to ask for, and he was sure he couldn't just turn up at the prison and ask if they had a fence he could visit. Courts were different. They were open to the public. A fence would eventually turn up at court. At that stage he had thought far enough ahead to realise he would find a fence at court, but not far enough ahead to ask himself how he would make contact once he found one.

The following days allowed him to develop his plan further. He did not think it would be wise to contact a fence directly whilst they were at court. Other people would see them together and wonder what they were talking about. If a fence was in court, maybe the family of the fence would be there giving them support. Ernie thought he could pass a message to a fence via their family.

Like most of Ernie's ideas, this was not as simple as he first thought. He had never previously been inside a court building, and the nearest he had ever got had been to watch Judge Judy and Judge Rinder. He knew where his local magistrate's court and crown court were, and he thought the magistrate's court dealt with less serious cases. He was not sure whether he would have to produce identification to enter, or whether there was a particular place he would have to sit once inside. There seemed so much to think about.

Eventually he decided to go in disguise, dressed as a woman in the same way as he had gone to the bank. If anything went wrong, it would be Ann Perkins everyone would look for and not him.

By this time Ernie thought his alter-ego ought to have a name and Ann Perkins seemed as good a name as any. If you had asked how he chose the name, he would not have been able to tell you, only that the name came to him in a flash of inspiration. Subconsciously Ernie had taken the first name of the Ann Summers shop and the last name of the Dorothy Perkins shop he had been walking past. His mind subconsciously thought of Ann Perkins but could just as easily have come up with Dorothy Summers. It could have been worse. He could have been walking past a Weird Fish and Banana Republic shop.

Ernie decided he would attend the magistrate's court. He imagined there would be less scrutiny entering Tameside Court on the outskirts of Manchester than there would be entering the Crown Court in the city centre. He had sometimes passed the Crown Court when trials had been taking place and had occasionally seen armed police outside. The local magistrates' court seemed a safer prospect. He had already decided to go in disguise, but there was still the problem of how to get there.

He didn't want to leave his flat dressed as a woman. He knew it would embarrass him if he met any of his neighbours, and it seemed pointless wearing a disguise if everyone could see him entering or leaving his home address. He needed somewhere near the court to get changed into his disguise in the same way he used Debenhams before going to the bank. The problem was that there were no large stores near the court.

Even if he found a nearby building to get changed in, that was not his only problem. He was sure he would have his bags searched as he entered court and he, or rather she, would have to explain why she was entering court with a bag of men's clothing. That would take some explanation, but he couldn't think of anything convincing.

He needed somewhere to change into women's clothing, but where he could also leave a bag of his own clothes to change into afterwards. He needed a room he could enter as a man carrying a bag, and leave as a woman without a bag, and a room to where he could later return as a woman without a bag, and leave as a man carrying a bag. His mind was in a whirl which was taking him around in circles, and he could not immediately think of anywhere suitable.

It was just after he woke up the following morning that his breakthrough occurred. It had been several years since Ernie had been able to afford a car, but he still had his licence. He could rent a van and park near the court. Then he could get changed in the van and leave his change of clothing inside for when he returned.

His primary concern was the cost, and it took several phone calls before he found a company that would rent a van to him at a price he wanted to pay. Eventually he found somewhere about a mile from home, and the only additional cost was the price of any petrol used. That didn't bother him as he only intended driving the couple of miles to court and back.

Ernie already had a decent mobile phone, but he bought a cheap pay-as-you-go phone so he could provide an untraceable phone number if anyone asked him for one. He found a mobile without a touch screen at a local supermarket for just over ten pounds, and it came pre-loaded with a free SIM and a pound's worth of credit. He set the phone up as if it belonged to Ann Perkins. He could use that phone to make calls to the fence and keep his original phone for personal use. He began thinking of Ann Perkins as his criminal name and Ernie Wright as his non-criminal name.

He could barely afford to hire the van, but believed it was a good investment. Ernie knew the fence would want a hefty fee, but he intended stealing more than a million pounds worth of jewellery and hoped to still have a million after paying any commission to the fence.

Chapter Five

On the Monday of the following week he took a bus to the van hire company and arrived around half-past eight. He produced his driving licence and two utility bills, and within minutes was driving away with a full tank of petrol. By a little after nine he had driven the couple of miles to Ashton-under-Lyne and had parked in June Street, a quiet area with no parking restrictions only a short walk from the court.

The first cases started at ten o'clock, so he had almost an hour to get ready. A transit van would have given him more room, but cost more. The small van lived up to its name, and when he crawled into the rear he couldn't stand up. Even sitting down, his head barely cleared the roof.

Ernie struggled to get undressed in the gloom but struggled even more to get dressed again as Ann Perkins. His tights gave him the biggest problem, but he knew they would and he'd brought extra pairs because he didn't want to draw attention to himself by going to court in laddered tights. He had difficulty putting them on whilst sitting on the corrugated floor of the van, and he put his thumb through the first pair before getting them fully over his feet. The second pair went on without mishap, but took him longer than expected. Pushing his bum off the floor with one hand whilst pulling the tights up with the other was not an experience he wished to repeat.

All the time he was getting changed he

monitored the front of the van. The semi darkness in the back was due to the rear doors having no windows, but anyone looking through the front windscreen whilst he was changing may have seen him semi-naked and phoned the police. For a moment an image flashed through his mind of a child looking through the windscreen and running home to tell their parents. He'd likely get lynched. At the very least he would have some explaining to do. Luckily, nobody looked into the van whilst he was undressed, and despite the lack of headroom he eventually completed his change.

The makeup was a different story. The last few times he had applied makeup he did so with little difficulty. He had experimented at home in front of a large mirror, and on the day he went to the bank he had put his makeup on in front of a large full-length mirror in the disabled toilet.

The rear of the van lacked a mirror of any sort so he had bought a small hand-held mirror with him. He was by then reasonably skilled at applying his makeup, but applying lipstick and eyeliner with one hand whilst holding a mirror in his other hand, and whilst having a pain in the bum from sitting on a corrugated floor, was a skill he'd not yet mastered. He had a small pack of wet wipes, but he lost count of the number of times he applied makeup, wiped it off, and then reapplied it, before he was happy.

He seemed to have taken a long time to get ready, and it surprised him to find it was only nine-thirty when he crawled out of the back of the van disguised as Ann Perkins. He wobbled along the first few yards of the footpath, but by the time he approached the court he had got his balance.

There were quite a few people standing around outside, so he stayed outside too. Most were in small groups, and the group closest to him comprised a man and woman in their mid-twenties talking animatedly to one another. He turned sideways on so as not to face them directly, but their raised voices made it easy for him to listen whilst keeping his distance.

"If that bloody copper hadn't come along with his dog, I'd have been home free." The man was wearing a hoody, with faded jeans torn at the knee as he took a deep drag from a self-rolled cigarette. "How was I to know the bloody alarm went straight through to the police station? I'd have been well away if it hadn't been for that bloody dog."

The woman was wearing slacks, trainers, and a cotton top with a heart-shaped hole cut in the top to display her cleavage. "It's your own bloody fault. You told me you were going straight." The woman had squared up to him with her arms folded and her foot tapping in time with her speech. Her lips pulled back to display gritted teeth as she spoke. "You don't care about me and the kids. If you did, you'd get a bloody job like everyone else. You're bloody useless. Can't bloody look after me. Can't bloody look after the kids. Can't get a bloody job. Can't even break into a deserted bloody warehouse. You're bloody useless."

"I did it for you and the kids," the man replied. His loud high-pitched whine caused several people in the crowd to turn their heads. "If you hadn't kept nagging me, I'd never have done it. Get me this. Get me that. Get me bloody everything we can't afford."

"Don't you bloody blame me. You're always trying to blame me, and it's not my bloody fault. I never asked you to get bloody caught. It's you. You're bloody useless."

They couple were so engrossed in their argument they hadn't noticed Ernie was anywhere near them. He heard no mention of a fence so moved away towards a larger group of three men and a middle-aged woman. This group appeared to be a husband and wife and two teenage sons. The men were all dressed in dark pinstripe suits matched with white shirts and striped ties, whilst the woman was wearing a smart cotton jacket and skirt. If he had seen the middle-aged man approaching court on his own, he would have assumed he was a solicitor or magistrate. He had that look about him, and all his family had taken time to dress smartly for their day in court.

The first couple Ernie had stood beside looked as though they hadn't got a penny to their names. The second couple looked like established pillars of society whose sons would soon go to university.

"Now don't forget," said their mother. "However much they provoke you, don't be disrespectful. Don't fidget. Don't put your hand over your mouth when you speak and don't look to us for answers. Stand up straight and don't put your hands in your pockets." She wiped a piece of dust off the collar of the eldest boy's jacket.

"It's all right mum, don't worry. We'll be fine." The oldest boy replied.

"What if they say they can identify us?" The younger one said.

His father gave him a pat on the shoulder and

smiled at him reassuringly. "You'll be fine. Apart from the snatch itself, everything you say will be true. Lots of teenagers ride mopeds, and there were lots of other teenagers about that day." He lowered his voice, unaware Ernie was still close enough to hear everything. "You had helmets on, so there's no way anyone can identify you. Besides, by the time they stopped you, you'd already passed everything to me. They found nothing on you, and they'll trace nothing back to you. I've already sold everything on. The police are sure it was you, but that doesn't matter. All that matters is whether they can prove it, and they can't. There's no evidence against you. It's all circumstantial. Just do as your mum says. Be polite, look the magistrate in the eye, speak clearly, and say you know nothing about it. Nobody can prove any different."

The two youths nodded in agreement, the elder one more vigorously than his younger brother.

"Take them in and get them seated," their father said. "I'll join you once I've finished this cigarette."

"Come along, boys. Let's get you inside. Don't forget, you never know who's watching. From when you go through those doors until you come out again I don't want you saying anything you shouldn't. You need to be on your guard the whole time. Look innocent, think innocent thoughts, say nothing incriminating, not even to one another." Their mother shepherded them towards the door, leaving her husband outside.

Ernie approached the man once he was alone.

"Excuse me. Can I have a quick word before you go in?" Ernie's brown wig had been straight when he had put it on, but unbeknown to him it had moved as he crawled from the van and it was now lying at a slightly odd angle to display wisps of greying hair at one side.

The man took one look at the woman and immediately saw her hair was obviously a wig. Her clothes seemed ill fitting too. Something about her rang a warning bell at the back of his mind, but there was nothing specific he could put his finger on. "Sure," he said uneasily. "What can I do for you? Make it quick. I've got to go inside in a minute."

"I heard you talking to your kids. Nice kids. They look very smart. They're a credit to you." Ernie thought a bit of flattery would do no harm.

"Thank you." His unease deepened as he waited for her to continue. She had obviously not approached him to complement him on his children, and he wondered how much she had overheard. He gulped at the thought she may be an undercover police officer and tried to remember if he had said anything incriminating before his wife entered the court.

Ernie hesitated and bit his lip. The man didn't look like a criminal. What if he really was a magistrate? He also went through the couple's conversation in his mind before deciding to continue. He had come too far already, so may as well come straight out with it.

"I'm looking for someone who can fence some stolen jewellery. Thought you may know someone."

The woman did not look like any undercover police officer he had ever seen, but the faint warning bells at the back of the man's mind had turned into a clanging gong screaming at him to be careful. There was no way this was not a set-up. People do not approach someone they don't know outside a courtroom and ask them to fence some jewellery. Something was definitely wrong.

"Do I look as though I know anyone who fences stolen goods? Sorry, but you've got the wrong person." He dropped his cigarette on the floor, stubbed it out with his foot, and walked away towards the building.

"If you knew a fence, I could make it worth their while."

The thought of making some extra money was irresistible and made the man pause. There was something different about the strange-looking woman and he was curious to know more despite his misgivings. He hesitated, then turned back. "I'm not a fence. I need to make that clear. I am intrigued though. Just for the sake of argument, if I was a fence, how would it be worth my while?"

"I intend robbing a jeweller's so you'd get your usual commission," said Ernie. "If the jewellery I'm selling is worth a lot, then your commission would be worth a lot, so it could be well worth your while." Ernie took a previously prepared piece of paper out of his handbag and held it out. "I've jotted down my name and phone number. If you know someone who'd buy the jewellery from me, I'd like you to pass my details on to them."

The alarm bells were still ringing loudly, but curiosity had trumped his concern. "I've told you I don't know anyone." He reached out, took the paper, and saw the name Ann Perkins and the number of the new pay-as-you-go phone that Ernie bought a few days before. Neither the name on the card nor the telephone number meant anything to him. He placed the paper into his inside jacket pocket. "I don't know why on earth you'd think I would know anyone like that. Sorry, but I don't. The idea's idiotic." With that, he strode away and entered the court building.

Ernie noticed the man had placed the paper into his jacket pocket before walking away despite protesting that he didn't know anyone he could pass it to. By this time, almost everyone had entered the building. Ernie considered entering too, but there were two security guards standing just inside the glass door who had been searching everyone and asking why they were attending. He thought back to the overheard conversations. He didn't think he needed to take the risk of entering the building. It seemed the boys had stolen something, passed it to their dad, and their dad had already sold it on. Ernie was sure the man was a fence himself, or knew someone who was.

He returned to the van and checked there was nobody about. There were no adults, just two young children playing at the other end of the street, so he climbed into the back of the van to get changed. Ernie had used most of the wet wipes when putting his makeup on, but did the best he could with the couple that remained before changing out of his disguise and back into his ordinary clothing. It was easier this time. He tore the tights off not caring if he laddered them, and he had no difficulty putting his socks on. It was still uncomfortable on the corrugated floor, but everything was easier with his own clothes.

He was not entirely successful at getting changed with no one noticing. The children at the end of the street had seen a woman climb into the back of the van, and a man climb out of it, but when they told their parents later, their parents thought they were making up stories. He had not been entirely successful in his lipstick removal either, and the remaining traces of lipstick were a source of amusement to the employee of the van hire company who later accepted payment for the petrol used.

Chapter Six

"I'll kill her." Alf Sidebotham's face was bright red, and he was projecting droplets of spit on those unfortunate enough to be closest to him. "I'll bloody kill her."

He had already decided the woman who caused Bob Hinchcliffe's arrest at the bank would have to pay for it. After the bank fiasco he had sent word for everyone to search for her, but despite intensive enquiries nobody found any trace. Nobody knew her name. Nobody knew her address. Nobody recognised her; not from the CCTV, nor from the newspaper description. She had just disappeared, and he had almost given up hope of getting his revenge.

Her appearance outside the court had unexpectedly intensified his anger. "Not only does she get Bob arrested, but now she's trying to fence some bloody jewellery. Who the hell is this woman? I'll bloody kill her."

The third floor office block on Camberwell Street was in the Cheetham area of Manchester to the north of the city centre. Outward appearances declared it to be the respectable headquarters of Sidebotham's Property Services, but it was mainly a front for his criminal activities.

The gang members knew it was best to stay out of Alf's way when he was like this but they had no alternative. They were there for various reasons, and postponement would only make things worse. Some had gone to pay their dues for crimes already committed, whilst others had gone to get his approval for crimes planned for the future. Whatever their opinion about Alf, they all acknowledged his system of pre-approving jobs had been a success. Burglars no longer targeted the same streets at the same time, drug dealers no longer fought over the patches allocated to them, and even online fraudsters avoided the scams of others.

They liked the advanced planning even though they were not so keen on paying for it, but they knew the payments were an essential part of the system. Some had tried to shirk their obligations in the past, but Alf's violent response always made them reconsider.

Alf's associates had all seen him angry occasionally, but few could remember him being as angry as he had been lately. Sid's message about being approached outside the court had put Alf into a foul mood where every word was being shouted, and where his face flushed into bright red as he spoke. They knew it was best to stay out of Alf's way when he was like this, but Jack tried to calm him down before he started taking things out on the rest of them.

"I don't know who she is boss," Jack said. "The woman approached Sid outside court and asked if he knew a fence. She gave her name as Ann Perkins and gave him a card with that mobile number on it, but apart from that we know nothing about her."

"Tell Michael I want to see him. I need him to sort this bloody woman out once and for all, and the sooner the better." Michael Carpenter was one of the primary reasons Alf had remained in business for so long. He was Alf's right-hand man. His fixer. They were roughly the same age and had known one another since their teens, but whilst Alf had schemed his way into becoming the boss and brains of the outfit, Michael's skills were more physical than cerebral.

Alf put up with Michael because he was no threat, and would never try to take over his business empire. Michael knew he was not clever enough, but he was not ambitious enough either. He remained happy for others to do the thinking and decision making. He did as he was told, and what he was told to do invariably involved brute force or violence.

Violence was Michael's speciality. It was uncomplicated and never touched him emotionally. He never asked why, never had sleepless nights, and never dwelt on the past. Once the violence was over, it was no longer his concern. For as long as they worked together, there had never been a task given to him that Michael refused to do.

Alf and Michael first formed a close attachment to one another when they were in their late teens and had done some jobs together. Michael watched Alf's back and got him out of a few scrapes, and in return Alf rewarded his loyalty. The thing that really cemented their relationship, occurred about eighteen months into their partnership. Michael got into an argument with a club bouncer, and the bouncer came off second best.

The fight was still going on when the police turned up, and whilst the paramedics took the bouncer to hospital for treatment to his broken jaw, the police took Michael to the police station and banged him in a cell. Ultimately, he got a six-month prison sentence for assault occasioning actual bodily harm. The fight had no connection to Alf, but because of their friendship he made weekly payments to Michael's mother for the entire period Michael was in prison.

Michael had an unusual childhood, but he was never fully aware how unusual it really was. He always believed his father died whilst he was an infant, and that his mother brought him up, but reality was the complete opposite.

It had been his mother who had died of cancer whilst he was an infant, and his father who struggled to cope. Things being what they were back in those less enlightened days, social workers rarely left a baby in the care of a sole male parent. They expected men to go out to work and women to stay at home and look after the family. In the absence of a mother, social workers felt it their duty to find a surrogate.

Michael's father feared they would take Michael away and have him adopted, so he pre-empted their expected action by doing a moonlight flit away from their Birmingham home. His father never knew whether social services would have actually taken the child into care, but once they moved away the family were no longer Birmingham's problem.

They moved to Manchester, where Michael's father dressed himself in his dead wife's clothes, and reinvented himself as Mrs Cynthia Carpenter. Their neighbours didn't know Cynthia was not who she claimed to be, and Michael didn't know either. For as long as Michael could remember his mother had raised him, and in Michael's eyes she could do no wrong. His father never told his son the truth, and he continued to live as a woman until his disappearance in unusual circumstances when suffering from dementia as a pensioner.

The support Alf gave to Michael's mother during the time Michael was in prison cemented their relationship in a way nothing else could. Michael felt a debt of gratitude to Alf, and from that day on he had always done whatever Alf asked him to do. Michael was the one person Alf could always rely on to give him one hundred percent unquestioning support.

Alf lost no time in telling Michael what he wanted. "I know you usually make things look like a bloody accident, but this time I want it to look like murder. I want no ambiguity. I need people to know I've had her killed for sticking her nose in where it's not bloody wanted. I want her dead, and the sooner the bloody better."

"Leave it with me, boss. I'll sort it." The only lead Michael had was the woman's name and phone number, and the knowledge she was looking for a fence. It was enough. He had no intention of meeting her, but he decided he could phone and set a meeting up. If she turned up at the meeting place, he would know who she was and he could follow her home and work out the best way of killing her. He intended killing her in such a way that everyone would know she was being murdered on Alf's orders, but he also had to arrange for both of them to have unbreakable alibis.

Michael had honed his craft over many years and had long since lost count of the number of people he had killed on Alf's behalf. The numbers were unimportant to him and he didn't think them worth remembering. The woman was just another job, and as far as he was concerned she was as good as dead. He would not have felt so confident if he had known his next murder would be his last.

Chapter Seven

"Hello! Is that Ann Perkins?" He could hear the person breathing, but they hadn't spoken to him and Michael needed to make sure he had not misdialled.

"Yes, I'm Ann Perkins. Who's calling, please?" Ernie remembered to speak in the high-pitched Ann Perkins voice he was getting used to. He'd only given his number to one person, but he couldn't be sure it wasn't a marketing call.

There was something recognisable about the voice that Michael couldn't immediately place. "I understand you contacted a friend of mine whilst you were looking for a fence. Could you tell me why you need one?"

Ernie had been expecting a call from the man he spoke to outside the court but this didn't sound like the same man. He needed to be as careful as possible. "A fence? Yes, that's right. I need to replace the badly worn fence in my garden. Can you help me find one?"

Michael had little time for game playing. He too was using a pay-as-you-go mobile nobody could trace back to him. "I'm not talking about a garden fence. My friend said you want to fence some stolen goods."

"Possibly," Ernie said. He didn't know who was phoning him, and he hesitated over whether to commit himself. He had no experience of this cloak and dagger stuff and had no idea whether anyone could trace his phone despite it being pay-as-you-go. It was all new to him. "How do I know I can trust you?" was all he could think of to say.

"You don't know you can trust me," Michael said, "and I don't know if I can trust you. For all I know, you may be the police, and this may be a setup. I hope not for both our sakes. What I do know is that you gave your phone number to a friend of mine and said you were looking for someone to fence some jewellery. That's why I'm calling."

"I see." Ernie's mind was working overtime. He needed to be sure he could trust the person he was speaking to, and he needed to know the man would not fleece him once he handed the jewellery over. He knew he could hardly complain to the police if he handed over the jewels and then the man refused to pay him. "Perhaps we should meet face to face," he said. "Somewhere public, with lots of people about. That way we can meet with less risk."

Michael didn't think Ann Perkins would be stupid enough to tell him where she lived, but he asked anyway. "All right. That's a good idea. Perhaps we can meet close to where you live. What part of Manchester are you from?"

The last thing Ernie wanted to do at this stage was to give his address on the East side of Manchester so he chose a North Manchester location instead. "Rochdale," he said, "but I don't know where you're from so it would probably be more convenient to meet somewhere central. Somewhere in the centre of Manchester convenient for both of us."

"Central Manchester?" The obvious central location would be Piccadilly Gardens, but there would be no cover if it was raining. Michael needed somewhere out of the rain, where there would be plenty of people about, and where he could have a good look at the woman without showing himself. "How about the food court in the Arndale Centre?"

"That's okay with me." Ernie said. "When should we meet?"

"How about tomorrow, about eleven? We could meet up over a coffee. How will I recognise you?"

"Tomorrow at eleven? Yes. Okay." Ernie decided he had better attend in character. The person was expecting to meet Ann Perkins, and he didn't want to confuse things by turning up as Ernie Wright. "It's mostly filled with young mums and toddlers mid-morning. I should be easy enough to spot as I'm almost fifty. I've got shoulder length dark hair and I'll be wearing a patterned brown dress. If it's raining, I'll carry a brown umbrella."

"Right," Michael said. "I'll see you tomorrow at eleven in the Arndale Centre Food Court."

As soon as he had hung up, Michael phoned Alf.

"It's sorted, Alf. I'm meeting her tomorrow." He didn't need to give the woman's name over the phone. Alf would know who he was talking about.

"Fine. I'll make sure I'm out of the way with plenty of bloody witnesses."

"It probably won't be tomorrow, but it's best if you do just in case. If it isn't tomorrow, then definitely within a day or two. You needn't worry. Whatever happens I'll have done it within forty-eight hours of the meeting."

"I'll make myself scarce for the next couple of bloody days then," Alf said. "Ring me when it's all over."

By the following day Michael had completed his preparations and had prepared a typewritten note just in case the opportunity arose to kill her that day. He didn't expect it, but if he got the chance, he'd take it. The woman said she was from Rochdale to the north of Manchester, but she would have no reason to tell him the truth and was probably lying. He thought she may even have to come into Manchester by train. The note he carried said the woman was being killed because she interfered with a robbery and helped the police arrest a robber. Alf told him he wanted her death to look like murder, so if she gave him an opportunity, he would slip the note into her pocket before pushing her off the platform on her way home.

Michael knew the police would grill Bob and try to discover which of his friends had been responsible for the killing, but Bob was in custody and could deny all knowledge. He couldn't give them any information about the death because he wouldn't know anything about it. They may suspect him, but could prove nothing.

Ernie also prepared for the meeting. He disguised himself as Ann Perkins and had stopped worrying about what the neighbours may think if they saw him entering or leaving. He was past caring what other people thought. When he'd gone to court to search for a fence, he hadn't wanted his neighbours to see him dressed as a woman so he'd forked out for a van. He couldn't afford to do that every time, but it wasn't just the money. Getting changed in the back of the van had been difficult and far from ideal.

Now faced with a similar problem, he had decided the expense and inconvenience were not worth it. He wanted to go to the meeting dressed as Ann Perkins, but he didn't want to go through the whole rigmarole of taking clothes with him and trying to find somewhere to change.

He persuaded himself it was nobody else's business what he wore or how he dressed. He was old enough to please himself, and getting into his disguise at home meant he could take his time and get everything right. If any of his neighbours saw him going out dressed as a woman, that would be their problem not his.

This was only the third time he had gone out in disguise, and he found it a lot easier changing in his own home than in the back of the van. It was easier, quicker, and he ended up with fewer wrinkles in his tights.

Once he was ready, he took a quick look out of his window towards the communal entrance. Ernie had told himself he didn't care if any of his neighbours saw him dressed as a woman, but it wasn't true. He knew he'd be embarrassed and wouldn't know what to say if they saw him. He'd have to deal with it if it happened, but thought it would be much better to get in and out without being seen. There was nobody in the communal area as far as he could tell, and listening at the door he could only hear the distant drone of traffic from the main road.

Opening his door, he stepped outside onto the communal landing at the same moment his immediate neighbour stepped out from his own front door. For a moment Ernie considered going back in his flat and closing the door, but his neighbour had already seen him and was staring at him. He only had a fraction of a second thinking time and hadn't been expecting to see anyone. He stared back for a moment before speaking, but his courage deserted him and the lie seemed easier than the truth.

"Hello," he said. "I'm Ann, Ernie's sister. You must be Colin, his neighbour."

"Yes, that's right," said the neighbour. "Pleased to meet you, Ann." Ernie breathed a sigh of relief as the neighbour walked away, but he suddenly stopped and turned back. "I didn't realise Ernie had a sister."

Ernie didn't have a sister until a moment ago. He had spoken without thinking, but now realised he would have to continue the deception. "We're twins, but we've not seen one another for years. I've been living in Australia, but I am staying with my brother for a while now I'm back in England."

"Well, welcome home Ann." He stretched out his hand, and Ernie shook it. "Should have guessed you and Ernie were brother and sister. You look so alike. Same build and same features, and you've still got your accent."

"We're not identical, but you're not the first to comment on how alike we are. Got to feel sorry for my brother, looking so much like his sister. He got teased about it no end when we were at school together."

"How is Ernie anyway? I've not seen him for two weeks."

"He's fine. He went out earlier."

"Where are you off to today?" asked the

neighbour. "Anywhere exciting?"

"Just going into Manchester to do a bit of shopping." As soon as Ernie had spoken, he realised he shouldn't have said what he had in case Colin was also going into the city centre and suggested they go together.

"That's good. Don't spend too much. See you later."

"Yes," said Ernie, "see you later." He watched as Colin walked down the communal stairway and out of the front door of the building and turned right. That had gone better than expected. Colin seemed to have believed he was Ernie's twin sister. If he ever had to provide his sister's date of birth for any reason, it wouldn't be a problem. Her date of birth would be as easy to remember as his own.

After leaving enough time for Colin to go in whichever direction he was going, Ernie made his own way down the stairs, out of the communal doorway, and towards the nearest bus stop.

Chapter Eight

Michael, as he had planned, arrived at the Arndale Food Hall a good half-an-hour before the time of the meeting, bought himself a coffee, and sat in the far corner from where he could see both entrances and all the seating area.

Being a little late for breakfast and too early for lunch, few people were eating full meals, but it was busy with people consuming drinks and snacks. There was a mixture of people. Some mothers with young children, several pensioners, and a whole mishmash of others of various ages. Michael looked at all the women sitting on their own, but none were wearing a brown dress. None of them wore a dress of any sort. They were all wearing trousers, so anyone in a dress would stand out and should be easy to spot. Michael bought himself a coffee and some fries and settled down to wait.

Ernie also arrived early, but only by five minutes. He had given his description to the Fence, but hadn't asked what the fence looked like. He knew the fence was a man from his voice, but not how old he was. Several men were sitting alone but the fence could be any of them. Ernie was a few minutes early and thought the fence may not even have arrived. Going to a counter, he bought himself a coffee and burger, found an empty table, and sat down to wait unaware he was already being observed.

Michael had little doubt the woman he was looking at was Ann Perkins. She was the only woman wearing a dress. That it was a brown dress was the clincher, but he would have been sure anyway. There were a more people in now, but she was still the only woman not wearing trousers or a hijab.

From where he was sitting he could tell her hair was a wig, and he wondered if her real hair was a different colour. If she took her wig off whilst he was following her it would be easier to keep track of her if he knew her original hair colour. He was also close enough to see she had stubble on her chin. Not a lot, but there was definitely some there. He looked at her legs and saw the wrinkled dark brown tights were not dark enough to disguise the thick dark hairs on her legs.

His scrutiny became even more intense when he thought he recognised her from somewhere before realising he was mistaken. She reminded him of his mother. Her physical features were different, but there was a resemblance. It was not one single thing, but a combination of several things. The way she seemed slightly unsteady on her feet as she walked in, the way her hair seemed slightly off centre, the way her stubble was already showing despite being only mid-morning, and the way her leg hairs were showing beneath her tights. None of those things on their own would have been enough to trigger the memories of his mum, but taken together they created an uncanny likeness.

Michael had never planned to approach the woman. He planned to identify her and then follow until an opportunity arose to kill her. He never intended to speak to her, but the resemblance to his mother compelled him to change his mind and he couldn't resist going to talk to her to see if the resemblance was as strong close up.

"Hello ... Ann?" He nearly called her mum and only just stopped himself in time.

"Yes," said Ernie. "Are you the person I'm meeting?"

She could almost have been his mother. The voice was similar. Deeper than most other women's voices. "Yes," said Michael. "I spoke to you on the phone."

Close up, even her facial features seemed familiar. Not the shape, but the unconscious twitches. It had been almost ten years now since she had passed away, but he still remembered the stubble on her chin and the wisps of grey showing under the wig she had worn to disguise her thinning hair.

"We're not related are we?" said Michael. "You remind me of someone." The uncanny resemblance had forced him to ask.

"Shouldn't think so," said Ernie. "My parents both died when I was a baby and my adoptive parents had me from a toddler." Ernie cursed himself. He had gone through the meeting several times in his mind. He had rehearsed the answers to all the expected questions, but that hadn't been one of them. He wanted to give away as little personal information as possible, but the stupid question about being related had caught him off guard.

"It's just that you look almost identical to my mother."

Ernie almost chuckled but put his hand to his mouth to disguise it with a fake cough. How could he look like the man's mother? It was ridiculous. He was a man in drag for god's sake. "My Mother had a sister I never met," he said, "but I met none of my birth family after being adopted. I was adopted in Manchester, but all I know about my real family is they came from somewhere in the midlands. Where are you from yourself?"

"Manchester." Michael hesitated. He had lived in Manchester for as long as he could remember, but he knew his mother originated from Birmingham. She never spoke about her family, and he had met none of his other relatives. "My mum was from the midlands. From Birmingham".

At that moment, rightly or wrongly, Michael became convinced Ann Perkins was a long-lost relative of his own mother. Perhaps even his mother's child. He knew his mother had a hard time before he was born, and he wondered if there was an earlier child she had given up for adoption. As he thought through all the possibilities, he knew for the first time in his life he had a contract he couldn't fulfil. It would be like killing his sister. Like killing the only other living member of his family.

Time seemed to lose all meaning as they continued to chat about family connections. They never conclusively established their relationship. Ernie, knowing he was a man, thought it unlikely. Michael, because he so desperately missed his mother, needed no convincing at all. He knew Ann Perkins was his sister.

It was a while later, once they'd exhausted all talk of any family relationships, before they eventually got around to talking about the reason they were meeting.

"What's all this about needing a fence. I understand you have some jewellery to sell."

"Not yet, I haven't," Ernie said, "but I'm planning to have some soon. I've got plans to rob a jeweller's, but I don't want to get left with jewellery I can't sell so I need to find a fence first."

"I could help you there." Michael had become engrossed and had cast aside all thoughts of killing her. "I'm not a fence myself, but I do know someone who'd buy some jewellery off you."

Talking about fencing the jewellery reminded Michael he was there to kill her, and he realised they would both be in danger if the robbery took place without Alf's permission. He would need to explain to Alf that Ann was a relative. Ann had annoyed Alf, but Michael and Alf were old friends and got on well together, so Michael was sure everything would be fine once he explained who she was to Alf. "Have you heard of Alf Sidebotham?" he asked.

"Alf Sidebotham? Don't think so. Is he a fence?" asked Ernie.

"Not exactly," said Michael. "I work for him, and he controls almost all the crime in Manchester. You pissed him off when you ruined a bank robbery and helped get someone arrested a few weeks back." Michael realised he should not have sworn in front of his sister, but she didn't seem to have noticed. "He was even more annoyed to hear you're planning to rob a jeweller's without his permission, and he sent me to warn you off."

The meeting had taken an unexpected turn when they had discussed their relationship, but until that moment Ernie thought things had gone well. "Warn me off?" he asked. "How do you mean? Do you mean he sent you to tell me I shouldn't rob the jeweller's at all, or that I can do it but need to get his permission first?"

"Neither of those I'm afraid. It's too late for that. He's pissed off because you foiled the bank robbery, and even more pissed off because you're planning a jewellery robbery. When I said he's sent me to warn you off, what I should have said was that he sent me to warn other people off by killing you."

Ernie felt the hairs on the back of his neck stand on end and a sudden chill down his spine. He got half out of his chair, realising as he did so that in ladies' shoes, he would hardly outrun Michael in his trainers. He kicked off his shoes and wondered whether to scream.

"Relax." Ernie felt a hand on his shoulder pressing him back into his seat. "That was the old plan." Ernie relaxed a fraction; but only by a fraction. He still didn't put his shoes back on, and he was still prepared to scream and run.

"I'm sure Alf will understand once I tell him you are family. He didn't know that when he told me to kill you. I didn't know myself, so he couldn't have done. I'll have a word with him and tell him, and once he knows I'm sure he'll let you rob the jeweller's. Once you've robbed it, we'll supply the fence and Alf will get his cut. Everyone will be happy."

Ernie was not so sure. He wondered what sort of man would order someone dead just because they had done what many others would have done in the same situation. He had intervened in the bank by accident, but even if it hadn't been an accident, it was only what any other person in the bank may have done. It appalled him someone would order a murder for such a trivial thing, but it also made him look at Michael in a fresh light and wonder what sort of man would carry out those orders.

"Are you sure he'll be okay about it?" Ernie asked.

"I'm certain," Michael said. He had convinced himself everything would be fine.

"Okay then. Perhaps it would be best to meet up again after you've spoken to him," said Ernie. "What about the same time and place in two day's time?" Michael's words had not convinced him someone who ordered a murder would so easily change his mind.

"Great," said Michael. "I'll go back and explain everything to Alf. He'll be fine once he knows you're my sister, and we can take it from there. See you here at the same time in two days."

"See you in two days then." Ernie put his shoes back on, stood up, and stretched out his arm to shake hands.

Michael ignored the outstretched hand and gave Ernie a hug. "A sister. I can't get over it. I'm really glad I found you." he said.

Ernie made his way quickly down the escalator from the food hall and into the Arndale Shopping Centre. Darting through the crowd he got himself as far away as possible as rapidly as he could. He realised Michael was a thug, and a weird one at that. Ernie had no intention of keeping the next appointment, but thankfully, Michael had only ever seen him dressed as a woman. Ernie consoled himself with the thought Michael did not know who he really was or where he lived.

He was careful on his way home and initially caught a tram going in the opposite direction to where he lived. A few stops later he got off the tram and got on the first bus that passed. A further bus ride took him back to the tram tracks, where he got a tram home mistakenly thinking nobody had followed him.

Colin smiled as they arrived at the communal door at the same time but from different directions.

"Hello again." said Colin. "You don't seem to have done much shopping. I should have reminded you our shops don't take Australian dollars."

Home safe, Ernie laughed as much from the release of tension as from the joke. "No," he said. "I was just window shopping. I thought everywhere took Australian dollars though. They do where I've been living. Just as well I saw nothing I fancied."

Colin had felt an attraction when they met earlier. There was something different and intriguing about the woman in front of him. Something alluring. "Perhaps you'll let me buy you a coffee sometime?" he said. "If we're going to be neighbours, we ought to get to know one another better."

Ernie was not sure how to answer. He just wanted to get into his flat as soon as possible and didn't want to spend time talking whilst in his disguise. "Er... Yes. I mean maybe. Er... Perhaps." By this time he had reached his door, and he quickly entered before closing it firmly behind him.

Colin smiled as he went into his own flat. He took Ernie's reply as a sign their feelings may be mutual. It had been obvious to him in the flustered way she responded when he invited her for coffee.

Chapter Nine

"You what?" Alf spluttered over his breakfast and almost choked on his toast as his face reddened with anger. "You bloody what? You bloody decided not to kill her?"

Alf got up late, and when Michael knocked on his door, he expected to hear he had already killed the woman. Michael always did whatever Alf asked him to do, so his disobedience came as a complete shock and he was angry and disappointed.

Michael had approached his boss with little apprehension, confident Alf would understand once he explained everything to him. His own experiences should have told him he was wrong, but his pleasure at finding a member of his family dulled his memory of how vindictive Alf could be when anyone upset or disobeyed him.

Michael could not have put into words exactly when the transition took place in his mind, but somehow Ann Perkins changed from being someone who reminded him of his mother, to someone related to his mother, and finally to someone who was his mother's child. His only sister.

Ann Perkins was his only living relative. The family resemblance had convinced him. Her dress sense, her hair, her stubble and hairy legs, her mannerisms, her voice; almost everything about the woman reminded him of his beloved mother.

"It was all a dreadful mistake boss," he said, desperate to calm Alf down. "She acted instinctively at the bank on the spur-of-the-moment so it wasn't really her fault. She couldn't help it." Michael could tell he had not convinced Alf. Alf's eyes were bulging and his face had changed to a brighter shade of red, but Michael ploughed on in his desperation to placate him. "She planned none of it, boss. It just happened. She's harmless."

Michael was hoping Alf would accept his explanation, but he had made things worse.

"Harmless! She got Bob bloody arrested. Ask Bob how bloody harmless she is. He'll tell you she's not bloody harmless. I was relying on my cut from the bank job, but because of her bloody interference it's all gone. I thought we had an understanding, you and me. Thought I could trust you. The woman's bloody dead, Michael. She's no more your bloody sister than I am. I'm bloody disappointed in you. I gave you a simple job to do, and you've let me down. If you won't do it, then I'll find someone who will."

Michael never gave up easily and Alf didn't intimidate him. He had to continue reasoning with Alf, not only for the sake of their friendship but also for the sake of his sister. He had only just found her and had no intention of losing her again. "Boss. Please. Be reasonable. She is my sister. I know she screwed up at the bank but she'll make up for it by giving you a cut from the jeweller's."

"The jewellers! I'm not letting her anywhere near any bloody jewellers," said Alf. "The bank was bad enough. She's threatened my bloody authority."

"She's no bloody threat, and she's learnt her lesson." Michael responded in kind and began shouting back. "The jeweller's is different, and it would be the first time she's ever done anything illegal. She knows she must ask your permission now, and she's okay with it. I know she didn't ask in advance, but I'm asking now on her behalf. She's agreed to give you your cut and she won't cause you any problems. She's no threat to anyone."

"No threat. No bloody threat. She's my worst bloody nightmare. She's screwed up one of my bloody jobs and I can't allow anyone to get away with that. I don't care who she is. The woman is dead. Dead and gone. You're with me on this, or against me, and from the sound of things you're bloody against me." Michael felt a sudden chill as Alf looked him straight in the eyes. "I thought I could rely on you, Michael. I've always been able to bloody depend upon you in the past. Don't tell me I can't."

Michael had never known his boss like this before. He had seen him angry enough to order people killed, but he'd never known him to be angry at him. They had always been friends, and this was the first time they had ever fallen out.

Michael saw Alf in a fresh light for the first time. He had always looked up to him, always done whatever he asked, and had always believed Alf knew best. It was finally dawning on Michael that Alf had never really cared about anyone but himself. Even giving his mother money all those years ago probably had an ulterior motive. Their friendship meant nothing to him. In all their years of friendship Michael had never asked Alf for anything. He never needed to, but today Alf had shown his true colours and dismissed out of hand

Michael's plea for clemency on behalf of his sister. Michael could feel the resentment welling up inside of him. He had always been Alf's strongest and most vocal supporter, but Alf was now treating him as though his past loyalty was nothing.

"Boss. Really. Let it go. Please. For the sake of our friendship. You know I've always done whatever you've asked. One-hundred percent. I've never let you down. I've never forgotten how you helped my mum out, and I've always been grateful, but this is different. We're talking about my sister. My only sister. Please, boss. Not her. I can't do it." Whilst Michael had been talking, he had imagined killing his own sister, and he knew he couldn't do it. The very thought of trying to kill her had caused his eyes to well-up. "Please. It's my sister. Anyone else. I'll kill anyone else, you know that, but not her."

Alf had calmed down a little after his rant, but that only made him more determined. It was unfortunate if the woman really was Michael's sister, but that didn't alter the fact that someone had to kill her. He had already announced her death sentence, and would lose more credibility if he allowed her to live. "No, Michael. I'm sorry. I've made my decision. If you can't do it, I'll ask someone else, but one way or another she has to bloody well go."

Alf's rage may have changed into steely determination, but Michael's emotions had done the opposite. He began the conversation feeling confident Alf would understand, but had ended it with a growing anger at the way Alf was treating him. He could so easily have given into his feelings and killed Alf at that moment. He considered it.

He was strong enough to strangle Alf with one hand and in his younger days he would have done. Only his experience persuaded him not to. He had long since learnt the easiest way of getting caught was to commit a murder impulsively. He would bide his time. "Fine," he said. "If that's what you think, do whatever the hell you like. But I'll tell you this, Alf Sidebotham, I won't let you touch a hair on my sister's head, not whilst I've a breath in my body." Michael stormed out of the house, slamming the door behind him, realising with his last few words their long friendship was finally and irretrievably at an end.

It was only later, in the quietness of his own home, that Michael realised the enormity of what had happened. Alf ordered people killed for far less, and the fact the argument took place in private would make no difference. Michael knew, because he had carried out such sentences himself, that Alf would want him killed for the way he had spoken to him. He knew the argument would have made Alf determined to take out two contracts, the original one on his sister, and another one on him.

Michael tried to put himself in Alf's shoes. He had done all Alf's previous killings as far as he knew. Alf had used no one else, so he wondered who Alf would find to kill him. A smile crossed his lips at the thought it would cost Alf more than the usual rate. Anyone coming up against him would demand a much higher fee because of the danger involved. He was no unsuspecting victim. He would be waiting for whoever was coming, so the killer would demand more money.

Despite the added cost, Michael knew it would not be long before someone accepted the contract.

Some youngster, perhaps, wanting to make a name for themselves. Michael thought it unlikely. Alf would not want to take the risk the person carrying out the contract would bottle it. He thought it much more likely the contract would go to an established killer. Someone with an already confirmed professional reputation.

Michael needed to be vigilant about the threat on his own life, but it was more important to him to do whatever it took to protect the life of his sister. Family came first, and he promised himself he would protect her from anyone who threatened her.

Outside of military forces there are few professional killers in the world, and of that select band of professional hit-men and women there are fewer still in Manchester. There are murders in Manchester just as there are in any large city, but most of these are spur-of-the-moment killings rather than professional hits.

Michael had only one major competitor, but there had always been enough work for both of them. They had a grudging professional regard that ensured they always kept a respectable distance between one another.

They worked differently, but they also worked with a different clientele. Michael had worked almost exclusively for Alf since being a teenager. The police listed most of Michael's murders as suicides or accidents, and he only used a gun on rare occasions. Sam Albright was the opposite. He worked for many people, and would work for anyone who payed his fees. He had no time for setting things up to look like a suicide or accident. He almost always used a gun. It was quicker, easier, and needed less planning.

Michael thought it was possible Alf may use someone from out of town, but it was unlikely. There were inherent risks involved in him using someone he did not know well. He was almost certain Alf would use Sam, and that gave Michael several distinct advantages. Unlike most victims, he knew someone was coming for him so he could make preparations. He had studied his rivals, including Sam, and had observed how they usually worked. Finally, Michael was far more experienced than Sam. Things would not end well for one of them, and Michael believed that person would be Sam. His own life, and the life of his sister, depended on it.

About the same time Michael was deciding his relationship with Alf was at an end, Alf was making a phone call to fill the vacated position.

"I've heard good things about you, Sam," Alf said, "even though I've never had cause to bloody use you myself. You come highly recommended and I've got a job for you."

Alf's call intrigued Sam. Although he knew Alf by reputation, they had never met or even spoken before. The closest they got had been at a dinner and dance when they nodded at one another from different tables. "I've heard about you too, Alf," he said, "but Michael does all your jobs doesn't he?"

"He has till now, but Michael won't do this bloody job. Thinks the target may be a bloody relative."

"I thought all his relatives were already dead," said Sam.

"They probably are," said Alf, "but he's got it

into his bloody head this person is a long lost bloody relative, and he's told me he just can't bloody well do it."

"If she is a relative of Michael's, she's no relative of mine. There's no connection between us so that won't be a problem."

Alf knew there was no family connection between Sam and Michael, but wondered if they were friends. He was on speaking terms with gang leaders in other cities, so he wondered if Sam and Michael had a similar arrangement. "So, the fact you'll be upsetting Michael won't be a bloody problem?" he asked.

Sam laughed. "Just the opposite. It'd be a bonus. He's always believed he was better than me, so it'll be an opportunity to prove him wrong."

Alf breathed a sigh of relief. If they had been friends, his phone call may have resulted in two killers gunning for him rather than one. "I've got two bloody jobs then if you're up for them," he said.

"I'm up for any jobs as long as the money's right," said Sam. "Just give me the details and I'll do them for you. One's a relative of Michael you said. Who's the other one."

"The other one is bloody Michael."

There was an audible intake of breath on the other end of the line. "Michael's the target?"

"Yes, he bloody well is. He knows too much about me. I thought I could bloody trust him, but his refusal to do the first job has made me question his bloody worth. I need people I can trust. People prepared to do whatever I bloody well ask them. Do these two and there'll be plenty of other work I can put your way."

Sam had been weighing up the implications of what he was hearing. "There's only one problem as far as I can see," he said.

"Which is?" asked Alf. Once he'd determined there was no connection between Sam and Michael he hadn't expected a problem.

"The first one you want me to kill is a woman. She'll be my usual fee. Michael's different. If you've fallen out so much that you want him killed, he'll know I'm coming for him. It'll cost you double to reflect the danger."

"Agreed," said Alf. There wasn't a problem. "I expected as bloody much. Double your usual fee for Michael. This is a one-off mind. All future jobs will be at your normal bloody fee."

"Are they urgent?"

"Yes. They're both bloody urgent," said Alf. "The woman's lived too bloody long already, so I want her dead first. She's planning to rob a bloody jeweller's and I want her dead before she does. If she goes anywhere near a jeweller's I want her bloody well stopped before she can rob it. Is that clear?"

"That's clear. How about Michael?"

"Do the bloody woman first. I want him to know I've had her killed. Michael can wait till after. Not too bloody long after mind. Couple of days at the bloody most."

"Right," said Sam. "I know Michael's details, where he lives, what he looks like. I just need details of the woman."

Alf passed on Ann's address, and the few other details he had.

"I want this done as soon as possible," he said. "She's making me look bloody weak, and I don't like it. If you'd killed her last bloody week, it wouldn't have been soon enough."

"OK... boss. Consider it done. Consider them both done."

"That's fine," said Alf. "I'll send the up-front money today. The rest on completion. Soon as you bloody can."

Alf hung up and sat there for a moment thinking about his approaching retirement. Michael had been his right-hand man for years and they shared a lot of history. This was the end of an era, and he knew things wouldn't feel the same without Michael by his side. Unaware how short his stay in Spain would be, he wondered for a moment if he should bring his retirement forward, before pushing the thought away.

Chapter Ten

Detective Sergeant Sarah Carter was in her favourite cafe. Coffee shop customers never got drunk in the way old time villains used to get drunk in pubs, but she had found the ambiance of a cafe in some ways even more conducive to gossip.

The Facebook generation was used to sharing personal details with friends, but many of them didn't know how to tweak their security settings and published intimate information to everyone. The same assumptions and indiscretions were taking place offline too. Smart phone users would speak as though they, and the person on the phone they were calling, were the only ones able to hear the conversation. That was untrue for at least one side of the conversation, but the tendency to use speaker-phone and hold a phone in front of them ensured nearby listeners could often hear both sides of a conversation.

Sarah had got into the habit of sitting in one of the city centre cafe's every morning before going to work. Once she was sitting at a table with a coffee cup in front of her, it was as if she was invisible. Nobody seemed to notice as she sat quietly listening to the conversations taking place all around her. Everyone was so used to customers fiddling with their phones as they ate or drank, that even taking out her phone and recording the more interesting conversations would draw no attention to herself.

She had always worked slightly differently to her colleagues, but those differences had frequently paid dividends. She had the happy knack of being able to befriend those she arrested when she saw them later.

She was not averse to getting drunk herself occasionally and didn't begrudge others getting drunk either even if she had to arrest them. Whatever foul language they shouted at her the night before, she never held a grudge. They would have to go to court and pay their dues, but the sober person she spoke to in a morning was not the same person as the drunk who confronted her the night before. When they sobered up, they had changed and she always respected that difference.

She was the same with the parents or partners of her prisoners. Sarah was always polite to them, always listened to them, and always seemed to understand their problems. When she later saw them in the city centre, she always acknowledged them with a nod or a word of welcome, and it was not long before her approach bore fruit. People remembered her for all the right reasons and frequently stopped to chat.

They knew she had a job to do, and sometimes her arrest of a drunken partner was just the kick up the backside the partner needed to sort themselves out. Sometimes she passed on information about a drug referral scheme or pointed them towards some charity or other. Family members of those she arrested had often thanked her.

Some of them had other reasons to thank her too. If someone was putting their child or partner in danger through drink or drugs, sometimes a quiet word with Sarah would sort things out. Her detection and arrest rate were such that as soon as she completed her probationary period colleagues encouraged her to apply to become a detective.

Like most detectives, she worked most afternoons and evenings, but she found her most profitable time was the hour regularly spent in the city centre cafe. It was there she got a lot of the information she subsequently acted upon.

She knew many of the local families, and most of the local criminals. She had joined the police when she was nineteen, became a detective when she was twenty-two, and after passing her sergeant's exam at the first attempt she became a detective sergeant at twenty-six. She was now almost thirty, had already passed her inspector's exam, and had spent the past ten years arresting Manchester criminals.

Her early arrests were mainly drunken youths rather than hardened criminals, and most of those she arrested early in her career became more responsible as they got older. Those who didn't change their ways, she continued to arrest in their twenties for more serious offences including robberies, thefts, and burglaries.

It would have been surprising, given the number and quality of her informants, if she'd never come across the name of Alf Sidebotham. She had heard of him and knew him by sight, and she knew colleagues had arrested him twice without ever having charged him. The information against him was always vague. There was usually enough evidence to convince the police he was guilty, but never enough for the Crown Prosecution Service to prosecute him in a court of law.

He was a major player. Everyone knew it. His name cropped up in connection with many crimes but he always seemed to be on the periphery of things. Somehow involved, but always with an unbreakable alibi. Despite all the villains Sarah had put away, and despite all the interviews and all the conversations she had overheard, she had never received any usable information about Alf Sidebotham himself. She didn't know it yet, but today would be different.

There had been nothing unusual about the start of Sarah's day. The cafe she most regularly made use of was in the Manchester Arndale Centre. Not the top floor food court where most of those seeking refreshments often ended up, but one of the smaller establishments on the ground floor.

To afford the centre's high rental fees, the proprietors needed to maximise income from the smaller floor space. As a result, the tables were much closer together than the ones upstairs, and more suitable for Sarah's purpose of eavesdropping on other customers.

Sarah had finished her first coffee and was considering calling it a day, but the cakes in the display cabinet persuaded her to stay a little longer. Once she got to the station, there was no telling how long she'd have to work before she took a break.

She purchased a cake with her second coffee and sat down again at her favourite table from where she could eavesdrop on the largest number of others. As she ate the cake, she listened briefly to a man on a business call, and to a woman phoning her daughter.

She heard no conversations of any consequence

from the surrounding tables. There were always other tables behind her whichever way she faced, but that did not matter and was often beneficial. Customers' seemed to assume that, if she couldn't see them, she couldn't hear them, and her best information often came from the tables immediately behind her.

She intended leaving after finishing her coffee, but someone spoke as she placed her mug on the table.

"Don't turn around. I want you to listen, but I don't want you to see me."

"I won't turn around if you don't want me to," she said. The man had been speaking directly to her, and she knew better than to turn around even without him asking. If he had wanted her to know who he was, he would have sat beside her.

"I have some information about Alf Sidebotham."

Michael had whispered, and despite their closeness, after being told not to turn around, Sarah could only just hear what was being said.

"Did you say, Alf Sidebotham? What about him?"

"Yes, Alf Sidebotham. You know who he is?"

"Everyone knows him. What's he done?" Sarah asked.

Michael was unsure how to begin. He had rehearsed nothing specific. He wanted to tell her that Alf intended to kill his sister, but he still felt disloyal. He had killed others in the past for what he was about to do. "It's not what he's done," Michael said. He couldn't tell the police about the past without incriminating himself. "It's what he's going to do. He's going to have someone killed."

Sarah's heart was already beating fast in anticipation, but it suddenly went up another level and for the second time she forced herself not to turn around. Being told about a killing in advance was not just unusual, it was unheard of, at least in her experience. She picked up her phone from the table and set it to record.

"Who's he going to kill?" she asked.

"It's not Alf that's doing the killing. He'll get someone else to do it. Did you hear about the woman who stopped the bank robbery off Piccadilly Gardens last week?"

"Yes, I heard about her. We've been looking for her." Sarah had spent several days looking for the woman, but without success. She had trawled through CCTV footage and saw her leaving the bank and entering Debenhams. After that. Nothing. Hours of searching had found no trace of her leaving afterwards. "What about her?"

"That's who's being killed. She got a friend of Alf's arrested so he's having her killed."

"We don't know who she is," said Sarah, "and we've not been able to find her."

"He knows who she is and where she lives, and he's determined to have her killed."

"Who is she?" A hand holding a small piece of paper appeared over her right shoulder. She took it without turning around and saw Ann Perkins name and address. "Is this who she is?"

"Yes. That's her."

"And he's asked someone to kill her?"

"Yes. He's asked a man named Sam Albright to do it."

"Are you sure?" asked Sarah.

"I'm one hundred percent sure he wants her

killed, and I'm ninety-nine percent sure he's asked Sam Albright to do it. I'd stake my life on it."

"So what's your angle in all this? How did you find out, and how come you're telling me?" When there was no immediate reply, Sarah thought the man was just taking his time and considering his response. "Why do you want the contract stopped?"

When there was no further response, Sarah waited a minute or two before turning around, but the man had already gone. She looked at the throng of people walking past. There were quite a few men, some alone and some with partners, but she didn't recognise anyone.

She got up and left, made her way to Central Park Police Station in time for the start of her shift, and played the recording of the conversation to her boss.

"Do you think it's legit?" Information often came Detective Inspector Jones' way, but like Sarah, he had never received a tip-off before a murder.

"Can't say boss. May be a hoax, but he sounded genuine, and I can understand his need for anonymity. I think this Ann Perkins at least deserves a visit. If she is the woman from the bank, I can see why she may have upset enough people to get herself killed. Perhaps we ought to offer her protection and keep her under wraps for a while."

"I'm not sure," the detective inspector said. "Why would anyone want to kill her? There seems no point. She tackled Hinchcliffe to the ground, but her evidence isn't vital. There were loads of witnesses, so killing her won't change anything.

They'll still find him guilty."

The identity of the woman from the bank seemed important to the detective inspector straight after the event, but things had moved on since then and it was no longer so important. Information about new crimes crossed his desk every day, and priorities were constantly changing. He considered what to do and almost convinced himself someone was having a joke and laughing at the police for not discovering who the woman was. He considered doing nothing, but then reconsidered. He ought to do something, just in case it turned out not to be the hoax he thought it was. If the woman turned up dead, he could at least say he had done something. "Just mention it to uniform. Ask them to drive by from time to time and keep an eye out on her home and tell them to report anything suspicious."

"Will that be enough?" Sarah hoped her boss would at least warn the woman, or even set up a covert observation.

"It's probably nothing. I shouldn't worry. Just pass it on to uniform."

Sarah was still not prepared to give in without a fight. Something about the matter-of-fact way in which the man had given the information to her made her think there was something in it. "Can I at least visit her? Make sure she is the person we think she is and get a witness statement for the bank job?"

"Look. I don't want you busting a gut over this. It's too far-fetched that anyone would take a contract out on her. There would be no point. Mind you, we could still use her written statement, so check her out, but not today. We've got other things on today, so check her out tomorrow morning as long as nothing more important comes up in the meantime."

"Thanks boss," said Sarah.

Chapter Eleven

According to Michael someone had taken out a contract on his life, but Ernie didn't understand why anyone would want to kill him. He had been responsible for the arrest of the man in the bank, but that hardly seemed a good enough reason to him. He'd killed no one, and the arrest wasn't planned. If things had gone according to plan, it would have been him being arrested not the other man.

That someone did want to kill him had a profound effect on him. He jumped at every little sound in his flat, and when he went out, he crossed over whenever anyone walked too close to him. Eventually he got so scared that he wouldn't go out at all.

Sitting in his flat gave him time to think about how he had considered suicide in the days immediately following the death of his wife and unborn child. Now death seemed more likely, he wanted to live. The thought of his imminent death did worry him, but amid his fear and confusion he recognised other emotions too. Ernie knew his past life had been depressing, but recent events had been intense and exciting.

He realised his fear had come before the death threat, and the threat itself had only intensified the feelings he already had. His new unfamiliar experiences, and even the danger of being caught, had brought him an excitement he had never previously experienced, and he'd found the adrenalin rush, the thrill, and even the fear, unexpectedly enjoyable.

He may not have robbed a bank, but he had planned to rob one, and had intended to rob it when he had gone in. Instead, he had become a crime fighter, a caped crusader. He realised he had never actually worn a cape, but he had foiled a violent bank robbery and looking back on events now he found the entire thing invigorating. He, who had barely been in a fight his whole life, tackled a gunman to the ground and had been responsible for getting him arrested. He hadn't meant to do it, but that was beside the point. He had saved the day and become famous.

Almost famous, anyway, given that everyone thought he was someone else. Nobody knew who he really was, but the local newspapers had plastered his CCTV image on their front pages, and the images even appeared in two national newspapers. His life had become a roller coaster of dramatic events in which he planned to rob a bank, planned to rob a jeweller's, almost changed publicly in the back of a van, tried to find a fence, disguised himself as a woman, told his neighbour he was his own twin sister, and had a contract taken out on his life.

The latter thought brought him up short and stopped his fantasising. So much had happened to him in such a brief space of time, and he was really excited, but on the minus side, someone wanted him dead. He was excited, but also terrified, and knew he'd be in danger as long as he remained in Manchester.

He already planned to move away from Manchester once he had enough money. That had been one of the primary reasons he had planned the bank robbery. Once he became a millionaire, he intended to move to a warmer climate, but the talk of someone wanting to kill him brought everything to a head. His first inclination was to move as far away as possible straight away, but he hadn't got enough money to go to a warmer country. He thought about the south coast of England. He may just be able to stretch his money out far enough to move. He could start again if he kept his head down until he knew it was safe. He could rob a jeweller's somewhere on the south coast just as easily as in Manchester.

It was at this point in his deliberations that Ernie realised he could still rob the Manchester jeweller's before disappearing to the south coast. He had already planned the robbery and already chosen the store and worked out how he would do it. If he robbed the jeweller's in Manchester, the police would look for him there, but he would be miles away on the south coast.

He'd put things off whilst he looked for a fence, but he now decided he didn't need to wait any longer. He could rob the jewellers and take the jewels with him to the south coast and find a fence there. He had told people he intended to rob a jeweller's, but hadn't told anyone which jeweller's. Nobody knew except him. He hadn't mentioned the name or location of the jeweller's to the man he met outside the magistrate's court, and he hadn't given details to Michael.

In that instant, he made his mind up. He believed there was no point delaying things and decided to rob the jeweller's the following day. He would then jump on a bus to London and be well away by the evening. He was sure the police would expect him to get away in a car and would never expect a getaway by bus. He knew a train would be a faster option, but until he found a fence for the stolen jewels, he knew the fare would be too expensive. A bus would take longer, but he would still be the other end of the country before the end of the day. Rob the jeweller's tomorrow morning, be in London late that afternoon, a night in a cheap London hotel, then another bus from London to Brighton. Sorted. Nobody would ever find him, and nobody in Brighton wanted to kill him. Once he was safely there, he could use the money from the sale of the jewellery to move somewhere warmer.

His mind made up. Ernie started putting his plan into action.

He already had a bag into which he could put all the jewellery after the robbery. He also still had a bag suitable for his change of clothes, and for his gun. He didn't intend using the gun to shoot anyone, but he'd use it to threaten members of staff. Now he had a real gun, he could even fire it into the ceiling to prove he meant business. The gun would keep them quiet during the robbery, but he also needed some way to stop them raising the alarm as soon as he left. Once he was out of the door, they would be free to call the police, and he needed some way to prevent it. He realised he needed time to get away, and time to change from his disguise and into his own clothing.

When he first moved into his flat, he had bought a packet of cheap cable ties, and he still had some long enough to go around wrists and ankles. He also had some masking tape. Used together, they would give him all the time he needed to make his escape and get changed before they raised the alarm.

That evening he stayed in watching the television, but by the end of the evening he had little idea about what he had watched. His eyes may have been constantly on the screen, but his mind was constantly elsewhere, flitting between the jeweller's, the bus, the south coast, and his eventual warmer climate. He hardly slept, but lay in bed with his eyes closed whilst constantly going over all his plans. The darkness passed excruciatingly slowly, but it did eventually pass, and the day of the robbery eventually arrived.

He got up early. Five o'clock was far too early, but he hadn't been asleep anyway, and could see no point in going over the plan again for the umpteenth time. The jeweller's didn't open until nine, and Ernie planned to get there about nine thirty. He had thought of everything and convinced himself nothing could go wrong.

Dressing as Ann Perkins, he took his time to put his makeup on and made sure he got everything right. He didn't feel hungry. He was too excited to eat, but forced himself to have a bowl of cereal because he didn't know when he would next have the time. He washed, dressed, and had his breakfast before six o'clock, and then sat watching the clock, willing the hands to move faster. Everything he needed to take with him was in the two bags at his feet. His breakfast, although slight, lay heavy and undigested in his stomach. It was taking all his willpower to sit still, but there was nothing for him to do. He did eventually stand up and began pacing the room. Backwards and forwards, constantly watching the minute hand move excruciatingly slowly past each mark of the clock until he eventually sat down again. He hoped in vain that his change of posture would cause the fingers of the clock to move quicker, but eventually it was time. He picked up his bags, turned off the electric and gas, closed the door behind him, walked down the stairs to the communal entrance, and went to catch the next available tram into central Manchester.

Detective Sergeant Carter parked her car on the main road outside the block of flats only minutes after Ernie left. She had worried all the previous day, half expecting every phone call or radio message to be the one that would inform her someone had found a woman's body. She obeyed her boss despite her misgivings but made her way to Ernie's flat as early as she dared. Like her boss, she half believed it was a hoax, but she didn't like taking chances with someone's life at stake.

She had used some of her spare time the day before to check out the voter's roll and council tax records and discovered they listed Ernest Wright at the address. The records were often out of date, so she assumed Ernest Wright was a former tenant and Ann Perkins had moved in since. She had also discovered the flat was on the first floor facing the front, so she sat in her car for a few minutes and examined the front of the building.

The entrance to the flats appeared to be around the back, but she could see the first floor curtains were open, so it looked as though the occupier was up and dressed. That was a relief to her at least. She had spent many hours as a younger constable knocking on doors early in the morning and had found people generally gave her a lot less aggravation if they were out of bed before she called.

She drove around the building to the rear car park and walked to the communal entrance. There were several bells beside the locked door, most of which had hand-written names inserted into the name plates. She quickly identified number seven, but the name card still displayed the name of the person she had assumed was the previous occupier. She wondered if Ann Perkins was their partner, or even a sub tenant.

The unexpected name caused her to hesitate for a moment before ringing the bell, but she couldn't tell if it was working. She couldn't hear it ringing, and nobody came to the door. She tried again. Nothing. If she had been outside one of the flat doors she'd have knocked, but there seemed little point knocking on the communal door. She waited a while and then tried number eight. That also brought no response. She was just about to try a third number when an elderly couple opened the door from inside.

"Are you looking for someone?"

Sarah could have said she was a detective, but experience had taught her it was sometimes better to keep that information until later. "I'm looking for an old friend of mine, Ann Perkins. I believe she lives at number seven, but she's not answering the door."

"Can't be this block love. Must be one of the other blocks. There's no Ann Perkins here." It was the woman who spoke, but her partner nodded in agreement.

"Are you sure? I'm sure she said she it was this block. Number seven. First floor front."

"No love. You've got the wrong block. I know everyone in this block and there's no Ann in the block at all. There's only four flats on the first floor. There's Tom and Mary in one, Alice in another, and the other couple of flats have single men in them. Ernie and Colin."

"Maybe she's staying at number seven with a friend?"

"It's a man at number seven. Ernie Wright. Never seen him with a woman."

"Ernie Wright? That's the name on the bell."

"Would be love, being as it's Ernie that lives at number seven. Colin lives next door to him. The only single woman is Alice, and the only other woman is Tom's wife, Mary. There's no Ann."

"Have you lived here long?"

"Lived around here all my life love and lived in this block for the past four years. Don't know any Ann Perkins around here."

"Okay. Thanks. I must have the wrong address." Sarah concluded it was a hoax, and was about to leave, but as they had been speaking, a man walked downstairs and Sarah held the door open for him. She considered entering and giving number seven a knock from inside but decided against it. There would be no point. The couple were adamant Ann Perkins didn't live there.

"Did I hear you asking about Ann Perkins?" the man said.

"Yes," said Sarah. "Your neighbours told me she doesn't live here."

"She didn't," said the man, "but she does now."

"This is Colin," the woman said to Sarah.

"Lives next door to number seven." "I've not seen anyone new, Colin," she said.

"She's not been here long," Colin said. "She's Ernie's sister from Australia. Living with him whilst she looks for her own place."

"I didn't even know Ernie had a sister," said the woman.

"Neither did I till she turned up," said Colin. "Twins apparently. There's a definite family resemblance."

"Sorry about that," the woman said. "Seems there is an Ann Perkins living here, but I didn't know."

Sarah had been standing listening to the conversation. At least the information about her name and address was right, so maybe the information about someone taking a contract out on her was right. Perhaps it was not a hoax.

"Thanks for that," she said. "I'll give her a knock."

"You'll be wasting your time," said the man who had come down the stairs. "You've missed her by ten minutes. Saw her going out earlier."

"Any idea where she went or what time she'll be back?"

"No idea. Could have gone anywhere but I'm sure she'll be back later."

Sarah eventually settled for putting a note through the door of number seven asking Ann Perkins to phone her as soon as possible.

On her way back to the police station she went over everything she knew.

It seemed to be true that a woman named Ann Perkins was living at the address, but she didn't understand why Alf Sidebotham would want to kill her for foiling the bank robbery. Sarah knew the woman tackled Hinchcliffe in the bank, but any bystander may have done the same The more she thought about it the more unlikely it seemed. Ann Perkins had not been the only one in the bank. Sarah's boss was there too. There would be no point in Sidebotham killing the woman.

After all her deliberations, Sarah Carter decided it was a hoax after all. Someone had read they were looking for a woman witness and thought it would be fun to waste police time by giving the name of a woman who had just arrived back from Australia. The hoax annoyed her, and she wondered who had so easily duped her. She took a bet out with herself that Ann Perkins was not even the name of the woman in the bank. When she finally got around to talking to her, she didn't think she'd know anything about it. The thing that pissed her off more than anything, was the fact her boss would ask how she got on, and she could imagine the smirk on his face once she told him it was all a hoax.

Detective Sergeant Sarah Carter may have thought differently if she'd arrived a few minutes earlier and seen Ernie leaving dressed as a woman. She may have even stopped the woman and asked her name, and Ernie was so hyped up he may have thought Sarah was the assassin who was looking for him. Anything may have happened. Ernie may have turned on Sarah and assaulted her or frozen up and stood there saying nothing. He may have run away as fast as his heeled shoes could carry him.

Any of those scenarios would have resulted in the day's remaining events turning out differently, but by the time Sarah arrived back at the police station, Ernie was already walking towards the jeweller's he intended to rob.

Chapter Twelve

Ernie had left his flat carrying a bag and disguised as Ann Perkins. The bag was for the jewels, and inside the first bag he had another bag with his spare clothes. Just below the top layer of the clothes he'd hidden the wrist and ankle ties, masking tape, and his gun.

Once the gun was in his hand, he planned to force the salesman and doorman to lie on the floor, preferably in a back room, whilst he put ties and gags on them. He could then put the closed sign up, lock the door of the shop, and take his time emptying the most expensive jewels straight into his bag in the knowledge nobody would disturb him.

Whilst on the tram to the city centre, he wondered whether he should have travelled by bus. Both forms of transport passed the block of flats where he lived but the trams were marginally quicker and that had been his foremost consideration. Once on the tram, he was not so sure he had made the right decision.

On a bus he would have been facing forwards and looking at the backs of the heads of people in front of him, and passengers behind him would only see the back of his head. Trams were different and designed with half the seats facing forwards and the other half facing backwards. There were few places to sit where he was not facing other passengers.

The seating arrangements never bothered him

in the past and had even proved to be a distraction helping to pass the time away during a boring journey. Ernie had often wondered about the passengers he faced. He liked to make up imagined backgrounds for them, and wonder whether they were single or married, local or visitors, undercover police officers or international terrorists, or whether they had more mundane occupations. When bored, his imagination turned to their baggage, and he tried to match their imaginary content to their imaginary occupations.

It was those thoughts that troubled him on this morning's journey. He imagined everyone facing him playing the same game, and he felt as though everyone was scrutinising him and wondering where he was going and what was in his bag. He kept looking at the top of the bag to make sure they could not see the gun or anything else showing he was on his way to commit a robbery. He was sure nothing incriminating was showing, but by the time the tram arrived at Saint Peter's Square he was almost paranoid, felt as though everyone was staring at him, and got off the tram expecting someone to challenge him at any moment.

"Excuse me, love." Ernie turned at the tap on his shoulder to come face to face with a man he just knew was an undercover detective.

"Is there a Wetherspoons near here?" the man said.

"There's a couple," Ernie replied, "and they're both close. There's one over there just across the square, and there's another one just around the corner."

"Thanks love," the man said as he hurried off.

Ernie had been so convinced the man was an undercover detective it took him a few seconds to realise the man wasn't coming back. He stood there watching, expecting him to turn back and arrest him at any moment. Ernie's legs felt weak, and the man was almost across the square before he gave a sigh of relief and felt the strength returning to them. Ernie remained on the platform as he watched the man turn the corner toward Wetherspoons, by which time Ernie's emotions had calmed down. He was still anxious, but nowhere near as afraid as when the man had tapped him on the shoulder.

Leaving the platform, he walked across the square, past Manchester's Town Hall, and towards the jeweller's. At first, his confidence increased with every step. He thought the man may have done him a favour by causing him to remain on the platform as everyone else left. If anyone on the tram had any suspicions about him, they would have gone by now. Lots of people were walking in the same direction as he was, but he didn't recognise anyone from the tram, and as far as he could tell nobody was paying him any attention.

He concentrated on the jeweller's as he approached, and could see the doorman standing in his usual spot in the doorway. Ernie considered walking straight in, but as he got closer, he realised the sunshine was reflecting off the glass windows and preventing him seeing if any customers were inside.

He stopped as he reached the window and looked through as though admiring the display, but focused his eyes beyond the display and into the shop itself. He would put things off for half an hour if there were any customers inside, and go to the nearby cafe and have a coffee until they had left, but through the glass he could only see the shop assistant standing behind the counter.

Ernie's whole concentration was now on the two members of staff as he stood at the window going through his plan for a last time. Nothing else mattered, and he was paying no attention to anyone else in the street. He mistakenly believed he had arrived undetected and was safe from interference.

He knew his address had never been in the newspapers, and he believed nobody had followed him home from the previous day's meeting, but he had been nowhere near as diligent as he thought he'd been. Even whist considering all the people facing him on the tram he had given no consideration to anyone sitting behind him. He had been alert, but not alert enough.

Ernie had not been the only person not paying attention. Sam had been so intent on following the woman he knew as Ann Perkins, that he was unaware that Michael was also following him.

All three had got off the tram at Saint Peter's square using different exits, and Sam and Michael had walked to different sides of the square and watched Ernie on the platform. They followed when Ernie moved off. Ernie, at the front, with Sam following some distance behind, and with Michael bringing up the rear.

Ernie had been totally focused on the job in hand, and oblivious to anyone behind him, just as he was now completely focused on running through the plan in his mind for the last time.

Sam had also been oblivious to anyone behind

him. His focus had been on the woman as she approached the jeweller's. His instructions from Alf had been to ensure he killed her before she entered any jeweller's, and he would have shot her already if there had not been so many people about. His only concern was how to kill her before she entered the jeweller's whilst escaping unscathed and unrecognised afterwards.

Michael knew Sam planned to kill his sister, and he knew Sam's usual weapon was a gun. Michael had brought his own gun, but the last thing he wanted was a public shoot out. He desperately wanted to stop Sam, but wanted to do it without drawing attention to himself. As he saw his sister approach the jeweller's he quickened his pace to close the distance between them.

Ernie took a final deep breath and prepared to enter. He strode towards the recess and turned in to approach the doorman standing outside the door but the next few seconds merged into a blur of confusion as several things happened in rapid succession.

"Damn!" Ernie, who was still a relative novice in the art of walking in high heels, had not seen the slight step his heel came into contact with, but he certainly felt it. His foot came to a complete standstill as his heel hit the step, but the rest of his body continued its forward trajectory, causing him to fall headlong into the doorman. Propelled by the momentum of Ernie's body, they both fell against the glass door which shattered under their combined weight, and they fell through the doorway onto the glass scattered floor of the shop.

"Sorted!" Sam saw Ann fall as soon as he fired his gun, and he made the not unreasonable assumption she had fallen because he had shot her. A momentary smile crossed his lips as he watched the scene for a second before turning away whilst putting his gun and silencer back into his jacket pocket.

"Stop!" Michael saw his shout had been too late to save his sister from being shot, and he reacted with anger, determined to get his revenge. He stepped towards Sam whilst taking his own gun out of his pocket.

Sam was already turning away from the door when he heard Michael's shout and initially thought the sound of breaking glass had drawn the attention of a bystander to what had happened. Almost immediately he realised his initial assumption was wrong as he turned to come face to face with an angry-looking Michael. Sam's gun was almost back into his pocket by this time, but he could see Michael was taking his own gun out. Sam quickly reversed the motion of his hand and withdrew his own gun again too.

There was a split second when Michael and Sam both realised their speeds were matching and they were both withdrawing their guns simultaneously, and another split second when they realised they were both aiming at the same time. Those split seconds merged into an eternity as both guns fired, both bullets drove deep into their respective targets, and both men fell to die before either of them hit the ground.

Chapter Thirteen

The doorman lay on the floor beside Ernie, but didn't understand what had happened. One minute he had been standing outside, preparing to open the door for a customer. The next minute, she fell against him and they had both fallen through the glass door. He looked at the hole in the front of his jacket. His first thought was that the glass had ruined it. It was a new jacket, and he'd paid for it himself. It was whilst he was looking at the hole that the pain hit him. He opened the front of his jacket, saw the growing red stain soaking into the front of his white shirt, and passed out as he stared uncomprehendingly at the stain.

The doorman was not the only person who didn't fully know what was going on. One moment, Ernie had been going into the jeweller's. The next moment, he had tripped over something. He remembered going head first into the doorman, and he remembered them both falling through the glass door and onto the floor. He didn't know the half of it and had no awareness of events outside the shop.

As he struggled to his feet, Ernie saw the growing pool of blood on the doorman's chest. He felt the conflict between nausea and faintness, and for a moment he wondered which would win out. Fortunately, both feelings went as quickly as they had come. He assumed the man must have cut himself on the glass as he fell through the door. The doorman seemed to be unconscious. Glass covered the floor so Ernie cleared some of it away with his foot and then knelt beside him to check for a pulse. An old employer had sent him on a first aid course, and although he only subsequently used his skill to put on a few plasters, he had become the designated first aider and earned extra pay.

He found the pulse. He still remembered some details from his first aid course and knew a fast and weak pulse indicated severe bleeding. It was so weak he could barely feel it, and he realised for the first time the man may die from lack of blood. Ernie pulled the doorman's jacket open and unfastened the shirt buttons. He had to stop himself gagging as his fingers slid on the man's blood, but he could see no glass. There was only a hole in the man's chest, towards his left shoulder, from which blood was spurting out.

Ernie assumed the glass had embedded itself so deep he couldn't see it, and he was unsure what to do. He remembered the treatment for bleeding was to apply pressure and raise the wound, but he instinctively knew he should not be raising the man's chest. He wondered if the wound still had glass in it, and he wondered if he would do more harm than good applying pressure. He looked at the spurting blood, and for a moment he even thought about applying a tourniquet, but thankfully for the patient Ernie could not think of a suitable tourniquet site for a bleeding chest wound. He didn't know what to do, but he knew he should do something.

In the end, for better or worse, he knelt next to the doorman who was lying on his back, and placed the palm of his hand over the hole in the man's chest. It didn't completely stop the flow of blood, but it considerably decreased.

All thought of robbing the jeweller's had gone from Ernie's mind the moment he fell. His initial thought was to prevent himself falling. His next thought was to prevent himself following the doorman through the glass door. His only current concern was to stop the bleeding from the doorman's chest.

As he knelt on the floor with his palm stemming the flow of blood from the hole in the man's chest, Ernie noticed two sounds reminding him of his real reason for being there. The first sound was an intermittent siren. The second sound was the noise of a heavy metal grill descending outside the jeweller's shop to cover the windows and door. Ernie needed to get away but also needed to help save the doorman's life. He was undecided what to do, but the downward speed of the shutters made the decision for him. Whilst he was still deliberating, the metal grill reached the ground and cut off his means of escape.

The shop assistant had remained behind the counter the whole time. He had seen everything, but even he didn't fully understand what occurred. He assumed Ann was a customer. He also assumed the two men outside, one of whom shot his doorman, were robbers. Almost instinctively he had placed his foot on the alarm button on the floor to activate the alarm and lower the protective grill before going to help his doorman.

As the man from behind the counter approached him, Ernie continued to place the heel of his hand over the hole in the doorman's chest and looked at the newly lowered grill. Through the grill, he noticed for the first time, the two men lying on the ground outside. The closest man lay face up in a growing pool of blood, but Ernie didn't know who he was or what happened to him. The man furthest away from the door was also in a growing pool of blood. He may have recognised him if he'd been lying face up and closer, but he was face down and further away, so he didn't recognise him either.

"What the hell just happened?" was all he could think of to say.

"Thank God you're all right." said the assistant. "I think we're safe now. One of those robbers outside shot Dave. They must have intended robbing us, but they seem to have got in each other's way and it looks like they shot one another by accident. Are you all right there for a minute?" Without waiting for a reply, the shop assistant took out his mobile phone, and asked for the police and an ambulance.

Ernie was feeling rather shell-shocked. He did not know what to do or say next. For someone who almost always had a plan, for once he was clueless. He stayed exactly where he was, to see how things panned out. Kneeling on the floor beside the doorman he just kept the palm of his hand pressed as hard as he could over the wound. The man's chest was moving up and down so at least he was breathing, and he didn't seem to be bleeding as much.

Ernie had planned to rob the jeweller's and to be well on his way before they gave the alarm. No hope of that now. Not with the siren going off, the grill blocking his escape, and a crowd already beginning to gather outside. He stayed where he was. Kneeling beside the doorman at least gave him time to think about what he should do next, but despite all the effort he put into his thought process, he still didn't know how to extricate himself from the position he was in.

It was only a few minutes before both the police and the ambulance arrived, and the jeweller opened the shutter to let them in.

One paramedic took over from Ernie and turned the doorman onto his side so he could treat the front and back at the same time. "You've done a good job there," he said. "You probably saved his life."

Ernie gasped. Once the man was lying on his side, he could see a much larger hole in the man's back that Ernie had not even realised was there.

As he heard Ernie's gasp, the paramedic looked up and smiled at him. "The exit wound is always larger than the entry one, but by pressing on his chest you pressed his back into the floor. That stopped a lot of the bleeding from the back too. Well done."

"It was nothing. Just glad I was here to help." Ernie couldn't drag his eyes away from the wound in the doorman's back. He stared without blinking, suddenly realising his vision was disappearing from the peripheries. He sat down on the floor before blacking out completely, and the tunnel slowly enlarged until he could see everything again. The hole he had pressed his palm onto seemed rather clinical. Small and round. The hole in the man's back was different. Larger, and jagged. He felt faint, but he also felt an idiot. Seeing the hole in the man's chest, he had plugged it with the palm of his hand but never considered the glass may have gone right through. He supposed he should have checked, but never gave it a thought. He had been too stunned by the suddenness of it all.

"You all right?" The paramedic realised how pale Ernie had become. "If you feel faint, just lie down for a moment until you feel better. Don't go collapsing on me."

"No. I'm fine now. It was just seeing his back. Felt faint for a minute. Didn't realise the wound was so big."

"If it hadn't been for your prompt action, he may have bled out before we got here. He was lucky the bullet didn't go through his heart. It was only inches away." Whilst the paramedic was talking, he had applied large dressings to cover the whole of the doorman's front and back chest whilst his companion had inserted a plasma drip into the man's arm. "He's stable enough for us to take to hospital now. Nicked a minor artery, but missed all the major ones. He should be fine."

When the paramedic mentioned a bullet, Ernie became convinced his gun must have caused the injury by going off accidentally as they had fallen. He felt sick. He hadn't intended to shoot anyone. The most he'd intended doing was firing a shot into the ceiling to convince them he was serious. Ernie was aware of the loaded pistol in his bag. He looked towards it, expecting to find an incriminating hole where the bullet had passed through, but he couldn't see one.

By now, he had fully recovered from his nausea at the sight of the exit wound. The feeling had gone almost as quickly as it had come once he had sat down on the floor. The paramedics had covered the man's wounds and there was nothing more Ernie could do. His overwhelming urge now was to run, and he pushed himself to his feet. The jeweller had raised the shutter to allow the emergency services to enter, so it was no longer blocking his way. The doorman was safely in the care of the paramedics, and there was no reason for him to stay.

The growing sound of sirens gave evidence that more police vehicles would soon arrive. Only the first two police officers were on scene. One was talking to the shop assistant and taking details about what had happened, and the other was outside holding back a growing number of bystanders. The two bodies still lay on the ground, and the second policeman had his hands full trying to secure the scene and stop the crowd getting too close. If Ernie was to go before other police officers arrived he knew he must go immediately.

"I'm still feeling faint. Can I step out for a minute for some fresh air?"

The police officer who was talking to the assistant turned towards him. "That's fine, madam, but please don't go too far. I'll be with you in a minute."

"Okay. Thank you." Ernie stepped outside and saw that the solitary police officer outside was not yet fully in control of the situation.

"You okay, love?" the police officer said.

"Yes. Just shaken up. Came out for a bit of fresh air."

"I'd stay near the door if I were you until we've got more bodies to hold the crowd back." The police officer had turned his back to the crowd momentarily to speak to Ernie, but they surged forwards as he was speaking and he turned to face them again. He was constantly telling them to move back, but however much they may have wanted to comply, they were being pushed forward by those standing at the rear who wanted a better view.

Ernie could see the young officer had his hands full, and all his attention was on the crowd which he could barely control. Ernie walked along the front of the shop until he reached the edge of the crowd, pushed his way to the back, and walked away as quickly as possible in the opposite direction to the approaching sirens.

"Hello again." Ernie had been so intent on walking in the opposite direction to the approaching sirens that he hadn't noticed Detective Inspector Jones arriving with his detective sergeant. They were both within walking distance when they'd received the call, and Ernie bumped into them as he turned a corner in his anxiety to get away.

The detective inspector had spent a few minutes talking to him in the bank and recognised him straight away. "I've been hoping to find you," he said. "My sergeant has spent some considerable time looking for you."

Chapter Fourteen

"I'm sorry, I can't stop." Said Ernie. "I've got somewhere I need to be." The last place he wanted to be was near the jeweller's.

"That's as maybe, but I'd like you to come with us." The last thing Detective Inspector Jones wanted was to let the woman disappear for a second time. He knew that lot at the station would never let him forget it. He put his arm around her and gently steered her back towards the jeweller's before turning towards his sergeant. "Let me introduce you to Ann Perkins," he said, "the lady we've been looking for."

"Hello Ann. I've even been to your flat looking for you," Sarah said.

"My flat?" said Ernie.

"City Court, Droylsden. I was there looking for you this morning."

Ernie wondered how she knew Ann Perkins was living in Droylsden. He had not given his address to anyone, but she'd found out somehow. "That's my brother's flat," he said. He thought it prudent to tell her the same story that he'd told his neighbour. "I've recently come back from living in Australia, so I'm staying with my twin brother till I find somewhere of my own to live. Anyway, can't stop. Perhaps I can pop into the police station to see you later." Ernie tried to shrug off the detective inspector's arm, only to find it immovable.

"Sorry Ann," he said. "Not a chance. I can't

afford to let you disappear again. I need a statement about your part in the bank robbery."

He gulped. If they had found out where he lived, maybe they had found out he had intended to rob the bank too. He didn't see how they could have done, but he couldn't see how they found out where he lived either, "My part in the robbery?" He tried unsuccessfully to pull away again.

"Your part in foiling the robbery," said the detective inspector. "If it hadn't been for your bravery who knows what may have happened. I should have taken a statement on the day and not let you disappear, but better late than never."

By this time, they were almost back at the jeweller's. "Once we've found out what's happened at the jeweller's," he said, "we'll take you back and get a full statement. It's probably a false alarm. It usually is."

As they approached, Ernie saw the uniformed police officer holding the crowd back was now being helped by some others. The officer saw him returning with the detective inspector and his sergeant. "Wondered where you'd got to," he said. "Thought you'd got lost in the crowd. I see you've already met the detective inspector."

"Yes. We've met," said Ernie.

The detective inspector looked at Ernie inquisitively and instinctively tightened his grip on his arm. "Don't tell me you're involved in this too."

"She was a customer," said the constable. "Rendered first aid to the doorman and saved his life."

"Did you now," said the inspector. "That's quite a coincidence, and I don't believe in coincidences. Do you sergeant?"

"No, me neither," she said as she stared at him.

The detective inspector and his sergeant could see the two men lying dead in pools of blood on the pavement, but they didn't yet know who they were or what had happened.

"You stay here with me," said the Inspector. "My sergeant will get a full picture of what's been going on." The inspectors grip tightened still further, conveying to Ernie that the request was not one he had any choice about. "You seem to have a knack of being in the wrong place at the wrong time. How did you get involved in this?"

"I was just window shopping," said Ernie. "I'd been looking in the jeweller's window to see if there was anything I liked, and I went to have a closer look inside. I tripped as I went in, fell against the doorman, and we both fell through the glass door. I thought the glass had cut him, so I gave him first aid."

Sarah Carter returned. "Seems the two men outside were trying to rob the jeweller's, boss." she said. "One of them shot the doorman, and in the confusion, they also seemed to have shot one another. Apparently, our heroine gave first aid to the doorman. Kept him alive until the ambulance arrived."

The detective inspector was loath to let the woman go. He was at the scene of a double shooting, and she was his only prisoner. "Are you telling me this woman was not an accomplice of some sort?"

"Afraid so, boss. The guy in the shop said the doorman would have been dead but for her. Thinks she's a real hero. Knelt in the doorway despite the two gunmen threatening her from outside. Jeweller thinks they had been trying to shoot their way in past the doorman, but seeing her in the doorway confused them and caused them to shoot one another."

The detective inspector guided Ernie towards the still broken door and into the jeweller's shop itself. He was still loath to release his grip on her completely, but the evidence was stacking up in favour of her presence being wholly coincidental. "Perhaps you had better tell me exactly what happened," he said to Ernie.

Ernie was conscious he still possessed a loaded pistol in his bag. He was desperate to get away but there seemed little chance at the moment. "There's not much more I can tell you." he said. "As I went into the jeweller's I tripped and fell. By the time I'd picked myself up it was all over. The two men were lying on the ground outside, and the doorman was bleeding from a chest wound. I kept my hand over it to stop the blood and stayed there till the ambulance arrived."

"Right." said the inspector. "That's another statement I need. I'll arrange for my sergeant to take you back to the station in one of the police cars."

"That's not necessary," said Ernie. "I can get there on the bus to save you the bother."

"No bother," said the inspector. "I'm still not fully convinced you had nothing to do with this so I'm sending you with my sergeant." He turned to his sergeant. "I don't want her disappearing again. Make sure you stay with her at all times and keep your eye on her till you get back to the station. You can take a full statement about the jeweller's, and whilst you're at it take a full statement about the bank. I don't want her out of your sight until she completely satisfies us she's an innocent bystander."

"Right, boss. Come on Ann," said the detective sergeant.

"Oh dear. If I must. My poor bladder. I won't be able to get as far as the police station without going to the toilet. Are you sure I can't come to the station later?"

"Not a chance," said the sergeant. "We're not falling for that again. You heard my boss. You're coming with me, and if you wet yourself in my car, I'll do you for criminal damage, and then you'll be in even more trouble."

The jeweller overheard the conversation, and in his opinion there had been no need for that last remark. Ann was his hero, and the police ought to be more respectful towards her. "There's a toilet in the back of the shop," he said. "She'll be more comfortable if you allow her to go to the toilet first. I'll show you where it is."

The detective inspector nodded and allowed Ernie to go with the jeweller into the storeroom at the back of the shop. There was a doorway into a single toilet cubicle, but Ernie also noticed a bolted doorway leading out to the rear.

"Thank you." Ernie went into the toilet and closed the door. He was hoping there would be a large window he could climb through, but there wasn't even a small window, just a noisy expel-air fan. He didn't really need to use the facilities, so he just sat there and waited, wondering what to do and listening to see if there was still anyone outside. He was almost certain the jeweller returned to the shop. If he was quiet, perhaps he could leave the toilet, creep to the bolted door and make his escape out the back.

He put his ear against the toilet door but the only thing he could hear was the detective inspector speaking to someone in the main shop. He flushed the toilet hoping the noise would cover the sliding of the back door bolts and opened the toilet door as quietly as he could.

"Hello there." Detective Sergeant Sarah Carter had been patiently waiting for him. "Are you ready now? It seems we will be in one another's company for quite a while," she said. "My boss will never forgive me if I let you disappear before we've got your statements."

It was late by the time Ernie got home. True to her word, she gave him no chance to disappear. Detective Sergeant Carter had been a constant companion and not let him out of her sight. She took him to Manchester Central Park Police Station and sat him down in an interview room to write a full statement about what happened.

"I need to start with your full name, your full date of birth, and your address."

Ernie was not all that good at lying, but he knew the secret was to keep it as close to the truth as possible. That way, if he got asked the same questions later, he could still remember the answers. He gave the name Ann Perkins, gave his own date of birth, and gave his real address.

"You do live at seven City Court in Droylsden then?"

"I do now. I told you. I've been living in Australia, but I'm staying with Ernie, my twin brother, whilst I look for somewhere of my own."

"Most of the people I spoke to had never heard of you."

"That's because I've not been there long. Ernie's lived there for years. Everyone knows him, but I keep myself to myself. Many of the neighbours won't have even seen me."

"That explains it then," she said.

If Ernie had been a suspect, the Detective Sergeant would have made more checks. Ernie was a witness not a suspect, so she accepted the information at face value before guiding Ann Perkins through the rest of the statement.

She knew there was something different about Ann Perkins, and she took her time taking Ann through the statement whilst examining her. She didn't need to be a detective to wonder about the gender of the woman in front of her. Detective Sergeant Carter could not help notice that Ann tottered when she walked, as though she wasn't used to walking in heels. She also noticed Ann's hair was obviously a badly fitting dark brown wig with wisps of grey showing underneath. It was getting late in the day by this time, and there was also a noticeable five-o'clock shadow; stubble that had appeared since they first met outside the jeweller's. There were other things too. The stance, the gait, the movements; there was something different about her. Even how she was writing her statement whilst seated with her legs wide apart seemed wrong.

Sarah was loath to put her conclusion into words as it was too easy to leave herself open to a criticism of political incorrectness. Eventually, although concluding Ann Perkins was probably transsexual, she decided to not ask directly. She tried to get the information by a less direct question. "Have you ever been known by any other names?" she asked.

Ernie realised there were advantages to being a woman. If he had dressed as a man the police would have assumed he was one of the robbers. They would have questioned him as a suspect and found the gun. They hadn't found it because, apart from the few minutes the detective inspector kept hold of him, they had always treated him as a witness. He felt compelled to remain in character.

"Other names? Yes, dear, of course. My maiden name was Wright, same as my brother. Perkins is my married name." It seemed disloyal to his late wife to change her gender, but he continued anyway. "My husband died from a stroke several years ago. That's why I've moved back to England."

It had entered Detective Sergeant Carter's mind that Ann may be transgender, but it had never entered her mind that the woman in front of her may be a criminal. The woman was a hero. She saved the doorman's life. Heroic at the bank too. The woman was a little strange, but she'd met many strange people during her time in the police and thought no more about it. She completed the statement and asked Ernie to read it through.

He took the form, and read from the top, confident that the detective had written everything he had said. The first sentence pulled him up short. 'This statement is true to the best of my knowledge and belief and I make it knowing that, if it is tendered in evidence, I shall be liable to prosecution if I have wilfully stated in it anything I know to be false, or do not believe to be true.'

He fixed his eyes on the phrase about being liable to prosecution, and it took an effort of will to continue reading down the page. Everything the detective had written was true. All the action was there exactly as it had happened. There was just the minor matter of his name, gender, and motive. The facts were real. It was Ann Perkins who was a fake.

By the time he had read to the end of the statement, he had half convinced himself it was unimportant. All the events were true. He had omitted to say he had been entering to rob the jeweller's, but everything he saw and heard was true and had been recorded correctly. He was worried, and he wondered if he was doing the right thing, but he ignored his conscience, and scribbled Ann Perkins' signature below the first paragraph, and at the bottom of each page.

It was easier for him the next time. It was too late to change his mind once he signed the first signature. After he had given his statement about the shooting, the detective made him write another witness statement about the bank robbery. By the time he had finished he was desperate to go home, and he barely read the accusatory first paragraph as he again signed as Ann Perkins.

Chapter Fifteen

MANCHESTER EVENING NEWS
Thursday 11 April 2019
Brave Woman Foils Jeweller's Raid
Second Robbery Prevented

A forty-nine-year-old woman is the toast of Manchester today following a triple shooting during an attempted armed robbery yesterday morning at Jonathan Jones Jeweller's in the centre of Manchester. Ann Perkins had been entering the jeweller's shop as two well-known members of Manchester's criminal fraternity tried to shoot their way past Dave Watson, the long serving doorman.

Perkins, realising what was about to happen, and with complete disregard for her own safety, pushed Watson out of the line of fire and saved his life. A bullet hit Watson in the chest causing severe loss of blood. It would have gone through his heart had it not been for the prompt action of Perkins, who having already prevented Watson from being fatally shot, treated his injury to prevent further blood loss and saved his life for a second time whilst waiting for the emergency services to arrive.

Ann Jones, of Manchester Ambulance Service was full of praise for Ann Perkins' action, "If it had not been for her prompt action, Mr Watson would undoubtedly have died before our ambulance arrived." Divisional Superintendent Philip Johnson of Greater Manchester Police also praised Perkins' bravery. "With no regard for her own safety she threw herself between the gunmen and Watson and saved his life."

Police are still investigating the circumstances,

and they particularly want to know how the two gunmen apparently fatally shot one another during the confusing first few seconds of the robbery. Both men were later pronounced dead at the scene, and police are appealing for anyone who may have been in the area at the time and who may have witnessed the incident, or filmed it on their mobiles, to come forward. The two gunmen are both known to the police but names are being withheld until they have informed their families. Mr Watson remains in a critical condition in Manchester Royal Infirmary, but his injuries are no longer described as life threatening. Mr Edward Fitzgerald, the manager, confirmed the men stole nothing during the attempted robbery.

Regular readers may recall this newspaper publishing an appeal for information about a plucky bystander who foiled an armed robbery at the Manchester Piccadilly Gardens branch of the Santander Bank in March. We understand that bystander was also Ann Perkins. On that occasion she tackled an armed bank robber and grappled him to the floor.

Despite having successfully tackled gunmen on two separate occasions Mrs Perkins remains modest about her part in foiling the robberies. She recently returned to England from Australia where she has been living, but she was born and bred in Manchester and typifies the grit and determination for which Mancunians are renown. In a statement to our crime reporter earlier today Perkins downplayed her bravery. "I'm no hero. I was just in the right place at the right time. Anyone would have done the same thing." This newspaper and its readers would beg to differ, and we salute her bravery and determination.

The days immediately following the raid on the jeweller's passed quickly for Ernie. So quickly in fact that the speed of events left him rather dazed. The national press picked up the article in the Manchester Evening News, and whilst none of the reporters offered to buy his story for cash, they were all willing to interview him over a meal or a drink.

The story was graphic enough, but Ernie embellished it with each telling, and by the end of the second day he had appeared on both local television channels and on one of the national channels. He had dressed as a woman each time, and Ann Perkins had become something of a celebrity. Things were going well for Ernie, but nothing lasts forever.

It was whilst he was going out dressed as Ann, that he next bumped into his neighbour. Ernie was on his way to do another interview, and Colin was taking some rubbish to the outside bins.

Colin smiled at him. "Hello Ann," he said. "You're looking radiant today. I've not forgotten about that coffee I owe you. How about later this afternoon? Perhaps we could meet up in town?"

The last thing Ernie needed was for his amorous neighbour to chat him up. "I'd love to, Colin," he said, "but not today. I haven't time. Next week perhaps."

Colin's smile got wider. She had remembered his name. He must have made an impression. "I'll hold you to that," he said.

Bob Hinchcliffe's plea hearing for the earlier

attempted bank robbery took place at Manchester Crown Court just three and a half weeks after his remand from the magistrate's court, and less than a week after the robbery at the jeweller's. Because they had caught him in the act, Hinchcliffe's solicitor and barrister both knew he had no option but to plead guilty. A long custodial sentence could immediately follow his guilty plea but his barrister would press for a pre-sentence report to give the solicitor time to find mitigating circumstances. It was clutching at straws, but anything was better than nothing. On the day, however, things did not go exactly as planned.

"Robert Hinchcliffe, you are charged with attempted robbery contrary to Section 8(1) of the Theft Act 1968, that on Wednesday 21 March 2019 you entered the branch of the Santander Bank at 130 Market Street, Manchester, with intent to steal, and immediately before, or at the time of doing so, and in order to do so, you used force on any person or sought to put any person in fear of being then and there subjected to force. How do you plead, guilty or not guilty?"

"Not guilty."

There was an audible gasp from the courtroom, not least from Hinchcliffe's lawyers.

"You are further charged with carrying a firearm with intent to commit an indictable offence contrary to Section 18(1) of the Firearms Act 1968, that on Wednesday 21 March 2019 you were a person who had with him a firearm with intent to carry out a robbery contrary to Section 8(1) of the Theft Act 1968. How do you plead, guilty or not guilty?"

"Not guilty."

Another gasp. This time a little quieter because the plea was not so unexpected.

"You are further charged with possession of a firearm whilst having previously been convicted of a crime contrary to Section 21(1) of the Firearms Act 1968, that on Wednesday 21 March 2019 you were in possession of an air pistol whilst being a person previously sentenced to a term of three years or more imprisonment. How do you plead, guilty or not guilty?"

"Guilty."

This time, as well as the audible gasp, his solicitor was scratching his head. All the charges related to the same incident, and he couldn't understand why his client would plead not guilty to the first two charges, and guilty to the third.

"My Lord." Hinchcliffe's barrister was on his feet. The last time they had spoken to Hinchcliffe was only a few minutes before the start of the hearing, when he'd told them he would be pleading guilty. "My client's pleas are different to the pleas I was expecting. I would like to request a short adjournment whilst I take additional instructions."

"Very well." The judge had also been expecting guilty pleas. "We will adjourn for thirty minutes."

His escorts took Hinchcliffe down to one of the holding cells under the courtroom where his barrister and solicitor joined him.

"I've changed my mind," Hinchcliffe said. "I know how it looks, but I'm not guilty. I'll hold my hand up to having the air pistol, but I never intended to rob the bank."

His lawyers both looked at one another; neither knowing what to say, and both waiting for the other to say something. The solicitor finally broke the silence. "You realise pleading guilty saves everyone time and money and you get a shorter sentence as a result?"

"Yes, I realise that," said Hinchcliffe, "but I'm not guilty."

"And you realise if you plead not guilty, but they find you guilty, you'll receive a longer sentence?"

"Yes," he said, "but I'm not guilty."

"But they saw you waving your gun about and demanding money from the cashier."

Bob Hinchcliffe had been expecting the question and had practised his reply. Time spent on remand had given him plenty of time to think things through and he had slowly decided to plead not guilty. So slowly that he only made his final decision as he was about to plead guilty that morning.

The events at the bank had happened so quickly it had taken him weeks to process everything. Yes, he had taken a gun out of his pocket, and yes, he had entered the bank with a loaded and totally illegally nine-millimetre pistol. But by some unknown quirk of fate it had changed into an unloaded air pistol by the time they arrested him. He could say he took the gun out because his wallet had slipped lower than the pistol in his pocket.

He had shown the cashier a note, but they hadn't searched him until he arrived at the police station. Whilst being taken there in a police car, he had shoved the note down the back of the rear seat, and as far as he knew they had never found it. Nobody had mentioned it.

He said 'this is a robbery, give me the money',

but the witnesses could have misheard. He could have said, 'this is no robbery', to stop the cashier being frightened by the pistol, and 'give me my money.'

The more he thought about it, the more he convinced himself he may just get away with it.

"I know it looks bad, but it was all a misunderstanding. I knew nobody would believe me because of my previous convictions. I'd been in Manchester to buy an air pistol to kill rats, and I took it out of my pocket to get to my wallet. I never intended to rob the place, but as soon as I took the gun out it was too late. The bank clerk immediately screamed, and as I tried to explain things someone knocked me to the floor and sat on me. They winded me so much I couldn't talk."

"Why didn't you say so sooner?" His solicitor did not believe the story. "That was weeks ago. Why leave it till today?"

"It was the shock I suppose," said Hinchcliffe. "It completely stunned me. The reaction of the cashier stunned me when I accidentally pulled the gun out. The woman stunned me when she attacked me and knocked me over, and I was stunned by the arrival of armed police, and by the arrest."

"But you said nothing at the police station either; not even to me," said his solicitor.

"Everything happened so fast at the police station. I didn't know what to say, so I said nothing. I knew they wouldn't have believed me anyway, and before I knew it they'd remanded me in custody."

"That still doesn't explain why you never mentioned it to me when I visited you last week to prepare for today's plea hearing, or even earlier this morning when we both visited you."

"I'm telling you now," said Hinchcliffe. "I never intended to rob the bank. It was all a mistake and very traumatic. The events at the bank. Being interrogated at the police station. The court appearance. Being remanded in custody. Everything was traumatic. I think I may have post-traumatic stress. I haven't been able to think clearly since the event, and I'm only thinking clearly now."

Lawyers are a weird breed. They cannot argue their client's innocence if the client tells them they are guilty. That would entail them lying in court. However, if their client says they are innocent, they must represent their client and present their client's arguments to the best of their ability even if they believe their story is a load of rubbish.

The solicitor and barrister listened with incredulity to Hinchcliffe's protestations of innocence, and to his reasons his protestations had been so slow in being voiced. They were ninety-nine percent sure Hinchcliffe was guilty, but they would give their client the benefit of that one percent. From here on they were duty bound to try and find evidence to back up their client's story, and to persuade the Crown Prosecution Service there was no case to answer. If they were unsuccessful at that first task, they would try the same argument on the judge. Finally, if both those attempts failed, and it came down to a full hearing, they were duty bound to convince a jury their client was innocent. In their heart of hearts neither of them thought their client had a chance, but their professional code of conduct meant they had to give him the benefit of the doubt.

All the talking had been between Hinchcliffe and his solicitor. The barrister had listened intently but hadn't spoken since entering the cell. He looked at Hinchcliffe, and then looked at the solicitor. "Right! We need a medical examination and a mental health report that highlights the amount of stress our client has been under, and we need to take another in-depth look at the bank's CCTV. The police only got statements from a few of the people in the bank at the time of the robbery, so we need to track down and get statements from every one of them, from the time he first went in until they took him out. If they can't remember the exact words he said, we need their statements to say that they can't exactly remember. We also need a statement from the shop where he bought the air pistol, and from now on we need to manage this case as a not guilty plea."

"The statement about the purchase of the gun may be difficult," Hinchcliffe said. He knew he had not bought it.

"Why difficult?"

"Because I didn't get a receipt," he said. "It was second-hand, from a guy on gumtree. We met in a pub in Ancoats. I gave him the cash, and he gave me the gun. If I'd known what would happen I'd have asked for a receipt, but he never offered one and I never asked for one."

"Don't worry about that for now," said his barrister. "Let's get back into court and get today over with first. We can go into all the details later."

Everyone returned to the courtroom, and the hearing eventually recommenced.

"Have you taken fresh instructions from your client?" asked the judge.

"Yes, my Lord. My client does not intend to change his plea. He has pleaded not guilty to the first indictment of robbery, and not guilty to the second indictment of carrying a firearm with intent to commit an indictable offence. He has pleaded guilty to the third indictment of possessing a firearm, and those remain my client's pleas. He has previously been sentenced to over three years in prison, and he admits possessing an air pistol. However, he had a good reason for having the air pistol in his possession, and did not realise it was classed as a firearm. He would like an opportunity of explaining his reasons to you before you pass sentence for that offence."

"I have no intention of passing sentence today," said the judge. "I will adjourn sentencing until I have dealt with the other two indictments at a full hearing."

"There is still the small matter of bail my Lord." The barrister thought he had no chance, but it was his duty to ask.

Judges should be impartial, but this judge had already read the pre-trial evidence, and already decided Hinchcliffe was guilty of all three charges. He did not know why the man was wasting his time by pleading not guilty, but he knew he did not deserve bail. "They have charged your client with robbery whilst in possession of a firearm. Given the serious nature of the offences I am refusing bail."

"Thank you, my Lord," the barrister replied.

Chapter Sixteen

"Ann Perkins?"

The voice seemed vaguely familiar. He didn't immediately recognise it, but assumed it was a reporter phoning for another interview. "Who's calling, please?" Ernie had become rather cagey by this time because he'd received quite a few crank calls due to the publicity. If this call turned out to be a crank, he could tell them they'd got the wrong number.

"Mrs Perkins. This is Detective Inspector Arthur Jones from Manchester Police."

"Oh, Hello!" Ernie immediately feared the worse. He assumed the police finally realised he had intended to rob the bank and jeweller's. He did not know how the detective could have found out, but in that instant, he was sure he was in deep trouble. Holding his breath, he waited for the inevitable request to give himself up at the nearest police station for further questioning. He even glanced towards the window to see if he could see any flashing blue lights or hear any sirens.

"It's about Bob Hinchcliffe, the robber you tackled at the Santander Bank. He appeared at Manchester Crown Court earlier today."

"Ah!" The word burst out of his mouth as he finally released his breath in relief. The detective wasn't phoning to tell him he was being arrested. He was phoning to tell him Hinchcliffe had already appeared in court and pleaded guilty. It was all over, and he could finally relax. "That's fantastic news," he said. "Thanks for telling me. It's very kind of you to phone me in person. I'm glad that's over with. I don't mind telling you I was nervous about attending court and giving evidence in front of everyone."

"I know what you mean," said the inspector. "I can still remember the first time I gave evidence, and it's always nerve-wracking if you've never done it before. That was many years ago now in my case, but I still remember what it was like. You've misunderstood me though. I'm not calling to let you know it's over, I'm calling to let you know you will have to give evidence after all. That's why I wanted to phone you straight away. You will have to give evidence I'm afraid. Hinchcliffe pleaded not guilty this morning."

"Not guilty! How can he have pleaded not guilty? We both saw him robbing the bank."

"We did," said the inspector, "and I fully expected him to plead guilty this morning, but he pleaded not guilty. They even adjourned so his lawyers could persuade him to change his plea, but he was having none of it and kept insisting he was innocent. They've had to adjourn the case for a full hearing and they'll be calling both of us as witnesses."

Ernie had been worrying about a lot of things lately but giving evidence in court had not been one of them. He'd worried about lying in his statement, but he'd been convinced he wouldn't have to repeat that evidence in court. "Sergeant Carter told me I wouldn't have to give evidence even if he pleaded not guilty," said Ernie. "She told me my written statement would be enough."

"She shouldn't have said that I'm afraid," said

the inspector. "Normally she'd be right, but we can make no guarantees. In many cases there's no need for witnesses to appear because the prosecution and defence agree not to challenge a written statement. I fully expected that to happen in this case. Our evidence is damning, but it's straightforward so there's nothing to argue about as far as I can see. Unfortunately, it's not down to me. Now Hinchcliffe's changed his plea, his defence team are challenging some statements so we have to attend."

"What! Everyone from the bank?"

"Er... no," said the inspector. "Just you and me. There are statements from everyone in the bank now. Most are unchallenged so those witnesses won't need to attend. Unfortunately, the defence do want to challenge our statements, so we both have to give our evidence orally so they can cross-examine us."

Ernie knew his statement was true and that he had nothing to worry about, but it still worried him. The statement may be true, but the person making the statement was a lie. He had made the statement in the name of Ann Perkins, and on the assumption he would not have to attend court and he found the thought of being cross-examined extremely worrying. To prevent being charged with perjury for lying about his name, he would need to attend court in character as Ann Perkins. He would also have to attend knowing he had entered the bank to commit his own armed robbery all the time he was in the witness box giving evidence against someone else who entered to do the same thing.

"Do I have to go?" he asked. The more he

thought about the consequences, the more determined he was to avoid going, If there was a way out of it, Ernie would take it.

"I'm afraid you do have to go," said the inspector. "My evidence is the same as yours, so you'll have nothing to worry about."

Not exactly, thought Ernie. "What if he changes his mind and pleads guilty?" asked Ernie. "Can he change his mind again?"

"He can do that any time, but it's not likely. If he pleads not guilty but then gets convicted, he'll get a longer sentence. I'm sure his legal team will have told him that already. I know you're anxious at the thought of giving evidence, but just stick to the facts and you'll be fine."

Ernie ran through the facts in his mind and was still unconvinced. "Is there any way to get out of it?" he asked.

"Afraid not," said the inspector.

"What if I just don't turn up?"

"I wouldn't advise it," said the inspector. "As things stand at the moment, they'll ask you to attend court. If you don't turn up on the day, the case will get adjourned and they'll send a witness summons ordering you to attend on the new date. If you don't turn up at the new date they'll issue an arrest warrant, arrest you and take you to court by force and order you to give evidence."

Ernie was still desperate to find a way out. "What if I still refuse to give evidence?"

"It's not worth it. I know you're eager to avoid it, but if you kept on refusing the judge could put you in a cell until you change your mind, and ultimately imprison you for thirty days."

"That's not fair. I could be sick and not able to

give evidence." said Ernie, already feeling ill.

"True," said the inspector, "but you'd need to provide a doctor's note, and that would only lead to an adjournment to a later date. There's no way of avoiding it I'm afraid. Nobody would ever give evidence if there was. You have to attend court. The whole legal process would break down otherwise."

"I see." Ernie did not really see. He did not understand how Hinchcliffe thought he would get away with saying he wasn't robbing the bank when he'd been seen waving his gun about. That's what he'd written in his statement, but Ernie really didn't want to attend court and say so. He'd not even wanted to give a written statement, but a written statement had seemed far better to him than giving evidence and he did not understand why that wasn't enough. From what the inspector said, it looked as though he had no choice but to attend court. "When is the hearing likely to be?" he asked.

"Not sure exactly," replied the inspector. "The average waiting time after an initial hearing is about six months. That would make it around the middle of October. Can't give a firm date because the plea was so unexpected, but we should know in a day or two. You'll be getting a phone call from the Crown Prosecution Service. Then a follow-up letter confirming the date."

"Okay. Thanks for letting me know." He thought things were far from okay.

"You're welcome. Sorry I was the bearer of unwelcome news, but I thought you'd want to know as soon as possible."

As he hung up, Arthur Jones could not help

feeling sorry for Ernie. He didn't envy him attending court for the first time. Jones had appeared so many times he was not at all nervous, but he still remembered how he had felt the first time. He may not have been nervous, but he was annoyed. There were so many other pressures on his time he could do without having to attend court for this one. He had been in the bank and had seen the offence and couldn't understand how Hinchcliffe could plead not guilty.

Chapter Seventeen

Detective Inspector Jones wasn't the only annoyed person in Manchester. The same feelings were being experienced on the opposite side of the law and order fence. Each day since the jeweller's debacle led to a deepening of Alf Sidebotham's temper. By the day Jones phoned Ernie about his need to give evidence, Alf was shouting at the other gang members and hammering on his desk.

"Your bloody useless the lot of you." He had lost his right-hand man, and for once in his life he didn't know who to turn to for help. He had always depended upon Michael, and when Michael had become troublesome, he had turned to Sam. Now they were both dead, and he was more determined than ever Ann Perkins had to die.

His authority was being increasingly questioned among his own gang and he felt the need to take decisive action. He knew he had made a mistake by announcing his intentions to have the woman killed in advance, and he should have waited until they had killed the woman before taking the credit. Announcing her death in advance had damaged his reputation, and he felt people were laughing at him behind his back. Not only was the woman still alive, but she was also the chief witness for the bank job, and Michael and Sam would both still be alive if it hadn't been for her. The word on the street was that the woman had got the better of him, and he knew only resolute action would save the day. He had lost the only two people he knew who would kill someone on his say so, and he reluctantly concluded he would have to do the job himself.

He would have been angry anyway, but his conclusion that he would have to kill the woman tipped him over the edge into an uncontrollable fury. It would not be his first murder, but his last one had been many years ago. He felt others should take the risks, and he should take a back seat, but there was nobody else he could trust. The only ones he trusted for such a job were both dead.

His diatribe continued as he blamed everyone but himself for the things that had gone wrong, but he eventually ran out of steam as he decided on his next course of action.

"Ann Perkins is bloody dead," he said. "She had Bob arrested in the bloody bank, and she's responsible for Sam and Michael shooting themselves at the bloody jeweller's. I can't rely on any of you bloody lot, so I will do the bloody job myself. I'll bloody kill her."

The men in front of him nodded their approval whilst trying to avoid the shower of spit that was being projected with his every statement. Many of them had been complaining about Alf behind his back, but none of them wanted to disagree with him to his face. Not whilst he was in his present mood, and probably not afterwards either. The other thing they were all sure of, is that none of them wanted to be in Ann Perkins shoes when he got hold of her.

"Get out of my sight," he shouted, and everyone but Jack disappeared as quickly as they could. Alf knew he needed to be alone, and he needed to calm down to give himself time to think. "You too," he yelled.

Jack was reluctant to go. The death of Michael had left a vacuum as Alf's right-hand man, and Jack was hoping Alf would ask him to kill Ann Perkins. Someone had to fill the vacuum, and Jack was hoping Alf would consider him as the man to take over the gang when he eventually retired.

"Get out!" Alf shouted again.

Alf's anger gradually dissipated and eventually he smiled to himself at the thought something good may come from it all. He had heard the whisperings, but the woman's murder would put an end to all talk of her getting one over on him. He would show everyone he was still the boss. He would stamp his authority on things and reassert his leadership by doing future killings himself. He realised he had become soft by depending on others and he determined it would end. Everyone needed to know he was still as hard as he had ever been and had to be feared and respected.

As Jack left the room, he wondered what he could do to persuade Alf he was worthy of stepping into Michael's shoes. It didn't take him long to decide on his course of action. Alf had said he would kill Ann Perkins, but Jack could save him the trouble by killing her first. Once he had killed Ann Perkins, Alf would have to consider him Michael's worthy successor.

Jack had done many things for Alf in the past. He had been especially good at persuading others to make payments they didn't want to make. He had never acted alone, and he had usually acted on the orders of others, but he was longing for an opportunity to step higher up the ladder. Killing

Ann Perkins was the ideal opportunity to show Alf how valuable he could be.

The extensive media coverage given to Ann Perkins meant Alf and Jack both knew a lot more about Ann Perkins than Michael and Sam ever did. They both knew how old she was and where she lived, and thanks to the local television news, they also knew what she looked like. Both of them wrongly believed the woman would be easy to deal with.

Chapter Eighteen

The earlier media frenzy had diminished considerably, and life had gone almost back to normal for Ernie. Nobody was buying him free pints anymore, but he was still dressing as a woman, still being recognised in the street, and still being asked for the odd selfie.

He had concluded the two gunmen who killed one another outside the jeweller's had been targeting him, and now they were both dead he mistakenly believed the danger had passed and all he had to worry about was giving evidence. He would have changed his mind if he had known there were two more murderers looking for him who knew where he lived.

Once it got to eight o'clock at night, Ernie rarely opened his door. There was no knocker or bell on the door to his flat, and the only means of contacting him was from the bell on the communal door outside. There were always kids playing around, and sometimes they would ring the bell and run away laughing, so Ernie invariably ignored any bell during the evening unless he expected someone to call. Whatever happened outside, Ernie felt he didn't need to know about it until the next morning.

The fact Jack was marginally less stupid than Alf, determined what they both did next. Jack planned to go to Ann Perkins home and weigh things up before deciding how best to murder her. Alf already had a plan. He intended going to Ann's home, ringing the bell, and stabbing her as she answered the door.

Jack got off the bus about nine o'clock at night opposite the block of flats and immediately realised none of the flats had doorways facing the road. Only windows faced him, most with curtains or blinds drawn. Walking along the front of the flats he turned into a cul-de-sac which took him to the rear where all the doors where, and the end of the cul-de-sac became a footpath taking him back to the main road.

He walked clockwise around the whole block, realising anyone who left the rear of the flats, whether turning right or left, would always end up on the main road. He found himself back at the bus stop where he started and it had a shelter with a seat from where he could see both ends of the block. He sat down to watch and wait before deciding how to proceed. If anyone noticed him, they would assume he was waiting for a bus.

During the next hour he saw someone leave to catch a bus towards Manchester, and someone else left to walk towards Droylsden. He recognised neither of them, and despite his hour long vigil Jack was unsure if Ann Perkins was at home. Something he had noticed during the past hour though, were the number of teenagers who disappeared around the side of the flats without reappearing.

Whilst Jack mulled over why so many teenagers where about, he saw Alf arrive in his car and park on the main road opposite him. After getting out of his car Alf concentrated on the flats and did not notice Jack sat in the bus shelter's shadow on the far side of the road. Alf walked around to the rear of the flats, and Jack followed at a discrete distance behind, staying back as far as possible whilst still keeping Alf in sight.

When Jack had entered the cul-de-sac earlier, he walked straight through without pausing, so as not to attract attention to himself. Alf's intentions were different. He was so mad that he didn't care who saw him. He was there to do a job, and nobody was going to stand in his way.

There were several blocks in the cul-de-sac, and the second block displayed a sign above the door indicating flats seven to twelve. Alf approached the locked door and pushed unsuccessfully before pushing the bell to number seven with his left hand. His right hand remained in his pocket, clasping the handle of his newly purchased knife. When nobody responded to the bell, he tried the door again before standing back to wait.

During the daytime it was easy to gain access to the flats as people entered or left, but at a little after ten-o'clock at night it was more difficult. Nobody was going in or out, and nobody was answering the bell to flat seven. Alf was unsure how to get into the block of flats, and he stood there waiting for some form of divine intervention. His inability to get at his prey did nothing for his mental stability, and he became even more angry and impatient as each minute passed.

The teenagers Jack saw earlier were regulars. They didn't live in the cul-de-sac itself, but in nearby streets. The local park gates were locked at dusk each evening, and there were no youth clubs in the area, so the teenagers just hung around. They had found the best place to hang around was the cul-de-sac at the back of the flats.

It was the ideal meeting place for them. No passing traffic, and hardly anyone about once it got dark. Nobody could see them from the main road, and few people entered or left the flats at night so there was nobody to chase them away. On the few occasions when someone did enter or leave the flats, they hid behind one or other of the large bushes growing on the opposite side of the cul-de-sac.

It became the recognised place to meet up, and nobody took any notice of them as long as they kept the noise down. Most residents didn't even know they were there. Whilst they could remain practically invisible, they could still see almost everything that happened around them. They melted into the bushes when Alf arrived and watched him try the door and ring the bell. That was nothing out of the ordinary. The youths usually kept the noise down until visitors either entered the building or went away, but neither of those two things happened and Alf just stood there.

These teenagers didn't consider themselves to be a gang in the usual sense. They were just a group of teenagers who enjoyed hanging around together in the way teenagers do, and they'd found the back of the flats to be the ideal place to do it. One or two of them had minor convictions for shoplifting or drinking under age, but most had no contact with the police.

They watched the man outside the door, and when nothing happened one of them eventually broke cover and approached him.

"Need any help mate?" Nobody had designated Chris as the leader, but he was the oldest and tallest, and he had the broadest shoulders and loosest tongue.

Alf nearly jumped out of his skin. His whole attention had been on the door and he hadn't seen the youth approach. Even now he was unaware of the other teenagers still hiding in the bushes. He half turned, saw the youth was no threat, and replied in his usual gruff manner. "Fuck off."

Alf was in the unfortunate position of believing everyone in Manchester feared him and knew him. They knew him well enough within Manchester's pub, club, and criminal circuit, but none of the teenagers knew him. None were old enough to enter pubs and clubs unchallenged, and they confined their drinking to cans of beer, and bottles of cider, purchased from nearby stores.

"What're you doing here?" Chris asked. "What're you hanging around for?"

Alf was already seething with rage, already felt his authority undermined, and already had his hand on his knife. "I won't tell you again. Fuck off!" To make his point, Alf withdrew the knife and waved it towards the boy.

Chris decided to go. He didn't like the look of the man in front of him, nor did he like the look of the knife the man was waving about. The sooner he could put some distance between them the better. If he had been on his own, he would have run away as quickly as he could, but he was aware of all the other youths watching and replied in kind before turning away. "Fuck off yourself you old bastard," he said.

Chris's reply tipped Alf over the edge. Already in a foul mood and intent on murdering someone, the boy had really annoyed him. "Don't tell me to bloody well fuck off. You're bloody dead you little prat." Alf held his knife out in front of him and lunged forward. In his day, Alf would have stabbed Chris with no difficulty, but today was not his day. Chris was younger, had been turning to go, and was sideways on as the lunge carried Alf past him.

It was only as he lunged past the boy that Alf finally realised they were no longer alone. Anticipating problems, the other teenagers had moved forward to support Chris, and Alf now faced a dozen of them. They were just kids, and he already had the forward momentum. Some of them did not even seem to be teenagers. Only ten or eleven. If only they knew who they were dealing with, he knew they would run a mile. He'd show them. He'd knife the first one he came to if they did not get out of his way. His heightened sense of excitement and anger, and his increased adrenalin, moved him forwards. He laughed at the power he had over them before his laugh turned to a grimace as his left knee gave way and caused him to fall.

In his determination to charge forward and take on the teenagers in front of him, he had forgotten about Chris. The blade had only missed his chest by a matter of inches, and Chris kicked out as Alf past him. The kick connected with the back of Alf's left knee, causing his leg to buckle and Alf to fall to the ground.

Alf kept hold of his knife as he fell, but he also put his hand out to prevent his head hitting the floor. He ended up lying face down, with his hand and knife, beside his head. Chris knew he had to stop the knife being used, so he stamped as hard as he could on the hand holding the knife.

The other youths surged forwards. They saw Chris stamp on the man, assumed he had kicked him in the head, and took that as an order for them to do the same. What happened next took only a few seconds, but seemed like several minutes from Alf's viewpoint. They charged in with kicks to almost every part of his anatomy. His head, his body, his arms and his legs; none of them escaped. Most of the youths aimed two or three kicks and then ran, scattering in both directions onto the main road, and then to their homes.

Jack hung well back, close enough to see what was going on but telling himself he was too far away to help even as some of the youths ran past him. He looked on as Alf received his beating and continued watching as Alf struggled unsuccessfully to get to his feet. Jack reached for his phone and made an anonymous call to the emergency services to tell them someone lay injured at the rear of the flats, and after finishing the call he made his way back to the bus stop as the first police car and ambulance arrived.

Jack's bus arrived just as the emergency vehicles turned into the rear of the flats, and he could see no good reason to hang about. Tonight's experience had taught him a few lessons. Alf was not the hard man he thought, and he no longer needed to impress Alf by killing Ann Perkins. He knew tonight's events would finish Alf, and someone else would need to take his place.

Chapter Nineteen

The ambulance arrived to find Alf still on the floor where the youths had left him. An examination revealed they hadn't broken his leg, and when the paramedics helped him to his feet he could stand, albeit painfully. They were more concerned with the kicking he had received to his head and took him to hospital for a full examination. His face was swollen, one of his eyes had closed, and the other was partly closed. His skull appeared to be intact, but as a precaution against him having some inter-cranial bleeding, they kept him in overnight for observation.

A police officer followed the ambulance to hospital and questioned him about the assault once the doctors said he was fit enough to interview.

The constable had taken statements from victims of Alf Sidebotham's henchmen before, but there had never been enough evidence to pin anything on Sidebotham himself. A wry smile crossed his lips as he considered the likelihood someone had got fed up waiting and had dispensed their own form of justice. As far as he was aware, this was the first time Sidebotham had been on the receiving end of a beating, and he thought it was not before time. "I understand from the paramedics that you were attacked," he said.

This was also an unfamiliar experience for Alf. He was used to making no comment when a police officer asked him a question, and this was the first time they had ever interviewed him as a victim.

There was no way he could admit children had beaten him up. "Yes, I was mugged," he said. "Two bloody men tried to take my wallet and phone, but I fought them off."

Shame they didn't do a better job, thought the officer. "Would you be able to recognise them again?" he asked.

"Yes, I'd bloody recognise them. Both well built. I'm six foot and they were both bigger than me." He'd been having problems with some Eastern European's lately, and this seemed an ideal opportunity to cause them some grief. "The one who demanded my wallet spoke with a Polish accent."

Both deserve a medal, he thought. "Any other distinguishing features. Hair colour, tattoos, clothing?"

"It was dark. All I know, is that they were bloody big and well built." He wished he'd had time to make up a better description. "There was quite a bloody scrap before I fought them off. They won't pick on me again in a hurry."

That's why you're in here and they're not, he thought. "And you'd never seen them before?"

"No. Complete bloody strangers."

"Leave it with me, sir," he said. "I'll circulate their details and we'll get back to you if we need any further information." The officer walked away with no intention of searching for the assailants. As far as he was concerned, they'd done everyone a favour, a public service almost.

After his night of observation, they dosed Alf up with prescription pain killers and discharged him. He remained at home for several days whilst the swelling around his eyes went down, and while his aches and pains diminished. He decided to tell his other gang members what he had told the police, that two Eastern European men tried to mug him but he fought them off. He'd half killed them, and they had been lucky to escape with their lives. He wondered if he should embellish the story to explain why they were both able to walk away whilst he needed hospitalisation, but he discounted the idea. The police had accepted his account, so he thought his gang would do so too.

Whilst Alf was hiding himself away until the discolouration had disappeared, the story was already being widely circulated about him being beaten up by a group of young teenagers scarcely old enough to shave.

The summons went out for all gang members to gather to elect a new boss. Some, who had not yet heard the details of what happened, attended out of curiosity. The rest attended because they knew they needed to sort things out. They couldn't afford to have a boss who was being so openly ridiculed, and they were determined to elect a new one.

An election may be too strong a word for what took place. They were all talking over one another. Within minutes everyone knew what happened, but everyone had a different idea who should take over as their new leader and there didn't seem to be a consensus. The arguments came to an abrupt end, and the election arguably took place, when Frank (the Bulldog) Wade forced his way to the front. Waving a gun in one hand he raised his other hand to command silence.

Bulldog had gained his name because he was an ex-boxer whose nose was almost flat. Few would argue with him when he was bare handed. None argued with him when he had a gun in his hand.

"Does everyone agree Alf has let us all down and needs replacing?" There were shouts of agreement, and lots of heads nodded. "In that case, I'm electing myself as the leader in his place. Any objections!" Some looked at one another, but nobody spoke. "Good. That's unanimous then. Thank you for your vote of support gentlemen. I'm glad I have your complete trust. I now consider myself duly elected and I will inform Alf about your unanimous decision."

Nobody felt brave enough to lift their heads above the parapet to raise the procedural point about them voting under duress. Some at the back took the opportunity of slipping out unseen, but the rest stayed in the meeting whilst Frank outlined his plans for the future.

Frank paid Alf a visit at his home the following day.

"Hello Frank. Come in," said Alf. Feeling secure in his own home he had opened the door in his vest, tracksuit bottoms, and slippers. "Sorry I've been out of bloody circulation for a few days. What can I do for you?"

Frank continued to train even though he hadn't boxed competitively for several years. His suit was tailor made to hide his shoulder holster whilst emphasising his bulging muscles. It was his working suit, and he was there to take care of business.

"I've come to say goodbye, Alf." He pulled his gun out and pushed his way in. "It seems you're taking early retirement." He had initially thought it would be best to kill Alf to ensure he would give him no trouble in the future, but Alf had been good to him in the past so he decided to let him live. Alf had never fully recognised his worth, but had always treated him well, so Frank intended to repay the debt. "You're finished Alf. I never thought I'd see the day a few kids would beat you up. There's no way back from that. You've got old, Frank, and soft. You're just not up to it anymore, and that Ann Perkins business didn't help either."

Alf didn't know what to expect when he went to the door, but he wasn't expecting to have a gun pulled on him. He'd told no one about the boys and wondered how Frank knew. Perhaps nobody else knew and he could still bluff it out.

"Bloody hell, Frank. Now look here..."

Frank prodded him with the gun. "No, you look here. Shut up and sit down. It's over. Everyone knows about the kids beating you up and the gang have already unanimously elected me to take your place."

Alf sat in his favourite armchair and looked at Frank standing with his gun at the other side of the room. His own gun wasn't nearby, and Frank was staying too far away to rush. He was certain Frank would shoot him. One of his legs began shaking uncontrollably, and he put a hand on the offending knee to keep it still.

"It's okay Alf," said Frank. "I won't kill you unless you do something stupid. But you are retiring today. I suspect you've got some money for a rainy day, and it's going to piss it down in Manchester. Relax. Enjoy your retirement. Take your money and go to Spain. But go quickly because you won't get another chance. You only have two choices, and I recommend retirement.

You don't really want to know about the other alternative. Do we understand one another?"

The realisation everyone already knew what had happened caused Alf to slump visibly in his seat. His head dropped as all the fight went out of him. Because of his aches and pains, he had slept little the previous couple of nights and felt more tired than he could ever remember. The old days were never like this. Gun or no gun, Alf would have killed anyone who dared to say he was finished. That this was happening in his own home made it worse but he was past caring. He had already considered early retirement. Not this early, but he had known for some time it was getting nearer, and he had looked forward to it. The kicking he'd received, the pain he still felt, the humiliation of facing everyone who knew about the kicking, and the thought of imminent death from Frank's pistol. They were all persuasive arguments for immediate retirement. "How long have I got?" he asked.

"A day would be best," said Frank, "but I'm not a heartless bastard and you've been good to me in the past, Alf. Shall we say one week? If you're still here in one week's time I'll come back to cancel the retirement plan and replace it with a funeral plan. Understand?"

The threat of violence was the one thing Alf understood only too well. He had based his entire career on it and had made his fortune from it. He understood it was time to move on, and for younger people to take his place. He had made his money and was at least being offered the opportunity to retire. "Sounds good to me Frank. One week at the most. I'll be gone long before then." Frank was giving him a lifeline, and he would take it as quickly as possible. If this morning had taught Alf anything, it had taught him things could change quickly. A few minutes ago, he had been in charge of the gang, but those few minutes had brought his departure and his retirement. Frank was letting him live this morning, but may just as easily change his mind this afternoon. Alf knew he needed to move quickly.

In the course of two days the gang had elected Frank as the new leader, and Alf had retired. From that day onward Alf never gave Frank, or Ann Perkins, another thought. They were history and no longer his problem. True to his word, within forty-eight hours he was on a flight from Manchester airport to enjoy his well-earned retirement in Spain. For the first time since his attempted bank robbery, the departure of Alf heralded an end to the current threats on Ernie's life. Unfortunately, there would still be others.

Chapter Twenty

The day of the trial came all too quickly and Ernie approached it with increasing trepidation. He was anxious in case anyone realised he had intended to rob the bank himself, anxious about giving evidence and being cross-examined, and anxious about wearing his disguise and committing perjury.

His more immediate anxiety revolved around what to wear. He only possessed one dress and thought he ought to wear something more up market for court. The first time he went looking for ladies' clothes he had dressed as a man and he found the entire experience difficult. Shop assistants kept giving him strange looks as he held dresses up in front of him and tried to guess which size would fit him. He thought buying women's clothes whilst dressed as a woman would be far easier, and less embarrassing. He could browse the charity shops to his heart's content with no one giving him strange looks. He spent a day looking around and eventually settled on a ladies' suit and jacket worn with a white blouse.

On the day of the hearing, he arrived at Manchester crown court early. He carried a handbag in case he needed to touch up his makeup, and as they searched the bag, he was desperately trying to think if there was anything distinctly male in it. He had packed scent rather than aftershave, but still had a nagging suspicion those searching the bag would know it belonged to a man.

He walked through an airport style security arch, followed by a hand-held scanner being waved all around him. The final security measure involved a physical pat down by a male or female security guard. He stood there impassively as she patted him down, and she finished by rubbing her hands down each thigh to make sure he had hidden nothing under his skirt. If she had started her searching an inch or two higher up, she would have found far more than she'd been expecting, and he would have had a lot of explaining to do.

Ernie was a nervous wreck by the time he passed through all the security measures, but his ordeal was only beginning.

"Would you tell me why you are attending court today?"

"Er, yes. I'm a witness."

"And the name of the defendant?"

"Hinchcliffe. Robert Hinchcliffe."

The security guard looked down his list and beckoned to a woman standing behind him.

"Can you take this lady to the witness suite please? She's a witness in the case against Hinchcliffe."

"Hello. Follow me, please."

The woman led Ernie through a door and down several long corridors until they came to a door with a plaque showing it led to the witness suite. She pressed the bell, and a man opened the door.

"This lady is giving evidence in the Hinchcliffe case," she said.

"If you would like to take a seat," said the man, "I'll let the barrister know you're here."

There were several small coffee tables, half of

which had people sitting at them. Ernie selected an empty table and about five minutes later, he saw Detective Inspector Jones walk in with a barrister.

"Hello Mrs Perkins," said Jones. "Would you like a coffee or anything? There's a machine."

"No. I'm fine thanks," Ernie replied. He was not sure his bladder was up to giving evidence, and he did not want to tempt fate.

"Do you need to read through a copy of your statement to refresh your memory before you go into court?" The barrister was a vision in black. Black shoes and socks. Black trousers with just the hint of a paler pin stripe, a black jacket over which he was wearing a black gown. His white shirt, and the white ribbons hanging down the front of his collar were the only things that lightened the sombre display.

"No thanks. I can remember everything." Ernie had gone over things in his head many times. Besides, he did not want to read the first paragraph. The bit about him being liable to prosecution if the statement was false.

"There should be nothing to worry about," said the barrister. "I'll just be taking you through the statement line by line and asking you what happened. I'll be in court when you see me next, but you'll be fine."

Ernie was unconvinced, but he just smiled meekly. Once the barrister left, he looked around to see if he could recognise anyone else from the bank, but the only person he recognised was Detective Inspector Jones.

"Where are the others?" asked Ernie.

"There's only the two of us," said the inspector. "I told you. The others are not coming. The defence accepted their statements and said they don't need to cross-examine them."

"But they want to cross-examine me?" Ernie still thought this was rather ominous.

"You and me both. You because you tackled him. Me because I arrested him. I wouldn't worry. It's quite normal. You'll be fine."

The barrister and the detective had both told Ernie he would be fine, but Ernie was still unconvinced. "That's easy for you to say. You'll be used to giving evidence. But why would they want to question me and not anyone else in the bank if we all saw the same thing?"

"That's just the way it is sometimes. Everyone else did see the same as you. I've read their statements. The only difference, is you were close enough to hear what the gunman said, and had the courage to stop him."

That made some sense, but didn't diminish Ernie's anxiety. "How long will he get if he's found guilty?"

"He'll be found guilty all right. He got a seven-year sentence last time, so he's facing at least a nine-year stretch this time."

Ernie sat in silence, reliving the morning of the robbery in his head and wishing someone else had tackled the gunman instead of him. He felt it unfair he was the only one giving evidence, and he would have gladly changed places with someone else.

"Ann Perkins."

He didn't hear the usher enter or hear her call.

"That's you." Jones gave him a dig. Jolting him back to the present.

"Ann Perkins," the usher repeated

"That's me." He said.

The usher smiled at him. "They're ready for you in court now. If you would like to follow me, please."

Ernie stood up, followed her out of the witness suite, and into courtroom two where she led him to the witness stand. As he walked through the courtroom, he had a sudden urge to go to the toilet, and realised he should have gone before they called him in even though he'd not felt the need until that moment. The butterflies were all taking flight at the same time, and were all battering against the walls of his stomach.

The barrister who had spoken to him in the witness suite was sitting closest to him, another was sitting a little further away, closer to a dozen people he took to be the jury. Both barristers had dressed almost completely in black. Black trousers, or in the barrister's case furthest away, a black skirt, and black jackets covered with a black gown. Both were wearing a white shirt or blouse, both with strange white ribbons hanging down from the front of their collars, and they were both wearing white wigs.

It was immediately obvious who the judge was. He was sitting at the front on a raised platform giving him an unrestricted view of the whole courtroom. Dressed in similar dark clothing to the two barristers, but with a bright red and blue sash to break the plainness. Immediately in front of the judge, but on the far wall, Ernie could see the man he had tackled in the bank, sat behind a screen with a security guard immediately behind him.

"Would you read the words on the card?"

Ernie took the card and looked at the words.

The butterflies were still screaming to be released. He was hyperventilating, and he considered making a bolt for the door even though he knew they wouldn't allow him to escape his ordeal. He made the mistake of looking up from the card, only to find that, without exception, everyone was staring at him. He looked back down at the card and tried to put everything else out of his mind. "I do solemnly and sincerely and truly declare and affirm that the evidence I shall give shall be the truth, the whole truth and nothing but the truth."

Several of the butterflies landed as he read the words. His stomach stilled, and by the time he had finished, his breathing had also calmed. He smiled to himself at the realisation that it did not matter he was not Ann Perkins, and it did not matter he was a man professing to be a woman. None of it mattered. He may be a fake witness, but the entire thing was a fake. The judge and barristers were all pretending to have white curly hair. The accused man was pretending to be innocent. The jury were pretending to be peers of the accused, but were probably all law-abiding citizens. Both barristers were faking certainty about the outcome whilst knowing only one would win the argument. It was all fake.

The judge smiled at him, and told him each of the barristers would ask him questions, but he should direct his answers directly to the jury.

The barrister closest to him was the prosecuting barrister who had introduced himself in the witness suite, and as he stood up to speak, Ernie tried to guess his age. Late fifties, early sixties, even late sixties. He oozed experience and confidence.

"Will you give your full name to the court

please," he said.

"Ann Perkins." The lie slipped easily off his tongue. His fear had almost evaporated, and none of the butterflies were in the air now. Only a few caterpillars still crawled around his stomach.

"Were you a customer in the Santander Bank on the corner of Market Street and Piccadilly Gardens Manchester on the morning of Thursday the twenty-first of March twenty-nineteen?"

"Yes. I was," said Ernie.

"Would you tell the jury what you saw and heard on that day."

Ernie took a deep breath. He was much calmer now he had navigated the initial difficulty of lying about his name. "I had just entered the bank when the man who entered just before me began robbing it."

"Objection!" The prosecuting barrister had risen from her seat and had addressed the judge.

Ernie had only said one sentence. He wondered if his new found confidence was misplaced. Surely the defence barrister could not be fully qualified. She didn't look old enough to have finished university. She looked inexperienced, and in contrast to the prosecuting barrister, her gown and wig looked brand new. He didn't fancy her client's chances despite her objection.

"Whether the person in front of you was robbing the bank, is what this jury is being asked to determine," said the judge. "Please confine your evidence to what you actually saw and what you actually heard, and not to what you surmise." The judge turned towards the jury. "You will ignore those last remarks of the witness," and he then turned back. "Please continue."

Ernie was still unsure what he had done wrong. He saw the man robbing the bank, and that was all he said. He tried again. "I had just entered the bank. A man entered immediately in front of me and I saw him pull a gun out, point it at the cashier, and demand some money." In other words, he thought, I saw him robbing the bank just like I said a minute ago.

"Can you see that man in court today?" The prosecuting barrister asked.

Ernie pointed to the man sitting in front of the security guard. "Yes. That man there."

"Could you explain to the court what happened after you saw the gun?"

"Yes. I saw the gun. I thought he was robbing the bank, so I tackled him."

"Is it true you tackled him to the ground, and you and others then held him until the first uniformed police officer arrived?"

"Yes."

"Thank you. I have no further questions for you, but please remain there as my learned friend for the defence will have some questions in cross-examination."

It was the phrase 'cross examination' that did it. Some butterflies took off fleetingly as the defence barrister rose to her feet.

"You have described my client pulling out a gun. How did he appear?"

"Sorry. I don't understand."

"Well, did he look surprised, startled, flustered?"

"He looked threatening. He had a gun."

"I fully accept he had a gun. That's not in dispute. What I am asking you is what expression was on his face. When you see someone with a gun, the tendency is to look at the gun. Did you look at his face, and if so, how did he appear? What was the expression on my clients face?"

Ernie thought back to the morning in question. He had repeatedly relived those moments, but his entire focus had been on the gun. When the man entered, he only saw the back of his head. He may have seen the man's face when he turned with the gun, but Ernie could not be certain. He saw him afterwards. That's how he could recognise him, but he couldn't be certain that he saw the man's face whilst he was waving the gun about. He saw the gun, and then everything happened so fast.

"I couldn't say. I'm not sure I saw his face until afterwards. I was concentrating on the gun."

"Quite so," said the barrister. "You gave evidence that he threatened the cashier. Can you remember his exact words?"

Ernie was on safer ground here. He vividly remembered what the man had said.

"He said, 'This is a robbery. Give me the money.'"

"I put it to you," she said, "that the words my client actually said were 'This is no robbery. Give me the money.'"

"No," said Ernie. "He said, 'This is a robbery.'"

"How many people were in the bank?"

"Pardon?"

"How many people were in the bank? We know my client was in the bank talking to the bank clerk. We know you were in the bank. How many other people were in the bank? How many were in the queue?"

"Oh! About half-a-dozen."

"And how far away from you was my client?"

"When he was talking to the bank clerk, about three metres."

"And how far away from you was the nearest person in the queue?"

"There was a woman and small child immediately beside me. Only one or two metres."

"So immediately beside you there was a woman and child, and immediately behind them?"

"Two women."

"Would it be right to say that the woman and child immediately beside you, and both women immediately behind them, were all closer to you than my client?"

"A bit closer at first, yes."

"And would it be true to say the mother was talking to her child, and the two women were talking to one another?"

"I'm not sure. I suppose so, yes."

"And amongst all this background chatter and noise coming from those close beside you, how can you be certain my client said, 'This is a robbery', and did not say, 'This is no robbery'?"

Each question increased Ernie's anxiety, and by this stage all the butterflies were flying again. She had confused him. His calmness had gone, and he was unsure how to answer. He had an overwhelming urge to agree and get the entire thing over with. "I couldn't be certain, but it sounded like, 'This is a robbery'."

"Thank you," said the barrister. "You could not be certain. You gave evidence that you tackled my client to the floor. How much time elapsed between seeing the gun and tackling my client?"

"I'm not sure. Not long."

"Five seconds, three seconds, one second? How many seconds?"

"One or two seconds at the most. I tackled him as soon as I saw the gun."

"So as soon as you saw the gun you immediately tackled my client to the floor. One or two seconds at the most?"

"Yes. That's what I said. I tackled him straight away."

"Thank you. So in summary your evidence is, my client pulled out a gun, that you did not see his expression, that you cannot be certain what he said, that he may have said 'This is no robbery', that he told the bank clerk he needed some money, and that as soon as you saw the gun you immediately tackled my client to the floor. Is that correct?"

Ernie was not sure he said that exactly, but he had said something like that. "Yes, that's right."

"Thank you. No further questions."

The judge dismissed him and told him he could leave the court. His part in the process finished. It had not been as bad as expected. They had asked him a lot of questions about what had happened, but nobody had suggested he may have been a man, nobody had mentioned he had disappeared straight after the robbery, and nobody had accused him of intending to rob the bank himself. It was over.

He made his way from the witness box towards an usher who opened the main door to the courtroom as he approached. Ernie had been desperate to leave the court as soon as possible, but another part of him wanted to stay to find out what happened next. His curiosity won out, and as he approached the usher, he whispered "Is it possible to stay in and watch?"

"Of course, Madam." The usher was whispering too. He pointed to an area just inside the door, towards the back of the court. "You can sit there, in the public gallery."

There was seating for about twenty people, but only five people were already there. The front row was empty, so Ernie sat in the chair closest to the door to watch the rest of the proceedings.

Chapter Twenty-One

They called detective Inspector Jones next, and after taking the oath he gave evidence similar in most respects to Ernie's. He was cross-examined about the expression on Hinchcliffe's face, but couldn't comment because Hinchcliffe's back was to him when he'd pulled the gun out. They also asked him about the exact words Hinchcliffe spoke, but he admitted he didn't hear them because of the noise from other people in the bank. He also gave evidence about his arrest of Hinchcliffe, and about Hinchcliffe's repeated refusal to comment when interviewed at the police station.

Whilst Jones was giving his evidence, Ernie took a more detailed look at his surroundings. Most of the things in the court seemed alien to him. The gowns, the wigs, the procedure. He looked at Hinchcliffe, and it surprised him how ordinary Hinchcliffe looked compared to his surroundings. The term armed robber brought many images to Ernie's mind, but the man in the dock did not seem to fit any of those stereotypes.

Hinchcliffe sat quietly, listening intently to everything that was being said. He appeared to be in his mid-forties, and smartly dressed in a dark suit, pale blue shirt and striped tie. Ernie couldn't help feeling how easily he could have been in the dock rather than Hinchcliffe. He considered himself a law-abiding citizen driven by events to rob a bank, and he wondered what the driving force behind Hinchcliffe's robbery was, and whether his life had been as depressing as his own.

The detective inspector was the final witness for the prosecution, and once his cross-examination ended it was time for the defence.

The defence barrister stood up to address the jury. "The prosecution has claimed my client went into the bank to rob it at gunpoint," she said. "The facts of this case, the events that occurred and even most of the words my client spoke, are not in dispute. However, the interpretation of those events is completely different when seen from my client's point of view. My client's case is that he entered the bank to make a perfectly normal withdrawal of his own money, and everything else that happened was as the result of a complete misunderstanding. I would like to call the defendant to the stand."

They escorted Hinchcliffe from the dock to the witness stand and swore him in. His barrister then asked what he had been doing in the hour immediately before entering the bank.

"I went to Ancoats," he said. "I went to buy an air pistol from a man who had advertised one second hand."

"And could you tell the court whether you bought the air pistol, the purpose for which you bought it, and what you did with it after purchasing it."

"Yes, I bought one. I've an old brick outhouse at the back of my house, and it's infested with rats. They got in when a nearby factory was demolished and I've not been able to get rid of them since. I've tried poisons and traps, but nothing seems to work so I got the air pistol to shoot them."

"And did you know," she asked, "that it was illegal for you to possess an air pistol?"

Ernie sat up and listened a little more intently. When he had bought his own air pistol, he'd been told it was fully legal and didn't even need a licence because it was such a low-powered gun. He couldn't understand why it was illegal for Hinchcliffe if it was legal for him.

"I didn't know it was illegal when I bought it," said Hinchcliffe. "I knew I wasn't allowed to buy a proper gun, but I believed an air pistol would be all right. I've since been told it's not. That's why I've pleaded guilty to possessing one. I only had it to kill rats though. I never intended to rob the bank."

They hadn't allowed Ernie in court until he entered to give his evidence, so he didn't know that, beside the robbery itself, they had also charged Hinchcliffe with two firearm offences. Nor did he know Hinchcliffe had no alternative but to plead guilty to one of those offences. Hinchcliffe's last sentence was for seven year's imprisonment, and that automatically barred him for life from owning any firearm, even an air pistol.

"Could you tell the court what you did with your air pistol once you purchased it that morning?"

"Yes," said Hinchcliffe. "I put it in my pocket, to keep it safe until I got home."

"And did you have anything else in your pocket?"

"My wallet. I wanted to draw a hundred pounds out, but I like to keep everything separate. So much for gas, so much for electricity, so much for food, and so on. The list was in my wallet, and my wallet was in my pocket."

"What happened," asked his barrister, "when you got to the bank?"

"I know I should have got into the queue," Hinchcliffe said, "but I was daydreaming and in a world of my own, and I went straight to the counter by mistake. When I went to take the wallet out of my pocket it had slipped below the gun. I took the gun out to make it easier. I did it automatically, and without thinking. The girl immediately screamed and thought I was robbing her, and I tried to explain it was all a mistake. Then everything happened at once. The man attacked me and ended up on top of me. I kept trying to get up but others piled on top and I couldn't move. When I was eventually helped up, they arrested me."

"Before you found yourself on the floor, when you first realised the bank teller was frightened and you tried to explain it was a mistake, what did you actually say to her?"

"I told her 'This is no robbery, give me the money.' I meant the money listed on the paper in my wallet."

"Did you intend to rob the bank?" asked the barrister.

"No," said Hinchcliffe. "Never."

The defence barrister asked no more questions, and it was the prosecuting barrister's turn to question him.

"What was the name and address of the person who sold you the air pistol?"

"His name was Barry," said Hinchcliffe, "but I don't know his address. He advertised it online. On Gumtree. We met outside the Shamrock Pub in Ancoats and I bought it from him there."

"You seriously expect the jury to believe you bought the gun from someone you don't know?" said the barrister.

"Yes. I only knew his name was Barry. I'd never met him before."

"When you were being interviewed at the police station, why didn't you tell the officers it was all a mistake?"

"I was traumatised," said Hinchcliffe. "One minute I was standing at the counter trying to explain myself. The next, I was being hurled to the floor and assaulted. To tell you the truth, when I was at the police station I was still stunned. Still traumatised."

"Isn't it the truth that you entered the bank to rob it?" asked the barrister. "That you deliberately took the gun out to threaten the bank clerk, and that you deliberately tried to scare her into handing money over?"

"No. That's not true."

Ernie couldn't believe what he was hearing. He had been certain Hinchcliffe had intended robbing the bank. Now, he was not so sure, and he wondered if he had acted too quickly.

Arthur Jones was also listening to the same evidence, but he had no doubts in his mind. Hinchcliffe's long list of previous convictions were enough to convince him he was guilty. Jones was anxious though. However implausible Hinchcliffe's story may seem; it was up to the prosecution to prove his guilt not the defence to prove his innocence.

In his closing speech the prosecuting barrister reminded the jury Hinchcliffe had entered the bank with a hidden pistol, pulled the pistol out at the counter and pointed it at the bank clerk. He also reminded them the bank clerk, in her written statement, said she feared for her life as he pointed the gun at her. He reminded them that all the witnesses in the bank believed Hinchcliffe's intention was to rob it.

His final reminder was in relation to the verbal evidence given by Ann Perkins and the detective inspector. Perkins, he said, only attacked the defendant because she was certain he was trying to rob the bank. The detective inspector gave Hinchcliffe several opportunities for him to explain what happened, but he'd failed to do so.

The defence barrister, in her closing speech, began by taking the unusual step of confirming to the jury that her client had a previous conviction for which he had received a seven-year prison sentence. She explained this was the reason it was illegal for her client to possess an air pistol. She urged them not to let past convictions influence them, but to determine her client's guilt or innocence solely on the facts of this present case.

She pointed out that her client had mistakenly believed the restriction about firearms did not apply to air pistols, and he only purchased it to kill vermin in his outhouse. Her client, she said, had a perfectly reasonable explanation why he possessed the air pistol. The resulting events were regrettable but understandable, and her client was sorry for any distress caused to the bank clerk or to any of the other customers in the bank. He was sorry for anything he did which gave the mistaken impression he was about to rob the bank, but that was exactly what it was. An impression. A mistaken impression. Her client was the unfortunate victim of circumstance and completely innocent.

The judge had taken notes throughout the whole proceedings, and he believed Hinchcliffe was guilty. He had listened to all the evidence and had come to his own damning verdict, but his opinion was now unimportant. The opinion of the jury was the only one that mattered. He gave a scrupulously even handed summing up and outlined the main legal points on both sides. After explaining the law on which they would need to decide, he sent them out to consider their verdict.

Ernie continued to hang around the court, eager to know the verdict. Having been certain Hinchcliffe was guilty, he now had doubts after having heard all the evidence and thought it could go either way.

The problem for the jury was Hinchcliffe's defence. It was not totally unbelievable. The jury discussed it throughout their two-and-a-half-hour long deliberation. They didn't believe what Hinchcliffe had said in his defence, but they could find no direct evidence to prove he was lying. They realised there may well have been proof if Ann Perkins had waited before tackling him, but she had acted straight away. They were being asked to decide whether a robbery would have taken place if Perkins had not intervened, and they found that impossible to answer.

By the end of their deliberations all the jury members believed Hinchcliffe was probably guilty, but they also concluded the prosecution evidence was insufficiently strong to counter the defence. They were reluctant, but concluded the prosecution had not proved the case beyond all reasonable doubt.

"Have you reached verdicts on which all of you have agreed?" asked the judge.

"Yes, my Lord," said the jury foreman.

"On the first count of attempted robbery, do you find the defendant guilty or not guilty?"

"Not guilty."

"On the second count of carrying a firearm with intent to commit an indictable offence, do you find the defendant guilty or not guilty?"

"Not guilty."

The judge listened to the verdicts impassively, and then directly addressed Hinchcliffe.

"The jury have found you not guilty on both of the counts I asked them to decide on today, and if those had been your only charges, you would be free to go. However, you have also pleaded guilty to a third count, the illegal possession of a firearm. I do not intend to sentence you for that offence today. I am ordering background and pre-sentencing reports prepared, in order for sentencing to take place at a later date. This is a very serious offence, and I am remanding you in custody whilst the adjournment takes place."

The not guilty verdicts surprised Ernie. He stood up to leave, but the judge had not finished.

"Before finally bringing this case to a close I would like to commend the bravery of the witness Ann Perkins. This jury have decided that no armed robbery was intended, but Mrs Perkins could not have known that at the time. Single-handed, and with no regard for her own safety, she tackled a person she believed to be an armed and violent robber and she deserves an award for her bravery. I am therefore instructing the High Sheriff of

Manchester to make a payment of one hundred and fifty pounds from public funds. It is not a great deal of money, but it reflects the thanks of this court for her brave and courageous action."

His words staggered Ernie. One hundred and fifty pounds may not be a great deal of money to the judge, but it was for him. One hundred and fifty pounds was nowhere near the million pounds he planned to rob, but it represented an unexpected windfall for which he was extremely grateful.

Chapter Twenty-Two

Four weeks later and Ernie was back for Hinchcliffe's sentence hearing. He had entered the same bank with an air pistol, so Ernie was curious to find out what sentence Hinchcliffe would receive for a similar offence. That curiosity had persuaded him to dress up and go through the entire security sequence once more; the scanner, the pat down, the search, and the request as to why he was attending. They directed him to court number four. It was about fifteen minutes to ten and the imposing courtroom doors were still locked. Beside the door was an equally imposing looking usher dressed in a black gown and carrying a clipboard.

"I'm here to see someone receive their sentence," said Ernie. "The person's name is Hinchcliffe."

"It's this court. I'll be opening the doors in a few minutes," replied the usher. "The public gallery is on the right as you go in."

Ernie stood beside the door and took the time to look around. There were two women standing at the far side of the door. A young woman in her early twenties, and another woman in her forties also waiting to go in. They looked familiar, but Ernie couldn't immediately put his finger on where he had seen them before.

"I remember you," said the elder of the two women. "You're the woman who tackled my Bob to the ground."

He was not giving evidence, so he had felt unconcerned about visiting court that morning, but as the woman spoke, he remembered where he had seen them. They had both sat some rows behind him in the public gallery at the original trial. He hoped they wouldn't make a scene, and he wondered if he had been wise to come. He could have read about Hinchcliffe's sentence in the local paper without having to face the man's wife. The judge would be sending Hinchcliffe to jail for a long time, and his wife was sure to blame him.

"Er, yes. Sorry."

The older woman smiled at him. "Don't be sorry love. He's the one who should be sorry. It's not your fault. It's not as though you were there to rob the bank. He was the one doing that, and he should know better after all this time."

Ernie was not sure how to respond, but as he was trying to plan a suitable reply, the usher unlocked the door. "You can go in now. Public gallery's on the right."

Ernie took a step back and allowed the couple to enter first to see where they would sit. He had no desire to continue the conversation. They may not blame him now, but things may be different once the judge passed a lengthy sentence of imprisonment. He watched as they sat down about four rows back, almost level with the dock. He sat where he had sat before. Well away from them, and at the front from where he could make a quick getaway through the nearby door if it became necessary.

He looked around the court. There were two reporters the other side of the room, and the two barristers from the original trial were already in court. He watched as they brought Hinchcliffe up from the cells and into the dock, and everyone stood as the same judge entered and the sentence hearing started.

The prosecuting barrister rose to speak first.

"The defendant has pleaded guilty to possession of an air pistol having previously been sentenced to a term of three years or more imprisonment. Your Lordship is aware of the circumstances of this case. You adjourned the case for pre-sentence reports, and there is nothing to add to those reports other than to draw your attention to the accused's antecedent history and the sentencing guidelines for this offence."

He then read out a long list of convictions. Hinchcliffe's first offence had been for burglary when he was only 17 years old, and they had sentenced him to 18 weeks at a young offender's institute. The final conviction was in 2008, also for burglary, when they sentenced him to seven year's imprisonment.

"The sentencing guidelines for the current offence is a mandatory sentence of five year's imprisonment," said the barrister. Ernie heard a gasp from the two women sat behind him. "Five Years!" he heard one of them shout out. He turned around to look at them. The barrister's words had visibly shocked them. Hinchcliffe's wife was shaking and was looking very pale as she was being comforted by the younger woman. Ernie understood how they felt. He had not been sure what to expect himself, but they had found Hinchcliffe not guilty of robbing the bank so he had not been expecting anything like a sentence of five years just for possessing the air gun.

Five years may have come as a shock to Ernie and the two women, but it had not noticeably shocked Hinchcliffe himself. He continued to sit staring straight ahead, his face displaying no emotion.

The prosecuting barrister took his seat, and it was then the defence barrister's turn to address the judge.

"My Lord. My learned friend has rightly drawn your attention to the mandatory five year's imprisonment for the offence my client has pleaded guilty to. I would respectfully draw your attention to the fact that your Lordship can depart from those guidelines in exceptional circumstances, and there are exceptional circumstances in this case. My client was not aware an air pistol was defined as a firearm. He purchased the pistol only to kill vermin, and not to facilitate a crime, so there was no criminal intent, just an ignorance of the law surrounding the legal firearm definition. My client would like to apologise to the court, and to assure the court that now he is fully aware of his legal responsibilities, nothing like this will ever happen again."

The defence barrister took her seat, and the judge cleared his throat and addressed Hinchcliffe.

"This is a very serious offence," he said, "with a mandatory sentence of five year's imprisonment even if, as in your case, you pleaded guilty. I have read all the pre-sentence reports, and I have listened to what your barrister has had to say on your behalf, but I cannot agree with your barrister's submission. The law is clear. An air pistol is a firearm, and the law prohibits you for life from possessing any firearm. Ignorance of the law is no excuse, so your belief that the air gun was not a firearm is irrelevant and in no way makes your case exceptional."

Ernie realised Hinchcliffe's prospects were not sounding good, and he looked towards the door to make sure of an unimpeded exit in case Hinchcliffe's relatives kicked off. If Hinchcliffe was going to get five years just for having an air pistol in his possession, God only knows how long he would have got if they had caught him with a proper pistol. He realised what a lucky escape he'd had by being thwarted both at the bank and at the jeweller's. He had enjoyed his period of notoriety. His life over the past few months had been far from dull, and despite his constant anxiety, he had really enjoyed himself. Ernie felt lucky and realised things may so easily have turned out differently for him.

Hinchcliffe had not been so lucky and was listening to the judge with increasing despair.

"I have examined the record of your previous convictions with great care," said the judge. Hinchcliffe knew there was no good news coming. The judge was about to send him down for a long time. The judge appeared to scrutinise his face, and sat there without speaking for what seemed to Hinchcliffe to be a long time, but which was only about thirty seconds. Thirty seconds in which Hinchcliffe could see his freedom drifting away. He looked towards his wife and daughter and wondered when he would see them again.

"I looked at your career," said the judge, "and I noticed an anomaly I do consider exceptional. Your career has been different to the career of most criminals appearing before me." That's it, thought Hinchcliffe. My previous convictions are worse than others. He will send me down for longer.

"We placed you in a young offenders institute following your very first criminal conviction, and we have incarcerated you for increasing periods of time ever since, the last time for seven years. Every single one of your sentences has been custodial. In your case, prison may well have been punitive, but it appears to have served no reformative purpose whatsoever. Neither has it served as the deterrent we meant it to be. The sentencing guidelines provide for a mandatory period of imprisonment of at least five years for your current offence, and I am only allowed to depart from those guidelines in exceptional circumstances. In determining whether there are exceptional circumstances I am directed to take a holistic approach and to consider every facet of your life, and I intend to do that in this case."

As the judge paused for breath, neither Hinchcliffe nor Ernie had followed what he was saying. They waited for clarity. Hinchcliffe and his family waited in dread. Ernie was waiting with increasing interest.

"In all your years of criminal activity you have never been offered probation, never been fined, never been given a suspended sentence, and never been sentenced to community service. I am mindful that your first period of incarceration was as a seventeen-year-old. These days we offer most seventeen-year-olds alternatives to prison and a chance to reform, but we never offered you that chance, so I am giving you that chance today. If you appear before me, or any other judge in the future, you should expect an extremely long prison sentence. To be clear, I must follow the sentencing guidelines unless it is contrary to the interests of justice or unless there are exceptional circumstances. I do not accept your lack of knowledge that an air pistol was a firearm as exceptional. However, I believe it is not in the interests of justice to imprison you today, and I believe there are exceptional circumstances in your case."

There was an audible gasp throughout the courtroom, and this time it appeared to come from everywhere. It was not immediately apparent whether it came from the public gallery, from the dock, or from the body of the court. Everyone had given an almost inaudible gasp, but the combination became audible.

"Your past custodial sentences have not been a deterrent. Neither have they been reformative. It is evident a further custodial sentence would have the same minimal effect and is not in the interests of justice. Similarly, your past sentencing history is exceptional. We give most first-time criminals a chance to redeem themselves and change their ways before we consider incarcerating them. We never gave you such a chance, so I am giving one to you now. In the interests of justice, and because of those exceptional circumstances, I am sentencing you to three-hundred hours of unpaid work which you must undertake in the community under supervision. Any breach of this community order may cause you to return to this court where I will rigidly follow the original sentencing guidelines and will send you to prison for a long time. This is a once in a lifetime opportunity. Do you understand?"

Hinchcliffe was so stunned he almost did not give the judge an affirmative answer.

Chapter Twenty-Three

Ernie left the court building and made his way along the busy Manchester streets towards the nearest tram stop. He was rushing to get away as quickly as possible and oblivious to anything else around him.

"Oi you! Hold on."

Hinchcliffe's shout caused Ernie to turn around. He had not seen Hinchcliffe and his family racing to catch up with him, and it alarmed him to see them rushing towards him. He wondered if they were a threat, and out for revenge.

"I'm sorry," panted Hinchcliffe as he drew level. "I didn't mean to startle you. I just wanted to catch you up and thank you." Hinchcliffe held out his hand and Ernie took hold and shook it gingerly, still very wary. "If you hadn't stopped me in the bank, I'd have been doing nine to twelve years by now."

Ernie still wasn't sure how to respond. He was still trying to work out in his own mind whether his rash action had prevented a crime or prevented a criminal from getting the sentence he deserved. "It was nothing," was the best he could come up with.

"No, it wasn't nothing," said Hinchcliffe. "It's given me a chance. You gave me a chance, and the judge has given me a chance, and I'm going to take those chances and turn my life around. I know I've got a terrible record and I know it's all been my own fault, but like the judge said, they never gave me a chance. I was lucky he never sent me down for a long time today, so I'm determined to take this opportunity of changing my ways and getting a proper job."

"He wouldn't have this chance if you hadn't intervened and stopped him robbing the bank," said his wife. "We can't thank you enough. I only hope he means what he's said this time. If he does, it'll all be down to you. Thank you."

"Really, it was nothing," said Ernie again. He knew he could so easily have found himself in a similar position. "We're all prisoners of circumstance. My life has had a few low periods lately so I can understand why anyone would want more money. I hope you find a legal way out of your own mess."

"I going to try working for a living." Hinchcliffe laughed. "I've not tried that for a while, so I'm out of practice, but something will turn up. I've always told Emma there's nothing she can't do if she puts her mind to it. It's time I took my own advice."

"Is Emma your wife?" asked Ernie.

Hinchcliffe laughed again and pointed to the younger woman. "My daughter," he said. "She's a student."

"What are you studying?" asked Ernie, surprised at how quickly his anxiety had dissipated. He had expected a lot of aggravation from a mafia like family, but they appeared to be normal.

"Computer studies," said Emma. "Just started my final year at the University of Salford."

"I envy you," said Ernie. "I learnt nothing about computers when I was at school, but now everything's computerised."

"She's lucky," said Hinchcliffe. "Entire life ahead of her. Mind you, I'm the lucky one today. We're all in your debt. If I can ever be of help to you, just call me."

Ernie couldn't imagine any circumstances in which Hinchcliffe could be any help to him, but he entered the number in his phone as Hinchcliffe recited it. "Thank you," he said.

"No. Thank you," said Hinchcliffe. "Don't forget. Just call if you need anything. I owe you one." Hinchcliffe held out his hand and shook Ernie's hand once again before he, and his family, walked away.

Ernie watched as the Hinchcliffe's disappeared down the road. He wondered how many times Hinchcliffe had previously promised his wife he would give up crime, and whether this time would be any different. Hinchcliffe was young enough to get a job and earn an honest living, and he could completely change his life around if he only kept his word.

His own position was unchanged. His celebrity status was already diminishing as fresh news stories emerged. He welcomed the financial reward from the judge, but he realised a hundred and fifty pounds wouldn't go far. He decided he'd buy himself a new television if he could get one for that price, but once he'd spent the money, he would be in the same depressing state as he was before.

He still sometimes found it depressing to think about the future, but when he did feel depressed, he forced himself to think about the recent past. Those thoughts always cheered him up. Nobody had guessed he intended to rob the bank or the jeweller's. The bank manager was happy because he had stopped a robbery. The jeweller was happy because he had stopped a robbery and saved the doorman's life. The police were happy because two murderers were off the streets. The media companies were happy because he had supplied them with several excellent stories. Hinchcliffe was happy because they had not sent him to prison, and the judge was happy enough with Ernie to give him a reward. It seemed to Ernie as though the entire world was happy with him, or to be more precise, the entire world was happy with Ann Perkins.

Slowly but surely the happiness of others was percolating into his own feelings. Ernie had enjoyed his recent experiences. As Ernie Wright his life had been boring, but Ann Perkins life was different. It was far more interesting and exciting. He imagined Doreen, his late wife, looking down with approval. She would not have wanted to see him depressed. Doreen had always been an outgoing person, and he wondered what she would have made of Ann Perkins. He was sure she would have approved. His Ann Perkins disguise had allowed him to come out of his shell. He had planned to rob a bank and jeweller's, he had a contract taken out on his life, he had foiled a bank robbery, saved a man's life, been present when two professional killers murdered one another, and been a witness in court. All those events had resulted in them writing articles about him in local and national newspapers, interviewing him on the radio, and on one of the local television channels. Ernie could not imagine a more fulfilled life than the one he was living as Ann Perkins.

The more Ernie thought about things, the more desirable Ann Perkins life seemed to be. It was the exact opposite of his own life, and yet it was his own life. He was the same person, but in his disguise he felt different, and people behaved differently towards him. He knew the future for Ernie Wright looked as bleak as ever, but he increasingly imagined a brighter future for Ann Perkins. He knew Ann Perkins would continue to live an exciting and eventful life, and he wondered how he could keep the deception going.

Ernie wasn't the only person thinking about Ann Perkins. She was also being considered by Detective Sergeant Carter. The detective sergeant couldn't get rid of the nagging feeling there was more to Perkins than met the eye, and she was sure Perkins was hiding something. Ann Perkins had no criminal record, and there was no trace of her ever receiving a caution or being flagged in any intelligence. She had been invisible to the police until recently, but her presence at the bank and jewellers seemed too much of a coincidence.

It had crossed Carter's mind that Perkins may have been an accomplice of Hinchcliffe's. Maybe the initial plan was for Perkins to help Hinchcliffe rob the bank, but she got cold feet and pulled out at the last minute. Sarah had questioned Hinchcliffe about the involvement of Perkins at some length but he had denied it. It was niggling away at her, and she still suspected Perkins was hiding something, and more involved than anyone thought.

Sarah couldn't solve the Ann Perkins enigma, so she put her on the back burner. There were more pressing matters, but she decided she would take another look at Perkins from time to time and review things in the light of anything new brought to her attention.

Two days after the court case, Ernie got an unexpected phone call.
"Ann Perkins?"
"Yes."
"My name's Jonathan Jones. I'm the owner of the Jonathan Jones chain of jewellery shops. I wanted to thank you personally for saving the life of one of my staff. I know my local manager thanked you, but I've been out of the country and have only recently returned. I haven't had the opportunity to thank you in person until now."
"It was nothing, honestly," said Ernie. "I did what anyone would have done."
"That's as maybe, but your prompt action saved the life of my doorman and prevented a violent robbery. The robbery would have been successful but for your intervention. I understand from my manager you're unemployed?"
Ernie had not meant to tell the world he was unemployed and short of money. His pride made him feel it was nobody else's business, but the journalists interviewing him were good at probing. That was their job, and it had eventually become an integral part of the story that an unemployed woman had been responsible for thwarting each robbery.
"Yes. That's right. I'm unemployed at present. I left my old job to set up my own business." Ernie was not sure why he said that, but it seemed better than saying they had made him redundant.

"I see. What sort of business are you setting up?"

Ernie had not expected the reply, and he said the first thing that came into his head. "I'm thinking of becoming a private detective."

"A private detective! What a splendid idea. From what I've read, you'd be a natural. Excitement seems to follow you around."

"Yes, it does rather."

"Anyway, to get back to the reason I phoned. Since my return to the U.K. I've thought long and hard about how best to thank you. We'd like to pay you a reward. We're a family company and not listed, so we don't have to get the approval of any shareholders apart from family members. We've all agreed to give you a reward of fifty thousand pounds. It will help start your business. It's the least we can do."

Ernie was staggered and lost for words. He stood holding his phone for several seconds before eventually answering. "Thank you," he stammered, not knowing what else to say.

"You're welcome. We're really grateful. The money will be far less than the robbers would have cost us. We would have lived with the loss if they'd succeeded, so we can live with it now. Our insurance would have gone sky high too. We're glad we can help."

"Thank you." Ernie still didn't know what else to say. Fifty thousand pounds. It all seemed rather surreal.

"I'll put the details in writing to you. All you have to do is let us have your bank details and we'll set up the payment."

Ernie immediately realised it was a scam.

Someone had read the newspaper articles or had seen him on television and decided he would be an easy touch. "You want my bank details? I'm not giving you those. It's a scam isn't it?"

The person on the other end of the line chuckled. "I can see why you may think so. I'm not asking for your details over the phone. I'm asking you to go to my Manchester shop. I'll send the paperwork there, then you'll know it's genuine. How about next Friday, about two o'clock?"

"Friday at two o'clock. That's fine. Anything I need to take?"

"No, only your bank details. I'll be at the shop myself then. It'll be nice to see you and to thank you in person."

"Right. I'll see you Friday."

The phone went dead. Ernie continued holding it as he calculated things in his head. Fifty thousand pounds was more money than he had ever owned.

On the following Friday he dressed as Ann Perkins and went to the jeweller's. Jonathan Jones had arranged for local media to attend, and they filmed Ernie being awarded with a certificate of appreciation.

"You're quite a celebrity Ann. Are you still looking for work?" The reporter from the Manchester Evening News was looking for a good quote.

"I was," he said, "but not now. I'm setting up my own detective agency."

"That's a great idea. A detective agency. When are you starting?"

"I have to find an office first, but I'll let you know."

"Do that," said the reporter. He handed Ernie a business card. "Let me know when you're opening your business, and we'll publicise it. It'll be a great story. Don't forget."

"I won't," said Ernie. "Thanks."

Later, in a more private ceremony with just himself and Jonathan Jones, he received a cheque for fifty thousand pounds made out to Ann Perkins. He explained he wanted to use the money to set up his detective agency, so he did not want it put directly into his personal bank account. He would open a separate business account for the agency to keep personal and business money apart.

Jones was so taken with the lady he saw before him, that he also gave her another cheque for ten thousand pounds from his personal bank account. A thank you from him personally as well as from the jewellery business itself. Ernie was not quite the millionaire he had hoped to become, but he thought sixty-thousand pounds would do very nicely.

Chapter Twenty-Four

Ernie still had lots of problems, but there were only two problems concerning the creation of his proposed detective agency. He needed to create a bank account in the name of Ann Perkins, and he needed to find a reasonably priced office.

His most pressing problem was the bank. He had received two crossed cheques in the name of Ann Perkins, so he needed to set up a business account in her name. He already possessed a bank account in his own name of Ernest Wright, but he decided not to open a new account at the same branch in case they recognised him. Disguised as Ann Perkins, he entered the branch of a different bank.

"I'd like to open a business account please."

"Could I take your name?"

"Ann Perkins."

"If you would like to take a seat for a moment Mrs Perkins, one of our business managers will be with you in a moment."

Ernie sat down for a few minutes before being approached by a young lady in a business suit displaying a discrete logo of the bank.

"Mrs Perkins?" The woman held out her hand. "If you would like to follow me, please."

Ernie followed as she walked to the far end of the bank and into a glass-walled cubicle. The woman sat behind the computer on the small desk and asked Ernie to take the facing seat.

"I understand you want to open a business

account. Can you tell me a little about your business?"

"I'm setting up a detective agency. The Ann Perkins Detective Agency. I need a separate account so I can keep my business money separate from my money."

"Ann Perkins? Are you the lady who stopped that bank robbery?"

"Yes, that's me. I'm setting up a detective agency."

"That sounds a wonderful idea. Do you already have a personal account with us?"

"No. I thought it would be simpler to use a different bank for my business account. Less chance of me getting confused and mixing them up."

"That's no problem. Will you be trading as a sole trader or as a limited company?"

Ernie had looked at the Companies House website. It seemed a lot of hassle to form a company. "Sole trader. There's just me."

"Fine. I'll just need to see some photographic identification, a passport, driving licence or something similar. Anything with your photo on as long as it is an official document in your name. I'll also need proof of your address. A utility bill, council tax or rental agreement with your name and address on it."

Ernie thought everything had been going fine until that moment. He had not expected being asked to prove who he was, and it seemed an unsurmountable problem. "Proof of identity and a utility bill?"

"Yes. Do you have those on you?"

"No. Sorry," he said. "I didn't think it would be

necessary, what with all the publicity and my picture having been in all the media. I just assumed everyone would know who I was."

The woman smiled. "I'm sure everyone knows who you are Mrs Perkins, but unfortunately I still have to see the paperwork. It's the law I'm afraid. Part of the money laundering legislation. I can make another appointment for you if it's easier. How about tomorrow at eleven?"

Ernie could not provide identity or proof of address in the name of Ann Perkins, but there was no way he could admit that to her. "Not tomorrow," he said. "I can't make tomorrow. Perhaps I could give you a ring once I've gone home and checked my diary? I'm extremely busy at the moment what with setting up the new business and everything."

"Of course," said the woman. "It'll be a busy time for you. That's why we'll always be here to offer help whenever you need it. Here's my card. It's a direct line so give me a ring once you've got everything together, and I'll arrange another meeting and have everything up and running straight away."

Ernie got up to go. "That's very kind of you. Thank you."

"Here, let me show you out." The woman accompanied him to the door of the bank before shaking his hand once again and saying goodbye.

As he travelled home, he felt a lot more uncertain about a business bank account. If there were similar requirements at all the banks, it seemed it would be impossible for him to open an account in the name of Ann Perkins.

He began browsing the internet as soon as he

was at home. Not sure what he was looking for, he began a series of general searches about opening bank accounts in someone else's name. All the websites he landed on were telling him the same as the woman at the bank. As far as he could tell, there was no way to open an account in the name of Ann Perkins without having some forged documents. Documents he didn't have and didn't know how to get.

His search for information about opening an account proved hopeless, but it did throw up other possibilities. Several websites suggested it was far easier to set up a limited company than he had first thought. It eventually dawned on him that not only was setting up a company relatively easy, but it may also solve the name problem.

A few hours later he logged into the Companies House website and read their step-by-step instructions about how to register a company. The last page displayed a large register now button. He was still not sure despite having read everything, but he clicked it anyway.

The first question asked him to confirm he was starting a new application, and the following questions were just as simple. Over the course of the next few minutes, he gave the name of his proposed company as the Ann Perkins Detective Agency Limited, gave his real name, Ernest Sykes, as the sole director and sole shareholder, and paid the twelve pounds fee.

The following day he received an email from Companies House confirming registration of the company and attaching his Certificate of Incorporation and Memorandum of Association.

Creating a bank account proved easy once he

formed the company. He used his phone to take photo's of his newly acquired company documents, together with images of his driving licence and utility bills. His searches the previous day led him to various banks operating almost exclusively via mobile phone apps. He registered with one of them and forwarded his documents. Their app compared the photo on his driving licence to the photo being taken on his phone, and within a few minutes they had created his business bank account.

When the debit card arrived a few days later, it displayed the name of Ernest Sykes and the company name of Ann Perkins Detective Agency and the bank had already agreed he could pay money in using an abbreviated version of the company name.

Having created the detective agency and bank account, his only remaining obstacle was to find somewhere to work from. He considered working from home, but discarded the idea as impractical. The business needed a professional image, somewhere he could receive clients whilst disguised as Ann Perkins. It did not have to be large, and a small office would be better and cheaper. The city centre was out. All those offices were much larger than he needed, and with much dearer rents than he could afford.

He travelled further afield whilst looking for somewhere easy to find, easy to access, and not too expensive. After lots of false starts he eventually found somewhere suitable in the Salford Quays area. The office was within walking distance of a tram stop to the city centre, close to Media City and the Lowry shopping centre, and fully serviced. The rent not only covered the small furnished office but also a communal reception area, a meeting room, and various utilities.

It was the third week in January by the time he moved in, and true to his word, the local reporter gave the new company some publicity in the form of a small article and photograph in the general section of the Manchester Evening News. The business editor also added a half-page spread in the business section a few days later. Ernie took out a small advert himself, but the articles provided far more publicity than the adverts.

There was an eclectic mix of businesses using other offices in the block, including accountants, IT companies, and business consultants. From his office window, Ernie could see the main entrance and private car park, and on his first morning he sat at the window and watched a constant stream of people entering and leaving, wondering if any of them were coming to see him, and wondering what sort of case his first client would bring. There was an internal telephone system connecting his office to the main reception area, but nobody called, and several times during that first morning Ernie picked up the handset to make sure it was working properly.

He didn't want to leave his flat every day dressed as Ann, but he knew it would be awkward to arrive every day at the office dressed as Ernie. The reception staff would soon get suspicious if they saw him arrive as Ernie, but later saw Ann in his office without seeing her enter. They would wonder where she had come from and where Ernie had disappeared to. The communal receptionists worked from eight thirty each morning until five thirty each evening, so on the first day Ernie took most of Ann's clothes and makeup, and stored them in one of his large storage cupboards. By arriving early and leaving late, he could arrive dressed as Ernie before the reception staff arrived, change into Ann's clothes for the rest of the day, and change back later for his journey home after reception closed.

Ernie's expected rush of clients never materialised, and by the end of January he was wondering if he had made a big mistake. He still sat at his desk looking out of his window at all the people entering or leaving, but he was no longer hopeful that any of them would be a client.

He ignored the initial knock on his door, assuming one of the maintenance staff carrying something along the communal corridor had accidentally banged against the door in passing. The second knock was louder and more insistent, and when he opened it he came face to face with a smartly dressed woman in her late fifties.

"Are you the detective? Ann Perkins?" Somehow, she had got past the receptionist without him seeing her.

"Yes," said Ernie. "Come in."

He showed the woman to his desk, and couldn't help noticing the styled hair, the manicured nails on her long slender fingers, the short tweed jacket and the pleated skirt. Sitting opposite her, he realised his demeanour was nowhere near as elegant. By this time he was used to wearing women's clothing, but he still found it difficult to hide all the male mannerisms gained by habit over the past fifty years.

"My son has disappeared," said the woman,

"and I'd like you to find him."

Ernie took a notepad out of the desk draw and placed it in front of him. He took his time selecting the best pen. Despite having sat day by day patiently waiting for his first client, he was unsure how to proceed and he needed some thinking time.

"When did you last see your son?"

"About a week ago, but he always phones me every day and I've not heard from him for three days."

"Three days." He immediately thought the woman was a bit of a drama queen. Ernie knew nobody would notice if he disappeared for three days. "Three days is not very long," he said. "Maybe your son has just gone on holiday without telling you. A last-minute bargain he couldn't ignore?"

"He wouldn't. Not without telling me first. Like I said, he always phones me every day, but I've not heard from him for three days and I'm anxious something's happened to him."

"Have you been to the police and reported him missing?"

"I have," she said, "but they're not interested. Told me to come back in a month if he still wasn't home."

"I see," said Ernie. "So, what would you like me to do?"

"I'd like you to find him. He's not at home, and he's not answering his phone. I've rung all the local hospitals, but none of them have admitted him. I know he wouldn't just disappear, so he must be in some sort of trouble."

"I can't promise anything." Ernie did not think

there was much mileage in the case, but it was his only case. Her son would probably turn up tomorrow. He thought her son had probably spent the last three days in bed with a new girlfriend. Still, if she wanted to pay him to look for her son, who was he to argue. "I'll make some enquiries for you," he said.

"Thank you. That's all I'm asking. It's so unlike him. I just need someone to take the fact he's missing seriously." The woman seemed composed up to this point, but Ernie could see the tears welling up in her eyes, and there was a tremor in her voice.

"Let me take a few details," he said. "Let's start with your name and address."

The woman gave her name as Jessica Smythe, and Ernie noted the address was in an area of South Manchester where homes were worth several millions of pounds. The woman saw him raise his eyebrows as she gave the address.

"It was my good fortune to marry someone very well off," she said. The woman's voice became steadier and tinged with a steely determination. "He was even richer by the time we divorced, so when he went off with his secretary I made sure I got my share."

"Is it possible your son's gone to visit his father?"

"No. His father's died since, and my son's never had anything to do with his father's floozy. Anyway, she remarried soon after he died."

"Right then. What I need is all the information you can give me about your son. Anything that will help me know where to begin looking for him," said Ernie.

Jessica Smythe gave her son's name as Timothy Armstrong, putting the different surname down to the fact that since her divorce she had reverted to using her maiden name. She supplied his full address, a land-line and a mobile number.

"You say you've been to his house?"

"Yes. He always rings me last thing at night, and when he didn't ring the first night I drove around the following morning but got no answer. I've got a key so I let myself in, but he hadn't slept in his bed."

"Were there any signs someone had broken into the house?"

"No, nothing like that. It was untidy, but that's all."

"How old is your son?"

"Mid thirties. Thirty-six."

"What about relationships?"

"A few girlfriends from time to time," she said, "but his last long-term relationship ended over a year ago. There's been nothing serious since. Nothing serious enough for him to tell me about."

"Would he have told you?"

"He always has in the past," she said. "Not one-night stands obviously, but he always phoned every day, and he always told me if a relationship lasted more than a day or two."

"So, nobody current that you know about," said Ernie. "What about his work? What does he do?"

"He studied hard and has a good job as a chartered accountant. I've phoned the company, but they say he's not been in for several days. They'd recently promoted him, so that's not like him either."

"Perhaps the stress of the promotion has been

getting on top of him so he's taken a few days off to recharge his batteries," said Ernie.

"No, nothing like that. He was enjoying the job."

"What's the name of the company?"

"Phimister's Financial Services in Levenshulme," she said.

"What about outside of work? Any hobbies? Interests? Local Pub?"

"When he's at the office, he sometimes has lunch nearby at the Blue Bell Inn in Levenshulme. I've been there, but nobody has seen him for a while. He's no real hobbies worth mentioning, but he does sometimes go clubbing in the city centre."

"Do you have a recent picture?" asked Ernie.

"Yes. I've several." She showed him some pictures on her phone. He selected the best head and shoulders shot and got her to send a copy to his own phone.

Ernie continued to ask as many questions as he could. He was not sure what was important and what was not, but he gathered as much information as possible. He still had no idea what he was going to do with all the information, and he was unsure how to go about finding a missing person, but he didn't intend telling the client that. He thought she'd probably find out soon enough, but meanwhile he held his chin in his hand and tried to look as though he knew what he was doing.

Once he'd completed all his questioning, it was time to turn his attention to the fee. The woman seemed well off, but he was still nervous about asking for money.

"I've got a standard contract," he said, "so I

only need to add the basic facts and print it out. Half the fee, together with an advance of expenses, is payable up front. If I can't find him, that's all you'll pay. If I do find him, or if he turns up, then the balance is due on completion."

"That's fine," she said.

He typed a summary of the case into the contract template on his computer, printed it out and handed her a copy. She gave it a quick scan, signed it, handed it back, and made the initial payment.

"Please keep in touch every couple of days to let me know how you are getting on," she said.

"Of course," he said. "I'll keep you fully informed at every stage." As the first client of the Ann Perkins Detective Agency left the building, Ernie found it hard to believe what just happened. He watched through his office window and pondered his good fortune as the woman walked through the car park to her car before driving away.

This was his first case, and he was excited even though he hardly knew where to begin. He had no idea where Timothy Armstrong was, no idea how to find him, and no idea if Timothy Armstrong even wanted to be found. This would not be easy, but at least she'd paid him some money up front.

Chapter Twenty-Five

Timothy Armstrong's mother had already visited her son's home and the place he usually had lunch when he was working. The one place she hadn't visited was his place of work. She'd phoned his office, but not visited.

At a loss about how to find someone who had disappeared, Ernie thought he'd begin by visiting Armstrong's place of work to find out when he was last there. Although his mother had phoned, she'd not been sure who she'd spoken to. It may only have been a receptionist, and Ernie thought one of the other chartered accountants may know something.

He checked the Companies House website and searched for the directors. There were two. Thomas Andrew Phimister born in 1958, and Andrew Thomas Phimister born in 1981. Father and son perhaps. He would go to their office and ask to see one of them. Maybe they would have some additional information. Perhaps one of them had even sent Armstrong away on a course or to a conference and he could wrap the case up quickly.

Ernie went in his official capacity, disguised as Ann Perkins.

Levenshulme is mid-way between Stockport and the centre of Manchester, but has kept its village like feel despite its proximity to the city centre. He travelled by bus the following morning and found Phimister's Financial Services on the main road between a barber shop and shoe repairers. The brickwork of those two shops was crumbling, the windows were dirty, and the doors were displaying closed signs despite being mid-morning. The Phimister's building was in better condition, but not by much.

Ernie felt something was not right. From what Armstrong's mother had been saying, Ernie had been expecting to see a top class chartered accountant's office. Instead, from the outside anyway, the office looked shabby and run down. Instead of going straight in, he walked a little further down the road before crossing over to the far side to have a better look.

The view was no better. From his vantage point on the opposite side of the road he could see the roof as well as the front. There were several tiles missing, and several of the upper floor windows were cracked. Ernie would have assumed the premises were empty and unused had it not been for the incongruous CCTV cameras. Contrary to his expectations, the cameras seemed new and out of keeping with the rest of the building's crumbling exterior. There were two on the front of the building, and when he walked around the block to the rear, he found there were also two cameras at the back.

He completed a full circuit of the building before entering to find himself in a small reception area. They'd hidden most of the interior behind a partitioned wall, with only a single doorway providing access to the rear from the reception area. The inside was as comprehensively covered by CCTV cameras as the outside, and there were three in the reception area despite its small size. One camera covered the main door, taking images of anyone who entered. Another covered the door to the rear, taking images of anyone who entered the inner sanctum, and the third camera covered the reception area itself. Someone was suffering from deep paranoia. Ernie wondered if the cameras were dummies, but the flashing lights seemed to indicate otherwise.

"Can I help you?" asked the receptionist.

"Yes. I hope so. Someone recommended Mr Phimister to me. Would it be possible to see him if he's free?"

"Is that Mr Phimister junior or senior?"

"They didn't say. I didn't realise there were two. My friend just said Mr Phimister."

"That's probably Mr Phimister senior then. I'm sorry, but he's not taking any new clients at the moment."

"That's a shame," said Ernie. "He came highly recommended. What about Mr Phimister junior?"

"He's not taking new clients either. They are both fully booked up for the foreseeable future I'm afraid."

"Is there just the two? Perhaps there are some other accountants available?"

"No. There's only the two of them," she said. "I'm sorry we can't help, but we are extremely busy. There's some other chartered accountants in the area that may have vacancies. Apart from that, all I can suggest is that you try us again in six months. Can't promise anything though, and to be honest we're still likely to be fully booked."

Ernie was running out of options, so he played his ace. "My friend said, if Mr Phimister wasn't available, to ask for Tim Armstrong."

The woman had been paying scant attention to

him up to this point. She'd answered his questions hastily, as if he was of little consequence. Now, she was definitely paying full attention. "I see. What's your friend's name."

Ernie knew something wasn't right. This didn't look like a chartered accountancy. It looked like a front. Behind the facade there was something more. Something dishonest was his guess. Something they needed to protect with the high spec cameras. He searched his mind for a criminal contact, and the only criminal that sprung to mind was the only one he knew.

"Bob Hinchcliffe gave me the name. Said to ask for Tim Armstrong if neither of the Phimister's were available."

"Bob Hinchcliffe? I'm sorry. Don't think I know him." The phone on her desk interrupted her. "Excuse me a moment." She picked it up without speaking. Listening intently to whoever was on the other end of the call.

Once she had hung up, she stood up, walked to the door and turned the sign from open to closed. "That was Phimister Junior on the phone," she said. "Seems he's just had a cancellation. If you'd like to follow me."

Ernie guessed someone must have been following the conversation on one of the cameras, and he followed her as she led the way through the door at the rear of reception. The change was immediate. The front office had been a perfectly adequate reception area. Spartan. Nothing exceptional. Just ordinarily adequate. The change as he walked through to the rear office was as spectacular as it had been unexpected. It was like a different building. She had led him into an office which appeared to have no windows, but which had panoramic views printed onto the full width of two walls. The impression was of a penthouse office overlooking the whole of Manchester. A man in his early forties was relaxing in a high-backed leather executive chair whilst seated at a matching leather-topped desk with a cigar in one hand and a cut-glass full of whiskey in the other.

"Thank you, Maud. Take a seat Mrs...?"

"Perkins. Ann Perkins."

Ernie thought he saw a definite twitch. An involuntary tic at the recognition of her name.

"Ann Perkins. What a pleasure to meet you," he said. "It is you isn't it? I recognise you from the papers. It's an honour to meet you. What brings you to our neck of the woods?"

Ernie got straight to the point. "You may have heard that I've set up a detective agency."

"I have heard," he said. "A ladies detective agency is sorely needed in this day and age. There are far too many husbands unfaithful to their wives and partners. Don't tell me one of my employees has been playing away?"

"No, nothing like that," said Ernie. "It's about Timothy Armstrong."

"He can't have been playing away. He's single I believe."

"He is," said Ernie, "but he's gone missing, and his mother's worried about him."

"Yes. I Heard about that," said Phimister. "His mother phoned and said he'd been missing a few days, but I've not seen him for the last fortnight myself."

"Doesn't he work here?" Ernie asked.

"Not exactly," Phimister said. "He works for

himself and has his own clients, but he comes in here occasionally and works from the office next door. Would you like to see it? We rent it out to other chartered accountants so he's not the only one who uses it, but it's not being used today."

He stood up and escorted Ernie along a corridor, and into an adjacent office. "He works freelance. Just pays us for the occasional use of the office when he has clients this side of the city."

The office was no less plush than the one Phimister occupied. The desk was similar, but with a picture of a couple with a child on one corner. At an angle, so clients and anyone seated in the main chair could see it. The picture confused Ernie for a moment as he thought Armstrong was single. The confusion must have shown on his face.

"This isn't his." said Phimister. "This picture belongs to the person who used the office yesterday. Hold on a moment." He opened the desk draw which contained several small picture frames. "This is Armstrong's," he said, pulling one out.

The picture had done nothing to remove Ernie's confusion.

"I know what you're thinking," Phimister said. "You're right. Armstrong's not married. It's an old accountant's trick. When you're married with children, clients are more likely to trust you with their money. I've no idea who the women and children are, but they've no connection to Armstrong. They've just been downloaded off the internet and he's been photo-shopped into the image to give the impression of a happily married family man."

Ernie looked around the office, but it was

sparse. Immaculately decorated with leather seating, oak bookcases, oak filing cabinet and the impressive but fake view over Manchester. "What about the filing cabinets?" he asked. "Will there be any clues as to his recent clients?"

Phimister laughed. "Doesn't even open. Just for show. We don't keep paper records any more. No need. All his client details would be on his laptop."

"Would you be able to tell me when he was last here then?" Ernie asked.

"Of course. Come with me." Phimister led the way back to the reception area.

"Maud. Will you check when Armstrong was last here?"

Her fingers were flying over the keyboard before he'd even finished speaking. "Nine days ago," she said. "A week last Wednesday."

"Thank you, Maud." Phimister turned back to face Ernie. "There you are then," he said, "we've not seen him for over a week. I do hope you find him. I don't know him very well, but I used to bump into him from time to time and his mother must be worried sick. Still, she's got you on the job now." He gave Ernie a pat on the back, but Ernie could not shake the conviction Phimister was insincerely patronising him.

Phimister accompanied Ernie to the door where Ernie noticed the receptionist had already turned the signs back to open. "One last question," he said. "Does Armstrong have a girlfriend or partner?"

"Not that I know about," said Phimister. "Never seen him with anyone. Have you Maud?"

"No. Sorry. I've never heard him talk about a partner," she replied.

"Right. Thanks for your help. If you think of anything else, please call me." As he left, Ernie handed Phimister one of his newly printed business cards.

The ride back on the bus gave Ernie plenty of time to think.

Armstrong's mother was familiar with her son's home, and a frequent visitor. If anything had been out of place, she would have noticed. The workplace was different. His mother had been adamant her son worked for Phimister and wasn't just using a desk at the premises. He was also supposed to have been promoted, and that wouldn't have happened if he'd been working for himself. Either her son was lying, or Phimister was lying. He'd put his money on Phimister being the liar, but couldn't think of a reason either of them would lie about where he worked.

Whoever was lying, and for whatever reason, Ernie was no nearer the truth. There appeared to be no current girlfriend, nothing out of place at home, no sign of a burglary or assault, and no trace of him at the office. He had exhausted all avenues of investigation, but he was loath to contact the client and tell her he was getting nowhere.

Ernie was half watching an inane quiz show on television, and half thinking about Armstrong when the phone jolted him back to the present.

"Ann. It's Bob. Bob Hinchcliffe." They had kept in touch since the sentence hearing and had met occasionally for a coffee in the city centre. Bob was still doing his community service, usually being supervised as he walked along some major highway picking up rubbish thrown out of car windows. In between the sessions of community service he had been unsuccessfully looking for a job. Things usually went well until he had to explain the regular gaps in his employment record, at which point interviews or phone calls would come to a speedy end.

"Hi Bob. How are you doing?"

"Fine. Sort of fine anyway. Community service is fine, but the job hunt is not going so well. At least I can look for a job and I'm not in prison, so things could be a lot worse I suppose."

"Something will turn up eventually," said Ernie. "How's the family?"

"They're fine. That's why I'm phoning. June wondered if you'd like to come around for dinner tomorrow night."

"What's the occasion?"

"No occasion. Just a normal dinner. June suggested I invite you. We're still grateful for the chance you gave me and she said she'd stretch to a bottle or two of wine if you come. Emma will be here too."

"Put like that, I can hardly refuse. Wouldn't like to deprive you of some wine. Two bottles won't be enough for the four of us though. I'll bring one. Red or white? And what time?"

"Either would be fine. We don't enjoy eating too late, so come for seven and we'll eat about half past if that's all right?"

"That's fine with me," said Ernie. "We'll catch up then, and I'll tell you all about my first case."

"You've got your first case? That's exciting. What is it? If you were Miss Marple, it'd be a murder."

"Nothing like that," he said. "Just a missing person. I'll tell you about it tomorrow."

Chapter Twenty-Six

The following afternoon Ernie closed the office early. He could think of nothing else he could do for his existing client but hadn't been able to concentrate as it was the anniversary of his wife's death. Hinchcliffe's home was only a short walk from his own, so he intended visiting the grave on his way.

As he sat on the bench with the two bunches of flowers, he was thinking how different his life could have. He'd had high hopes he and Doreen would have grown old together and his loneliness was almost palpable. He had never been one to say much, but her presence had always been enough to stop his depression deepening to unmanageable depths. Their temperaments had complimented one another. He had a tendency to overthink things and see all the potential complications, but she had always been unworried about the future.

He thought he'd learnt how to shun the thoughts triggering depression, but he recognised them now. He knew he should think of something else, but as he looked at the grave a short distance away he wasn't sure he wanted the pain to end. He missed Doreen, but at least they had a shared past. Doreen's stroke had snatched Daniel's future away. He sometimes wondered if it had been wrong to give the child a name but there had been so many hopes and dreams. Ernie had achieved so little but he would have ensured Daniel's life would have been different. All that potential was gone, and Ernie wondered what the point of his life was without the continuity that had been so cruelly snatched from him.

Ernie turned his attention to his client in a conscious effort to beat his depression and think of something else, but it didn't work. He realised he had done everything he could, but it hadn't got him anywhere and even his current venture seemed pointless. He had no idea what else he could do to solve the case, and the more he thought about it the more depressed he became. The earlier excitement about setting up his detective agency had faded, as had his anticipation about what his first case would entail. He had failed his first client, failed as a private detective, and as the grave in front of him so graphically illustrated, he had failed as a husband and father.

Other mourners were scattered throughout the cemetery, but he was physically and mentally alone. He lowered his head into his hands and broke down. Uncontrollably sobbing as his heaving body and mind gave up any semblance of restraint. Gradually the sobbing decreased until he eventually controlled it. The release made him strong enough to override most of the negative thoughts that still tried to intrude. He told himself Doreen wouldn't want to see him like this and imagined her scalding him. He wanted to be a strong father figure, and for his son to look up to him. He gave himself a few more minutes for his eyes to dry before rising and making his way to the grave.

He had known the anniversary of their deaths would be difficult, but the depth of his emotions had stunned him. Going into the flower shop and buying flowers had caused him no problems and his breakdown in the cemetery had been unexpected. Now alongside the grave it surprised him how resolute he felt.

His wife had been twenty-four weeks pregnant when she had the stroke that killed her. Their son was delivered by caesarean section after her death but he failed to take his first breath and they were buried together. "I've brought some flowers for you and Daniel," he said. He stood there for a moment in silence before speaking. "You mustn't worry about me. I've got new friends. They've invited me for dinner. I'm being looked after.... I'm looking after myself too.... I wish you were both here." He felt his eyes filling up again and stood in silence to compose himself before ending as he always did by reading the words on the gravestone. "Earth has no sorrow that heaven cannot heal," for his wife, "Born in the arms of angels," for his son, and "God bless you both".

Sarah Carter had been driving past the Cemetery when she had seen Ernie walk in, and the detective had parked on the road and watched as he sat on the bench and went to the graveside. She still had misgivings about Ann Perkins and still thought she had hidden something when they'd last met. She had found nothing about her on their own system. She'd even considered asking the Australians if they knew anything about her, but hesitated to make a fuss without at least some evidence to back up her gut feeling.

Sarah watched the person she believed was Ann Perkins walk away and waited until she had turned the corner before leaving her car and walking to the grave to discover it was for a woman named Doreen Sykes. She recognised Sykes as Ann's maiden name and thought the woman was probably Ann's mother. Then she saw the dates and realised she couldn't be because she was born the same year as Ann. She read the full inscription and realised the grave was for the wife of Ann's brother and their stillborn son.

After reading the inscription, she saw it was the anniversary of their deaths, and she immediately thought the two bunches of flowers were from Ann and her brother. She bent down to read the cards, and it surprised her to find they were both from Ernie Sykes, one for his wife and one for his unborn child. Ann had brought no flowers of her own, but there was no reason she should. According to Ann's interview she'd moved to Australia before her brother got married and returned after her sister-in-law's death so they couldn't have been close. Something didn't ring true. If they'd never met, then why was Ann so visibly upset at the graveside? And where was her brother if today was the anniversary of the death of his wife and child? What was so important that he couldn't come to the graveside himself?

There were no answers, only questions, but the growing number of unanswered questions about Ann Perkins had brought an increasing unease that Sarah was missing something important. She'd repeatedly gone through all the facts she knew about Ann Perkins and had found no evidence she'd committed any crimes, but Sarah trusted her intuition and there was definitely something intangible preventing her from giving Ann a clean bill of health.

Chapter Twenty-Seven

Short of any specific guidance, Ernie could not decide what wine to take so was taking one of each. One red and one white. They'd drawn the curtains in the semi-detached house, but as he approached, the porch had a warm glow from the escaping light.

Bob Hinchcliffe opened the door almost immediately after Ernie had knocked on it.

"Come in, Ann." he said. "We've been expecting you. I saw you coming from the upstairs window." Ernie held out the bag of wine. "Is that for us? You shouldn't have brought two bottles, one would have been enough, you must look after your money until your new business is up and running properly."

He led the way through the open plan living area to a large kitchen diner at the rear which was the full width of the house. They had already laid the large dining table and Hinchcliffe's wife was just putting something in the oven.

"Hello Ann," she said. "Right on time. Dinner will be about half an hour." She turned to her husband. "Bob, show Ann into the lounge. You'll both be out from under my feet."

"Come on, Ann," he said. "We're in the way here."

"Not too long mind," she said. "Half an hour."

Ernie and Bob retreated to the lounge where Bob took what appeared to be his usual chair. Ernie assumed the other chair was his wife's, so sat on the settee.

"I can't wait for you to tell me about your case," Bob said. "Better had though, or else you'll only have to repeat it all at dinner time. June and Emma are both dying to hear about it."

Ernie hadn't seen Emma. "Is Emma here, or is she coming later?"

"She's here. She still lives at home, and she's usually glued to her computer. When she's here she hardly ever leaves her room apart from meal times. Eats with us though, so the smell of cooking will entice her down once it's out of the oven."

They engaged in small talk until called into the dining room, where Emma joined them as her mother dished up a full roast dinner.

"You've got a lovely home," said Ernie, "and they say crime doesn't pay." He meant it as a joke, but could have kicked himself as soon as the words left his mouth.

Far from upsetting his hosts, his comment seemed to have the opposite effect. June Hinchcliffe laughed. "He was never that good at crime, Ann. He kept getting caught and there was no way he'd have ever got a mortgage for this place."

"She's right," said Bob "It's no thanks to me. I could never have bought it. June's the breadwinner. She's always earned more than I have."

"What do you do then June?"

"I'm a local government officer with Manchester City Council," she said. "Been there since leaving school. Started as an admin assistant and worked my way up. I'm the project manager for the council's disability plan."

"Sounds interesting," Ernie said.

"It is," she said, "and well paid. They keep coming up with plans for making everywhere disabled friendly, and my job is to ensure those plans get implemented."

"That's been half the trouble," Bob said. "I think I should be the breadwinner, but June's always brought in more than me. Depresses me sometimes."

"I keep telling you. It doesn't matter," she replied. "You don't have to prove yourself to me dear."

"You say that," he said, "but it's a man's job to care for his wife. It may be old-fashioned but it's how I was brought up. You keep saying it doesn't matter, but that doesn't stop me feeling that it does. That's the main reason I've gone out stealing. I should support you, not the other way around."

"And look where it's got you," she said. "You can't care for me from prison."

"I've never gone out intending to get caught," Bob said.

Emma had kept quiet up till this point, but now she joined in too. "Nobody goes out intending to get caught, dad, but you were never very good at it, it's about time you gave up and found something else."

"Well, thanks for your vote of support," Bob snapped. "It's different for those with degrees. I never had that chance."

Ernie was sorry he'd asked about June's job. It seemed to have touched a raw nerve.

"Still. All that's behind you now," Ernie said. "You've got a fresh start with a wife and daughter who both love you, and there's far more to life than any job title we may have." Ernie recognised his hypocrisy as soon as he had spoken. He remembered how it felt when they had made him redundant. The depression and the anxiety had become overwhelming. It was one of the first things he asked when meeting someone, and it was one of the first questions he asked June Hinchcliffe. His own job had defined who he was, and when they made him redundant he felt like a nobody. "How's your own job hunt going?" he asked.

"Not well," Bob said. "The job applications usually ask for a full work history with no gaps. Trouble is, my work history is full of gaps. I could lie and say I've been working abroad for all the years I've been in prison, but they'd probably ask what type of work I was doing and what countries I've worked in. I've found it easier to tell the truth on job application forms and say I've made mistakes for which I've paid my dues in prison. Kills the application process stone dead."

"What sort of things are you looking for?" Ernie asked.

"Some type of admin job," said Bob. "That's how I met June. I got a temporary job as an admin assistant at the town hall the same time as June started her permanent job. That's enough about us though. We're dying to know about your first client. A missing person case you said."

Ernie welcomed the change in conversation. "Yes," he said, "a missing person case. A woman came in and asked me to find her missing son."

"A missing child?" said June. "I've not seen anything about it in the papers."

"It's not a missing child," said Ernie. "Her son's

in his mid-thirties. He always rings his mother every night but hasn't phoned her for several days. The police aren't interested unless there's evidence of foul play, which there isn't, but the man's mother is convince something's happened to him. Says it's out of character for him not to contact her every day. His mother's been to his house and there is nothing untoward, and she's phoned his work but they haven't seen him for a while either."

"Probably just gone on holiday," Bob said.

"That's the first thing I thought," said Ernie, "but his mother's adamant he wouldn't have gone away without telling her first. I've visited his place of work, and it's weird. His mother was certain he worked there, but they told me he didn't. Not directly anyway. Apparently, he just uses their office from time to time. It was a strange place. Run down when you look at it from the outside, but inside it's rather plush, and bristling with CCTV cameras inside and out, as though they've something to hide. Anyway, I've been there, and it's a brick wall so I've no idea what to do next."

"What's his job?" June asked.

"Whose?" asked Ernie.

"The man that's gone missing. What's his job?"

"Chartered accountant," Ernie replied. "Works for a company called Phimister's, or more precisely doesn't work for them but uses their office from time to time."

"Phimister's! Do you mean Phimister's Financial Service in Levenshulme?" Said Bob.

"Yes, that's the place," said Ernie. "Have you heard of it?"

"They're the biggest crooks in the business," Bob said. "They do all the books for half the criminal families in Manchester. Phimister's is the place to go to if you have any money that needs laundering. They're accountants all right, but they've cooked so many books they've probably got a Michelin star."

"That would explain all the CCTV cameras," said Ernie. "I had a walk around the back. More cameras and what looks like a brand new lock on the back gate. Thought it was strange for a rundown building to have so many cameras."

"They're a bit stupid," said Bob. "They're in a rundown building so as not to draw attention to themselves, then they make it stand out by putting new cameras all over it. What's the name of the man that's missing? If he worked for Phimister's, I may know him."

"Timothy Armstrong," said Ernie.

"Tim Armstrong? I do know him," said Bob. "Don't think he's bent though. I think he does the books for Alf Sidebotham. Alf launders all his criminal money by investing it into legitimate businesses, and Tim does his books. The way I heard it, Tim only does the books for the legitimate part of the business, not his criminal activities."

"Could he have found out about the criminal side of the business and threatened to go to the police?" Ernie asked.

"Suppose it's possible," said Bob. "If he found out about it and it didn't bother him, that's one thing, but if it did bother him and he said so, he could well be in trouble."

"I spoke to young mister Phimister," Ernie said. "He's the one who told me Armstrong didn't work for him. I checked with the receptionist too. She confirmed he only used the office occasionally and hadn't been in for over a week."

"She would," said Bob. "It'd be more than her job's worth to contradict her boss, but that doesn't mean she was telling the truth."

"You say it's got lots of CCTV cameras?" Emma asked.

"Yes," said Ernie. "The front and back are both covered with them, and there's three cameras just in the reception area. Loads more in the back offices. I don't think there's any part of the building not covered."

"If they're that paranoid," Emma said, "there'll be a recorder somewhere storing the footage so they can access it remotely. If they can access it remotely, then I should be able to access it too. I could probably hack into it."

"Hack into it?" Ernie asked.

"Yes," she said. "The CCTV will stream to a hard drive probably in one of the back offices. They'll have set it up so Phimister can access it remotely to check the footage. If he can access it, then so can I, and I'd be able to look for the missing man and tell you when he was last there. If Phimister's lied to you, you'd know."

"And you can do that?" asked Ernie.

"If anyone can do it, my Emma can," her mother said. "I think I'm good with computers, but she's brilliant. If my Emma says she can do it, then she can."

"Isn't that illegal?" Ernie asked.

Emma ignored his question and asked one of her own. "Do you have a picture of the missing man," she asked.

"Yes," said Ernie. "I've got one on my phone.

Do you want to see it?"

He got his phone out, searched for the photo of Armstrong, and showed it to her.

Emma looked at it for a moment before sending it to her own phone. "Got it," she said. "Now, if you'll excuse me. I've got work to do. I'll get started on it straight away." She left the room, and Ernie could hear her climbing the stairs to her bedroom.

"May not see her now for days," said Bob.

It surprised Ernie how things were turning out. He'd been downhearted after his visit to the cemetery, not only because of his bereavement but also depressed at his inability to solve his first case. He had expected the evening would allow him to take his mind off things, and in the case of his wife and son that had been true, but not in regard to work. Talk about work had dominated the whole evening, but he understood more now than when he'd arrived. He knew Phimister looked after the books of criminals, and Armstrong looked after books for a criminal's legitimate business. Not only that, but if Emma was as good as her parents thought she was, she could check if Phimister and his receptionist had been telling him the truth when they said he'd not been there for over a week.

"Did you say you were looking for an admin job?" said Ernie.

"Yes," said Bob. "I've tried several things, but I've always enjoyed admin work. Photocopying, answering the phone, brewing tea for visitors, that sort of thing. Trouble is, most offices have confidential stuff of one sort or another, and it makes it difficult for them to use an ex-con. If something goes missing I'd be the first person to get the blame, but the company would also get a bad reputation for employing me in in the first place. It's easier for them not to take that risk."

"Fancy working for me?" said Ernie. The seed thought had travelled from the back of his brain to the front, and then straight out of his mouth. "When I went to Phimister's the other day, I had to leave my office empty. I don't want to do that as I get busier. I'll probably be out a lot, so I'll need someone at the office I can trust. Someone to do the basic admin and answer the phone whilst I'm away. How about it?"

"And you think you can trust me?" said Bob. "Despite my criminal past?"

"I do," said Ernie. "Your past isn't important. You've invited me into your home and made me welcome despite me giving evidence against you. I appreciate that, and I'm sure you won't let me down. I'm sure you won't let your family down either."

"So, would this be part time?" Bob asked. "Just for the time you're out of the office?"

"No," said Ernie. "Full time, and permanent. Well, as permanent as anything is these days. I intend making a go of my business and having you there will put my mind at rest whilst I'm out investigating cases. You can look after the office and make sure I don't lose any clients while I'm out."

"I'll do it," said Bob. He had not expected a job opportunity over dinner. He had applied for plenty of jobs but had got nowhere because of his past. Here was someone offering him a job who already understood all about his past without it bothering him. "When would you want me to start?" he asked.

Ernie laughed. "You haven't even asked me what your wages will be yet."

Bill laughed too. "Don't tell me. They're crap?"

"That's right," said Ernie. "I can't offer you much to begin with, but it will be at least a living wage, and it will be full time. As the business takes off, I'll review things every six months. You'll never get less than the living wage, but as soon as the business can afford it, I'll give you more."

"Sounds fair enough," said Bob. He would have taken the job, any job, without any talk of future pay rises. Anything was better than nothing. "Starting when?" he asked.

"How about tomorrow?" said Ernie. "Nine o'clock. Here's my card, and it's got the address on. Nine till five, with an hour off for lunch."

"Just one thing," said Bob.

"What's that?"

"Do I call you Ann or boss in the office?"

Ernie laughed. "Just Ma'am," he said. "Ma'am will do fine."

Chapter Twenty-Eight

Emma's bedroom was large, but only just large enough for her needs. It contained all the usual paraphernalia a young lady required, a bed, a large mirrored wardrobe, and somewhere to sit whilst she put her makeup on. These essential items weren't the problem. It was the other things which made the room look too small.

Her wider than usual desk contained three computers. There was a Windows laptop and a ten inch netbook both used for her university studies. The laptop contained presentation software for when she had to produce collaborative projects with other students, and word processing software for her assignments and final dissertation. The netbook had copies of her assignments, but she mainly used it for research as it was small enough to carry into lectures.

The third computer was a desktop. A large free standing system that took up too much of the vital floor space. This was her pride and joy. It had three separate hard drives complimented by impressively fast components. Two of the drives provided separate backups of the main drive, and the main drive itself contained a Linux distribution enabling her to work from a command line. She didn't need any slow or fancy graphics and the command line suited her just fine. She had connected the rig to a thirty-two inch wall mounted monitor ideal for displaying text, and a full size computer keyboard and mouse, both ergonomically designed to allow her hours of strain free repetitive use. The fake leather computer chair was the final component, and she could adjust it in several directions to provide ultimate comfort over lengthy periods.

Emma was in the final year of her undergraduate cyber security course at the University of Salford. She was in line for a first and had already decided she would study for a masters once her present course ended. There was a worldwide shortage of cyber security experts and her long-term goal was to earn the enormous sums of money her profession promised. Large multinational corporations had become depended upon computerised systems, and they paid substantial sums for security experts who understood the external threats to those systems, and who also understood how those threats could be prevented.

When companies employ cyber security experts, they give them permission to test their systems, identify any weaknesses, and make proposals as to how they can strengthen those weaknesses. Such permission is at the fulcrum between what is legal and ethical, or illegal and unethical. The UK's Computer Misuse Act makes it an offence to access someone else's computer without permission and there are no exceptions and no loopholes, not even for those taking cyber security courses. Authorised access to someone else's computer is legal, but unauthorised access is always a criminal offence.

Emma's course was both academic and practical, and the only way she could gain those practical skills was by testing the security of other people's computers. The university's computer science department had set up their own networked systems for that very purpose and had given students authority to test their skills by breaking into them. They were not alone. Some companies selling cyber security software also allow their customers to try out their software by attacking networks they have built specifically for that purpose.

Baz had been a significant help to her too. Emma had never met him in person, but they had gradually noticed one another's posts on a cyber security forum. She had been sceptical about him at first. There were plenty of posers on the forum bragging about knowledge they didn't have. She supposed it was the same for him. It took time for them to develop trust in one another's ability as they had watched one another develop over the past eighteen months. It was obvious Baz was more advanced than she was, but she had impressed him by the quality of her posts too. They eventually contacted one another via the forum's personal messaging service and later exchanged more detailed information.

Baz was doing a cyber security master's degree at the University of Oxford. They'd tested one another by authorising the hacking of each other's home computers, and this taught them a lot of vital practical skills. They also learnt a lot about each other. Despite never having met, they both knew almost everything there was to know about each other. They shared the intimacy that only comes from having accessed all the hidden personal files and images on one another's computers.

Because of her almost three years of study, and her friendship with Baz, Emma not only had a deepening knowledge of how to keep systems secure, but she also knew how to overcome the security of most of those systems.

Ann Perkins had helped her dad twice, and Emma was as grateful as her parents. Ann had tackled her dad in the bank before he had time to commit the robbery, saving him from a lengthy custodial sentence. Now she had offered him a job. Emma had no hesitation about showing her thanks by using her skills to help the Ann Perkins Detective Agency solve its first case.

She looked Phimister's Financial Services up on the internet and discovered it had its own website. There was only a single page giving brief details, but it was enough.

A search told Emma they hosted their website at a data centre in the south of England, with all emails from Phimister's Manchester office passing through that data centre's mail server. Hacking into the server gave her access to all Phimister's emails, and the header of those emails gave her the IP address of the router in Phimister's office through which most of the emails began or ended their journey.

Once armed with the IP address, the rest was relatively easy for her. In no time at all she had access to the router in Phimister's office, and through the router to the digital video recorder which asked for her username and password. She tried the default access details for that make and model of recorder and it surprised her when she didn't get access. Most users either don't know how to change the defaults, or don't bother changing them even if they do know how. Her set back was only temporary. She started a programme which tried thousands of regularly used passwords and usernames every second, and within a fraction of a second she was in.

Once she had access to the software in the digital video recorder, her monitor split into ten segments, one segment for each of the ten cameras. A list down the side of the main screen named each camera and clicking on a name displayed a long list of times and dates in half-hourly segments. She scrolled to the bottom of the list and discovered they kept the recordings for two weeks. She only needed images from a few days ago so knew those images would still be on the server.

Having achieved her immediate aim, she logged off.

Everyone had left the dining room, and they were all in the lounge, finishing the wine. "I'm in," she said. "I've got access to the cameras at Phimister's."

"That didn't take long," said Ernie.

"I told you she was good," her mother replied.

"So, what have you found?" Ernie asked.

"Nothing yet," said Emma. "I got access, and then logged off, but now I know the username and password, I can log in anytime. I can compare the image you sent to my phone with the images of those entering and leaving the office. I just need to narrow things down a bit. When did they say he was last there?"

"About nine days ago," said Ernie. "That would be ten days now."

"That's where I'll start looking then," said

Emma. "It looks as if they only keep things two weeks before over-writing everything. I'll save everything onto my computer then it won't matter if it gets written over as I'll have my own copy. It may take me a while to download and look through everything, but as soon as I find anything, I'll let you know."

"That's great Emma," said Ernie. "Thank you."

"No problem. See you later."

Emma disappeared back upstairs.

"Smart kid you've got there," said Ernie.

"Smarter than me anyway," said Bob. "I can use a computer, but I've no idea how she does all the things she does on hers."

"Me neither," Ernie replied. "She'll never be out of a job, that's for sure."

"First one of our family ever to go to university," said June.

"You must be very proud of her," said Ernie.

"We are." Bob said. "Very proud."

The evening continued with inconsequential small talk, and Emma never reappeared before it was time for Ernie to leave. He thanked his hosts for a wonderful evening and reminded Bob he expected to see him at the office promptly at nine o'clock the following morning.

"I'll be there," Bob replied. "Nine o'clock on the dot, and yours is milk but no sugar."

"I can see we will get along fine," said Ernie. "See you tomorrow."

By the time Ernie was leaving, Emma was already halfway through downloading copies of all the files from the remote recorder to her own computer. Once completed, she chose some files at random and played them through to make sure everything had downloaded with no errors. They all seemed to be alright.

Thomas Phimister had told Ernie Tim Armstrong had not been in for ten days, so she had a look at the files from the day he was last in. The recordings were in half-hour segments, and she began with the one starting at eight o'clock in the morning. She knew it would take a long time if she looked at everything in real time, but there was a danger she would miss something if she looked too quickly. She tried to find a middle ground, something fast enough to be speedy, but slow enough not to miss anything. She was not sure she had got the balance right, but she felt she could always go through things again later if she needed to.

The first person who entered the building arrived just after nine, and Emma assumed it was the receptionist. She unlocked all the inner offices, took a book out of a draw, and then spent most of her time sitting at the reception desk whilst reading. Only a single phone call disturbed her, and nothing else happened until ten o'clock when several people arrived in quick succession. They all walked into the largest of the rear offices and appeared to be having a meeting, but none of them looked like Tim Arnold. After fifteen minutes, all but one left, and she assumed the man who remained was Phimister. It was just before eleven when she eventually saw Tim Armstrong arriving. She stopped the tape and, holding her phone beside the screen, she compared the phone image with the CCTV image. It was definitely him.

Things became easier once she had identified him. She followed him from the outside camera at the front of the office, through the reception area where he offered a cursory greeting to the receptionist, and to the empty office at the rear. He sat at the desk using his laptop and she would have like to have seen the screen, but couldn't because the camera was at the wrong angle.

Emma kept her eye on Armstrong whilst still checking the main outside camera on a split screen. A middle-aged man arrived after about ten minutes, spoke to the receptionist, and she accompanied him through to Armstrong's office. The client stayed for a little under half an hour before leaving, and Armstrong then spent several minutes looking through some papers and entering details into his laptop. She followed him as he left his own office and entered Phimister's office. It looked as though they had an argument, but eventually Armstrong stormed out of the office, stormed through the reception area, and out of the main door.

Emma viewed the rest of that day's images, but there was no sign of Armstrong's return. She scanned the next couple of days images seeing no sign of him, but by then she was getting tired and it was late. It had been a long day and she could not be sure she had not fallen asleep during the last video. The university described the following day as a study day, but in the time-honoured tradition of students everywhere, she thought of it as a day off. She finished for the night, to resume her search the following morning.

Chapter Twenty-Nine

Ernie arrived early at the office the following day and had already disguised himself as Ann Perkins before Bob arrived at nine o'clock.

When Ernie's phone rang, it was the receptionist. "I've got a Bob Hinchcliffe here," said the receptionist. "Says he works for you."

"That's right, Dave," said Ernie. "He starts this morning."

"I didn't realise you were taking anyone on," said Dave

"Sorry," said Ernie. "I should have told you, but I wasn't taking anyone on till last night. It was a spur-of-the-moment thing."

The receptionist laughed, "Drunk where you?" he said.

"We'd downed a few," said Ernie, "but not that many. Bob's my new administrator."

"Right, I'll send him along. Do you want me to give him a key, and show him where the communal kitchen is?"

"Yes please," said Ernie. "All our stuff has our name on, so make sure he doesn't pinch anyone else's mugs, but can you ask him to bring coffee's back, one for me and one for himself."

"Will do," Dave said, as he hung up.

A few minutes later Bob arrived at the office carrying two cups of coffee.

"Here you are. Milk, but no sugar," said Bob. "What do you want me to do first?"

"I'm not sure," Ernie said. "I hadn't thought

that far ahead." Ernie had been bored before the first client had turned up, and he'd struggled to find things to occupy himself, never mind someone else. "I need someone to be in the office to make appointments and answer the phone when I'm away, but I hadn't thought further than that. As we get busier, there'll be many things need doing, but there's nothing specific at the moment. There's no filing to do, nothing to photo copy and no letters to answer."

"Tell you what," Bob said. "I'll keep supplying you with tea or coffee every hour until you've worked out what to do with me."

The phone rang. Ernie reached out to answer it but Bob beat him to it.

"This is the Ann Perkins Detective Agency. Robert speaking. How can we be of assistance?"

"Dad? Dad, is that you?"

"Oh, hi Emma," he said. "Yes, it's me."

"I almost didn't recognise you with your posh voice."

"Not posh, Emma. Professional. That was my professional voice."

"Whatever. Can I speak to Ann please?"

"Of course." Bob passed the phone over.

"Hello Emma. How are you getting on?" Ernie asked.

"I've found something interesting. Are you going to be in all morning? If so, I'll come and show you."

"Yes," he said. "We'll both be here all day."

"Right. I'll be there in about an hour."

"Okay, see you later," Ernie said, before hanging up.

"Wonder what she's found?" Bob said.

"She didn't say," said Ernie, "but she seemed very excited about something."

It was not long before Emma arrived with her laptop, placed it on the desk, and turned it on. Whilst it was booting up, she explained why she had come.

"I found Timothy Armstrong on the video. He went to the office ten days ago just like they said. A client visited him, and then he had what seemed to be an argument with Phimister before he stormed out. That appeared to have been the last day he was there. He never appeared again, but I continued looking at the rest of the footage and other people were coming and going all day."

"So, they were telling the truth," said Ernie, "the last day he was there was ten days ago."

"Not exactly," said Emma. "Ten days ago was the last day he was there, but once I'd checked all the day time footage I went on to scan through the night time footage. He was there four nights ago."

"Four nights ago. That's about the time he disappeared. Why was he there?" Ernie said.

"I'll show you." She turned the laptop towards her and selected a video. "It was dark, so you can't see all that well. It's timed at half-past one in the morning. I've split it up so you can view all four cameras at the same time. The action starts in a couple of seconds at bottom left. That's the camera outside the front door."

Ernie and Bob huddled around the laptop. A white unmarked van pulled up and three people got out from the front. Although the image was not clear enough to identify who they were, their dark silhouettes stood out against the white of the van. They moved to the back door of the van and carried something out. Something that was bulky and awkward to carry.

"What on earth's that?" Ernie said.

"You can't tell from this picture," said Emma, "but that's Timothy Armstrong."

"Are you sure?" Bob asked.

"I'm sure, dad. You'll be able to see for yourself in a minute."

They continued watching as two people held onto the bundle whilst the third opened the outer office door.

"Bottom right," said Emma, as the men entered the reception area.

"Top left," she said, as they passed through reception and into the back. Once through the door from reception, they dropped the bundle unceremoniously onto the floor. Someone turned the lights on, and the film showed Armstrong on the floor. His face was red and swollen, and he appeared to be unconscious.

"Blimey!" Ernie said. "What are they doing to him?"

"Just watch," said Emma. "You'll see in a minute."

The lights allowed clear images to be captured on the CCTV. "That's young Phimister," said Ernie. "I don't recognise the other two."

"I do," said Bob. "The one standing closest to him is his father, old man Phimister. The other one's Frank Wade. Bulldog Wade they call him."

Once the three men had got their breath back, two of them got hold of a leg each and dragged Armstrong's body along the corridor. As they got to the end of the passage close to the rear door, they appeared to go to the left-hand side of the corridor and then disappeared. "Where did they go?" Ernie asked.

"That's a good question," said Emma. "The entire place is bristling with cameras. Outside front and rear, reception area, offices and passageways. Everywhere except wherever they've taken him. You can't tell from the camera covering the passageway, but there's a room just off. On the CCTV footage the passage just looks continuous all the way to the back door."

"A hidden room of some sort?" said Bob.

"Looks like it," she said. "When you view the images of the offices, both seem to be the same size, but if you look harder, you can tell Phimister's office goes back further than the other one. There's just enough space behind the other one for another small room."

"Well done Emma," said Ernie. "What happened next?"

"That's just the thing, Ann," said Emma. "Nothing else happened. Two of the men leave, but Armstrong and the third man, Wade did you say? They remain in the hidden room. I've been through all the remaining tapes. Wade reappears eventually and others go in, but Armstrong never reappears."

"You mean he's still there? Still in that room?" said Ernie.

"Looks like it," Emma replied. "Doesn't seem to be any other way out. They've covered all the exits with cameras. If they'd taken him out, I'm sure I'd have seen him. I think he must still be there."

"Bloody hell," said Ernie. "Shouldn't we tell the police?"

"Hold on," Bob said. "Tell them what exactly? They'll ask how we found out. We can hardly tell them we've hacked into a private CCTV system. Anyway, even if we show them the footage, what does it show? It shows Armstrong being carried into his place of work by his employers. If there is another way out and he's not there when the police call, they'll just say they were helping him because there was an office party and he was drunk, and once he sobered up, he went on his way. We'll probably all get done for wasting police time, Emma will get done for illegal hacking, and I'll be back at court and have my community service replaced by a jail sentence."

"But we have to do something," Emma said. "The way they just dumped him on the floor and then dragged him along the corridor. He could even be dead."

"Are you certain there are no other cameras, Emma?" asked her dad.

"Dad, I've checked them all," she said. "As far as I can tell from the camera out the back, there are not even any windows in the room they carried him in to. If we hadn't seen them disappear to the left at the end of the passage, we wouldn't even know there was a room there."

"Could we break in?" said Ernie. "We could see if Armstrong was being held prisoner and phone the police anonymously once we're sure."

"There doesn't appear to be any alarms," Bob said, "but who do you think will break in?"

"I thought you'd do it," Ernie said.

"No way." Bob and his daughter replied in unison.

"There's no way that's going to happen," Bob

repeated. "If I get caught breaking in, everyone will think I'm a burglar. Nobody will believe me when I tell them I've broken in to rescue someone, and they'll throw the book at me. You could do it, Ann. You'd get away with it because you're a private detective. If you get caught, you could tell them you're on a case and they'd believe you because it would be true. You'd be all right."

"No way," said Ernie, echoing their own answers. "I don't understand the first thing about breaking into anywhere. I wouldn't know where to begin."

"Everyone has to start somewhere," said Emma.

"No," Ernie said. "I don't have to start anywhere. I've not broken into anywhere in the past, and I don't intend starting now." A small inner voice reminded him about the bank and the jewellers, but he discarded it. Neither of those had technically involved breaking into a building.

"Let's see the film again," her dad said.

They watched the film again from the beginning.

"Stop it there," Bob said. She stopped the film at the point Armstrong was being dragged along the passageway, and Bob studied it for a few seconds. "Can you enlarge the area around the back door?" he asked.

Emma zoomed in until the rear door filled the monitor.

"What have you seen?" Ernie said.

"There's no way of breaking in through the back door," said Bob. "It's only got a cheap lock on it like most back doors have, but it's got three strong bolts on the inside. It's my guess that nobody uses that back door and the bolts are always on. Top, middle and bottom. You'd need to use some serious force to get in there."

"That's out then." Ernie gave a sigh of relief. He had no qualms about asking someone else to break in, but there was no way he was going to do it himself.

"Not so fast," said Bob. "Have we got some images of the front door, Emma?"

"Sure. Do you want them up?" Without waiting for an answer, she switched cameras, and zoomed in to display a large image of the front door. "How's that?"

"That's better," Bob said. "That's more interesting."

Ernie and Emma both stared at the screen, but to them it just looked like an ordinary front door and not interesting at all.

"That's a five lever security mortice lock," said Bob.

Ernie had heard about five lever security locks. They always asked about them when he renewed his content insurance. He didn't know what sort of locks he had, and he'd no idea what a five lever mortice lock even looked like. A lock was a lock as far as he was concerned, but he knew they must be good if insurance companies recommended them. He couldn't break in through the back door and he couldn't break in through the front door. He did not have to break in at all. He breathed another sigh of relief despite realising he still had no idea what else to do.

Chapter Thirty

If Ernie thought he'd got out of breaking into Phimister's office, he was soon disillusioned.

"You'll easily get in there," said Bob.

"Eh? I thought that made it harder to break in," said Ernie.

"You'd think so, but you'd be wrong," Bob replied. "I could get in there easy. You'll be fine."

"You keep saying I'd be fine, but there's no way I'm breaking in there. No way," he said again. "Anyway, they'd catch me on camera."

"Not necessarily," Emma said. "I could sort it." She put another image on screen. "This is a different night, a night when nothing's happening. What do you see when I run it through at normal speed?"

Ernie and Bob both watched the screen.

"What are we supposed to be looking for?" Ernie asked after a few minutes. He hadn't seen anything unusual.

"What can you see?" she replied.

"Nothing," Bob said. "Just the front of the building."

"Exactly," said Emma. "Nothing moves when there's nothing happening. I could replace the live feed with a still image, and nobody would be any the wiser. You could break in through the front door, but if anyone checked the cameras, they would see nothing out of the ordinary."

"That's all well and good, but I still don't understand how I can get in," said Ernie.

"I can help you there," said Bob. "Are you going home now, Emma? If so, I'll come with you. I've got some things I need to collect. I'll be back in an hour or two."

It was almost two hours before Bob returned, and Ernie spent most of that time trying to think of a good reason to avoid breaking into Phimister's office. He could think of no better excuse than he would be scared stiff.

When Bob returned, he was carrying a backpack.

"What have you got there?" said Ernie.

"This," said Bob, "is a five-lever security mortice lock," he reached back into his bag, "and this is a tensioner," he reached in again, "and this is a lock pick."

Ernie explained something that was glaringly obvious to him, but which did not seem to be as obvious to Bob. "I can't pick a lock," he said. "I've no idea how to even begin picking a lock."

"You may not know how to do it, but I do," Bob said, "and I will give you the benefit of my experience. You don't need to know how to pick lots of locks. Just this one. It's the same type that's on the door of Phimister's office. I can get through this in seconds, and within a couple of hours you'll be able to do the same."

"I'm not so sure about that," said Ernie.

"I'm sure," Bob said. "I'll show you the inside first." He undid the screws holding the lock together. "Normally, you can't take the side off because it's fastened in the door, but look at these levers. Cheap locks only have one lever, but this model has five. You can't force the bolt back because all five levers are in the way."

"Yes. I can see that," said Ernie.

"Each of the levers have a slot. The slot's called a gate. When all five slots line up, it creates a single gate allowing the lock to open." He put the key in and turned it. "When I turn the key all the levers move up slightly and once all the slots are in a line, the bolt slides back."

"Easy enough with a key," said Ernie.

"Easy enough with a pick too, usually," said Bob. "The levers lift in a certain order, all you have to do, is put the pick in and pick each lever up one at a time until you've lifted them all. Unfortunately, with this lock they've made it harder."

"How's that?" said Ernie. Intrigued now despite his misgivings.

"It's a security lock. Got three features to prevent picking. The first one's here, where the key goes in. It's called a curtain. When you put the key in, the first movement of the key moves the curtain round so the head of the key can move the levers. If you put a pick in, the curtain is still in the way, and the pick can't reach the levers. The second security feature is the gates. The slots in the levers. Each lever has a false gate as well as the real gate, a smaller slot too small for the bolt to pass through. If you try to pick the lock and line up one of the false gates instead of a real one, the lock still won't open it."

"Sounds good to me," said Ernie. He was growing more confident every minute. The lock seemed impregnable.

"The final security feature is this bar above the top of the levers. You can use brute force on some locks and move the levers right up into the lock casing and away from the bolt altogether. Not all locks have this, but this is a decent lock and the bar stops brute force attacks. It stops the levers from being pushed too far up."

"Well, that's it then," said Ernie. "Even you couldn't get into this lock."

"You'd think so wouldn't you," Bob said. He put the screws back into the side of the lock and assembled it fully before locking it with the key. "This pick moves the levers, but the security curtain stops it. This tensioner moves the security curtain out of the way. Neither of them is enough on their own, but put them both in together and you turn the tensioner to get rid of the curtain and use the pick to move the levers." As he had been talking, he had been following his own instructions and inserted both the tensioner and pick into the lock. "The pick needs to lift each of the levers in the right order. One. Two. Three. Four. Five." He pushed the pick further into the lock after each click until the bolt sprang back into the casing and unlocked. "It's as quick and as easy as that," he said.

"Wow!" said Ernie. "That was quick. It's fine for you though, you'll have had lots of practice."

"Not as much as you may think," said Bob. "You'll soon get the hang of it too."

Ernie spent the next few hours in Bob's master class. At the beginning he convinced himself it was impossible and his attempts confirmed his belief. It was difficult for him to hold the tensioner and pick together and he was reminded of the times he had tried patting his head with one hand and rubbing his belly with the other. Even when he had mastered moving the curtain out of the way and getting the pic past it, he still found it difficult to feel the difference between the real and false gates.

"It's always difficult at first," Bob said, "but you're doing fine."

"I don't think I can do it," said Ernie. "The lock's not even close to opening."

"You're closer than you think," said Bob. "It may feel as though you're not getting anywhere, but sometimes there's only one gate between you and success. You're getting most of the gates lined up each time, but it only takes one to stop it opening."

Suddenly, almost fifteen minutes later, the lock sprung open. "Well done," said Bob. "If you can do it once, you can do it again."

Ernie failed the next time, and the time after that. He was successful again the next time though, and a few minutes later he was succeeding more often than he was failing.

"Listen for the clicks," said Bob. "You'll hear each lever click into place. You're still finding some false gates, but the real gates are larger and move more than the false ones, so you should feel for the movement too. You don't need your eyes. Just listen and feel. Feel for the movement and listen for the clicks."

Slowly, but surely, Ernie got better at it. He was still anxious about the break in, but he found the lock picking exercise strangely satisfying. There was a definite buzz every time he heard a lever click into place, and a sense of achievement as the bolt finally slid back.

"It's actually easier than it looks." Ernie was taking a break and drinking a well-earned coffee.

"Don't tell the insurance companies," said Bob.

"I told you it was easy. It takes a bit of practice, but once you've got the hang of it, you could do it blindfolded. You don't have to see what you're doing. It's all about the feel of the gates and the noise of the levers."

"I'm still far from sure about tonight," Ernie said.

"You'll be fine. There can't be any bolts on the inside of the front door because it's the door everyone leaves by. That's why they bought an expensive lock. In most cases an expensive lock works fine on a front door. I'm sure a neighbour would ring the police if they saw someone picking my front door one night. The office is different. It's a commercial building with no houses overlooking it. You'll be in and out before anyone even knows you're there. Emma will replace the live footage with the static image, and she'll put the live image up on her own screen. If anyone does come along the street whilst you're breaking in, or comes to the building whilst you're inside, we can phone you and tell you. That's not going to happen though."

Ernie hesitated before answering, not totally convinced. "I suppose not," he said eventually.

"There you go then," said Bob. "Once you're inside you can check the back room. If Armstrong's there, ring and tell us and we'll ring the police anonymously once you're out. If he's not there, just come out the same way you entered. Once you're out, Emma will return the cameras to their normal settings and nobody will be any the wiser."

"I'd feel happier if you were with me," said Ernie. "If there's no chance of me getting caught, I can't understand why you can't do it yourself."

"I would if I could," Bob replied. "Trouble is, I'm too well known. You can walk about the streets all night and nobody will ever ask where you're going or search your pockets. They'll just assume you've been out for the evening and you're on your way home, or you're working nights, or any of a million reasons people need to be out and about at night. But as soon as a copper sees me, they'll use any excuse to search me, and if they find a pick on me I'd be in court the following morning for going equipped for stealing, and I'd be sent to prison the same day. I just can't risk it."

Ernie didn't think he could risk it either, and he intended saying so, but somehow, the message got muddled between his brain and his mouth. "I'll do it," he said. "I'll break in tonight."

"Thanks Ann," said Bob. "You'll be fine."

Chapter Thirty-One

Ernie was visibly shaking. His teeth were providing a tuneless drumbeat to accompany his breathing and the freezing wind cut through him like a knife as it drove the rain into his face. He had already made a mental note to buy Ann Perkins some warmer winter clothing. He'd worn a dress when he went to rob the bank because he wanted no one to make a mistake about his gender. He needed to ensure police looked for a female robber not a male one, but his priority now was to stay warm rather than to look feminine.

He wore an anorak, but although it kept the wind off his body, it did nothing for other parts of him. His ears felt cold enough to snap off, and he had never before realised that his nose stuck out so proudly into the wind and rain. All the rain that landed on his waterproof coat had run straight off onto his tights and shoes, and his feet were sodden. He told himself he only shook from the cold, but he also shook from fear.

Being scared was not a new experience to him. He'd been scared when he went to rob the bank and jewellers, but tonight's fear was different. There was street lighting, but it threw large shadows across the road, and left large pools of impenetrable blackness at the edges. His overactive imagination saw dark uniformed police officers lurking in the shadows, just waiting to pounce as soon as he started breaking in.

The earphones gave him some comfort, but not

enough.

"We have you in view now," they said. "Emma's got you on camera. She's already changed the picture so you don't appear on the recording, and we'll keep our eye on things from this end."

"Right," Ernie replied, hoping they understood what he said through his chattering teeth. "I'm going now."

As he approached the door, he looked at the lock. He couldn't tell if it was identical to the one he had practised on. He couldn't be sure because he could only see the keyhole, and even that was in his own shadow, but he had come too far to turn back now and would just have to take Bob's word for it.

He listened, but there was no sound other than the wind and the rain. No alarms. Nobody crying out, and nobody asking why he was standing in front of the door.

Taking the tensioner and pick out of his pocket, he lined them up as Bob had taught him and pushed them into the keyhole. The protective curtain moved out of the way as he added pressure to the tensioner. He moved the pick and immediately heard the click as the first lever moved out of the way. "That's the first one," he said.

"Well done, Ann. I knew you could do it." Bob's voice said in his earphone.

"Long way to go yet," Ernie replied.

Ernie now realised why Bob told him he could do it blindfolded. He couldn't see the lock properly, never mind the working end of the pick. Click. "That's the second."

He had kept his hands in his pockets until he got to the door, but his fingers were getting cold now and finding it hard to hold the pick and tensioner together. He had only been at the door a matter of seconds, but it seemed a long time. "I'm going for the third lever now, but my fingers are freezing."

"You'll be warm once you're out of the wind," Bob said, "and you'll be in inside in a minute."

The clicks from the remaining levers came in quick succession. "That's the last," he said. "No! Wait! It's not opening. I've done all five, but I still can't open it."

"Don't panic," said Bob's voice through his earphones. "You've probably got a false gate, that's all. Remember what I taught you. Come out in reverse. Move all the levers back then start again. You've got bags of time. You've only been there about two minutes and there's nobody else about."

Ernie heard another voice from further away. "I'm monitoring the front and rear cameras," said Emma. "The streets are empty. There's no rush."

"Thanks Emma," Ernie said. "I'll start again."

Ernie took his time, reversed what he had done, and then began again.

The second time, all the levers moved to the correct gate, and as he moved the fifth lever, the pressure of the tensioner moved the bolt back into its casing and the pressure on the lock caused the door to open.

"I'm in," he whispered.

"We're with you, Ann. We'll follow you through on the cameras. Put the latch on if there is one, so the door appears to be locked if anyone tries it. Nobody will tell from outside that the full lock isn't on, but you'll be able to get out in a hurry if you need to."

"Thanks Bob. I'll do that."

Ernie followed Bob's instructions and closed the door behind him on the latch but without locking it. He had been in the reception area before, but it looked very different in the dark. Out of the wind and rain, he stood still for a few minutes rubbing his hands until his teeth finally stopped chattering and the circulation to his fingers was restored. By then he had got his bearings, and he crept across the room towards the door giving access to the offices.

He opened the door, closed it behind him, and felt for the light switch on the wall. The light blinded him for a moment, but he soon adjusted to it. Looking down the passageway towards the rear door it looked exactly like it had done on the images, and there didn't seem to be a room off.

He walked down the corridor, and as he did so an opening came into view on his left-hand side. "There's only a small recess, then a door. You won't be able to view me on any of the cameras once I've gone through the door, so I'll put my phone on face-time so you can enter with me."

"Be careful," said Bob. "We don't know what's in there."

Ernie started filming and held the phone in front of him as he stepped forward and pushed open the door.

"Bloody hell!" he exclaimed.

There was only a small emergency light on in the room, but as light flooded in from the passageway he could see a mattress on the floor near the far wall. The person lying on it stared up at him, cowering and wide eyed with fear. His hands were handcuffed together and his chained and manacled left foot was fastened to a cast iron radiator. The man was curled up into a foetal position with his arms wrapped protectively around his head.

"It's okay," said Ernie as he stepped into the room. "I'll not hurt you."

The man still looked wide eyed and apprehensive, and Ernie was wondering what else he could say to reassure him when he felt a sudden blow to the back of his head. For a split second he felt his vision blurring and his legs buckling beneath him as he dropped his phone. Then there was nothing.

The light returned slowly. At first it was only a faint glow through his closed eyelids. As it grew in intensity, he opened his eyes only to shut them again immediately as the light hit him. He didn't know how long he'd been unconscious. A splitting pain at the rear of his head was the first thing to return after the light. His hearing followed some time later when he heard a distant voice asking how he was. His vision returned in stages, initially rather blurry before being able to open his eyes and focus fully again.

"Are you all right?" the voice asked again.

He turned towards it, realising he now lay on the same mattress as the man who had spoken to him. Ernie went to rub the pain at the back of his head, but found his hands handcuffed. He tried to stand up and discovered his left leg shackled to the same radiator.

"What's going on?" he asked.

"I wanted to ask you the same question," said

the man.

"Are you Tim Armstrong?"

"Yes! How did you know? Who are you?"

"My name's Ann Perkins," said Ernie. "I'm from the Ann Perkins Detective Agency and your mother sends her regards. She asked me to find you and rescue you. Don't worry, everything will be fine."

"You bloody idiot. You've not rescued me. You've just got yourself captured. We're both in trouble now."

"What hit me?" asked Ernie.

"Frank," Tim said. "Frank Wade. Used to be a boxer. Packs quite a punch, doesn't he?"

"Where the hell did he come from?"

"He didn't come from anywhere. He was already here, sitting just behind the door as you entered. He was amusing himself by tormenting me, but you caught him by surprise entering the way you did. As soon as he got his wits back, he smacked you one."

There was nobody in the room apart from the two of them. Ernie looked at the handcuffs, and then at his ankle. There didn't seem any way to escape.

"What happens now?" he asked.

"My guess is, Frank has gone to phone Phimister, the owner of the building. They'll decide what happens, but I know what's in store for me. I'd be dead already if they'd got what they want. I've got a copy of their accounts, but they don't know what I've done with it. That's my insurance policy. They may torture me but won't dare kill me till they've got their hands on it. You're different. You've got no insurance policy.

They've no reason to torture you, but they've no reason to keep you alive either."

Ernie looked around for his phone. He'd had it when he entered, but he'd dropped it when Wade hit him. He couldn't see it, but it was possible Wade may have found it and taken it away.

"I'm sure I'll be all right. I've got a little insurance policy of my own, and I've some friends who will send some help."

Tim Armstrong didn't look convinced. "That's what I thought at first," he said. "I contact my mum every night so thought they'd free me as soon as she realised I was missing. Trouble is, nobody knows where I am. You'll be the same. They may miss you, but nobody will look here for you. How did you find me anyway?"

Ernie decided not to tell him. Bob and Emma wouldn't know exactly what happened in the back room, but they would have seen Frank leaving and they'd know something was wrong.

A noise caused them both to turn their heads and stare at the door as it opened.

"Two of you to bloody contend with now," Frank said as he entered. "You're dead love," he said to Ernie. "I don't know who you are and why you'd want to break in here, but you've picked the wrong place."

Ernie suddenly realised Frank thought he was a common burglar and didn't know why he'd broken in.

"I thought it was an empty office," said Ernie.

"Well, you made a mistake," said Frank, "because it wasn't, but you'll be wishing it had been when we're finished with you."

Chapter Thirty-Two

"Who the hell are you?" Thomas Phimister was unhappy someone had broken into his office, and he was even more unhappy about being called out in the middle of the night to sort things out. He believed chartered accountancy was a nine-to-five job with at least a two-hour lunch break and a three-day weekend. He didn't do nights, and would rather have been in bed.

Ernie didn't recognise Phimister as he had only met his son. More importantly, Phimister hadn't recognised him, and Ernie thought he may get away with it if he continued acting the part of a burglar. Given they were crooks themselves, he thought they may understand it was all a mistake and let him go. "I saw the empty office," he said, "and thought there'd be nobody in. Gave me a right scare when your man found me. I caused no damage and stole nothing. I chose the wrong office that's all. If I'd known it was your office, I'd have gone somewhere else. Sorry."

"Sorry! You're sorry! You will be sorry," said Frank. "And for the record I'm nobody's man. He may work in this office and have his name over the door, but he doesn't own it. I pay his salary and he works for me not the other way around."

"Sorry sir," Ernie said.

"A bloody woman," Frank said. "You should be at home looking after your man. You shouldn't be out in the middle of the night breaking into places like this. That's men's work."

Ernie thought that was sexist, but he thought it best not to say so. "Sorry," he said again.

"Has she been anywhere else?" asked Phimister. "In any of the other offices?"

"Not as far as I can tell, but we can check the CCTV."

"We'd best do that then. What's Armstrong said to her?"

"I've said nothing," said Armstrong. "For all I know, she's a plant to get me talking but I'm not talking to anyone. I'm not talking to you and I'm not talking to her. My information's safe, but the person who's got a copy of it will take it to the police if I'm not out of here soon."

"You'll be out of here soon enough," Wade said. "If you don't answer our bloody questions, you'll be going out in a box."

"I've no idea what you gentlemen are talking about," said Ernie, "but no harm done. If you'll let me go, I'll be on my way." He got hold of the chain that was fastening him to the radiator and held it up to show he'd have been on his way already if he'd been able to.

"Not yet," said Frank. "Let's check the video and see where she's been since she broke in. We'll have a better idea what to do with her once we've seen if she's been rummaging about. I'll come with you whilst we have a look. They're not going anywhere."

Frank double checked the handcuffs and manacles to make sure everything was secure, before he and Phimister left to check the CCTV in Phimister's office.

Ernie listened to the receding footsteps and spoke to Tim Armstrong as soon as they disappeared.

"I wouldn't put too much faith on them not killing you," he said. "It may delay things not telling them, but it sounds like they'll kill you anyway once you've told them what they want to know. They'll probably kill me too. It's the only way they can be sure I won't go to the police."

"I've sent a copy of their hard drive to someone I can trust," said Armstrong. "If I'd told them who I'd sent it to she'd be dead by now too, but at least delaying things has given her a chance to get right away."

Whilst Ernie and Tim Armstrong were discussing their fate, Frank and Phimister were having a somewhat similar discussion in Phimister's office.

"There's no sign of her on the video," said Frank. "Between you leaving yesterday afternoon and arriving early this morning nobody else arrives. It's as though she's come from thin air."

"That's odd," said Phimister. "How can that happen? There are no gaps in the tape, she's not a ghost, and there are no windows broken. You found a lock pick when you searched her, so she's definitely come through the front door, but I don't see how she could have done. Unless..." He looked at the camera in the corner of his office. "I wonder... I wonder if she's hacked into the CCTV."

"She can't have. We'd have noticed."

"Not necessarily," said Phimister, "and I can't think of any other way she could just walk in here without being picked up on camera. All the cameras seem to work properly and they appear to have been working all night, so there's no other way I can think of for her picture not being on any of the images."

"What does that mean?"

"It means she's bloody dangerous, that's what it means. She could be an undercover cop. Fraud or even serious crime. We should cut our losses, kill both of them and deny they were ever here."

"What about the copies of the hard drive Tim's got?" asked Frank.

"I know he's made copies of some files, but I don't know what he's done with them. If he's given a copy to someone else for safekeeping we'd have heard by now and had a more official visit from police with a warrant to search the premises. The fact she's had to break in to search the place means the police haven't got enough evidence for a warrant so we should be all right. I think Tim's bluffing and playing for time. I'll let you do the honours."

"Me! You work for me, remember. Why me?"

"I'm strictly a cerebral person," Phimister said. "I'm an accountant and I'm good with figures, but I look after the paperwork and that's all I want to do. If you can give me half an hour before you kill them it'll give me time to get back home. I'll come in for work as usual in the morning by which time you'll have cleaned everything up. You're the boss now Alf's gone, so the physical stuff's your domain. If I were you I'd call someone in to help you move the bodies after you've done them."

Frank was going to argue. He was new in the job and it didn't feel right for Phimister to be telling him what to do. On the other hand, Phimister was right and there was no need to be churlish about it. Someone did have to kill

Armstrong and the woman, and Phimister wasn't the right person for that. He decided to let it go. He'd have plenty of time to put Phimister in his place once he had dealt with the current situation.

After Phimister left, Frank made a phone call for one of his gang to come and help move the bodies. "Get the polythene," he said. "We'll kill them on that, then roll them in it to keep the room clear of forensics. There'll be no trace they've ever been here."

Frank loaded his gun and played with it whilst he was waiting. He had killed someone before, but that had been in a street shootout with another gang trying to take over their territory when Alf had been the boss. Despite his hard-man image and reputation for violence he'd never killed anyone close up in cold blood. Whilst waiting for the other gang member to turn up he was thinking about the best way of killing the prisoners. He had a knife and a gun, and he'd initially decided it would be easier to shoot them. He thought it would be less disturbing, and give him fewer nightmares, if he could kill them without being within arm's reach.

His dilemma was how to shoot them without leaving forensic evidence. He had a silencer, so noise was not an issue, but the blood and bullet holes were concerning him. If he shot them after he had wrapped them in polythene there would be no blood splatter, but there would still be a bullet hole in the floor or wall after it had passed through them. If he shot them before he put them in the polythene there would be a hole and blood splatters. Either way, if the police turned up with a warrant, they'd find traces of the murders. There seemed to be no option. He finally decided he would stab them whilst they were on the polythene. There would be no blood splatter and no damage to the floor or walls.

Ernie and Tim were aware their time was running out, but unaware of the finer details of what Frank was planning. If they'd been aware, they would have been shouting, screaming and struggling to escape, but it wouldn't have made any difference to the outcome. They were both secured, and there was no way to escape.

When they next saw Frank, he was not alone. Another man accompanied him, and together the two men dragged in a large sheet of polythene, and opened it out onto the floor. They covered all the room apart from the area close to the mattress and then dragged the mattress on top of it before opening it fully to cover the remaining floor area.

Ernie and Tim were not sure what would happen next, but they both rightly guessed Frank was preparing to kill them. The polythene sheeting gave them a clue, but the real clincher was when Frank returned with a large knife that had a serrated blade. Frank passed the knife from one hand to another as he looked at each of them in turn.

"This can be quick and easy, or slow and painful," he said. "It's up to you. Who's first?"

Both Ernie and Tim moved away as far as their chains would allow them. "You're first," he said to Ernie. "Last in, first out. That's what they say."

Ernie knew Bob and Emma would be watching the CCTV footage, and would know what was happening, so he'd not been unduly worried until now. He'd been assuming that someone would turn up to rescue him at any minute, but as each minute had past with no one coming his anxiety had steadily increased to an almost unbearable peak.

As Frank approached him, Ernie's nostrils flared, and he snorted as he backed away. "Get away," he shouted. His wrists were on fire as his struggles wore the skin away beneath the handcuffs. His eyes were stinging from his tears and he was sobbing and gasping for air as his body prepared for a fight he couldn't win and a flight his chains were preventing him from making. The ankle of his left leg was still shackled to the cast iron radiator, and as Frank continued advancing Ernie continued backing away until the chain was as tight as it would go. He was sure he was going to die, and he closed his eyes for a split-second to convince himself it wouldn't happen if he couldn't see it coming. It didn't work, and he snapped them open again in time to see Frank lunging forward. For another split-second he considered trying to head butt him or kicking him with his unshackled leg, before bowing to the inevitable and turning his head to one side so he didn't have to see what was about to happen.

"Got you," said Frank, as he lunged forward.

There was an almighty crash. The sound of splintering timber. Shouting, and the sound of running feet. "Armed police. Put down your weapon."

Frank had been oblivious to what was going on around him. Focused on the tip of the blade as it lunged towards Ernie's chest, the noise had only fractionally put him off, but it was enough. The lack of concentration, combining with Ernie writhing to escape, resulted in the blade slicing through Ernie's clothes and causing little more than a flesh wound.

Frank was still holding the knife as he turned towards the noise and saw the two armed police officers just inside the doorway.

"Armed police. Put the weapon down," one of them shouted again.

Thankfully for Frank, the police themselves saw they were in no danger. He had left his own gun in the office and only taken a knife into the room. He was within range of their guns, but they were safe from his knife. It was a stabbing knife not a throwing one, but for a moment he did considered throwing it. The police officer closest to him saw the warning signs and was preparing to shoot, but his considerations ended abruptly as Ernie concentrated all his pent up fear into a kick that thudded into the area between Frank's legs.

Frank dropped the knife and turned back toward Ernie. "You bastard," he said, before dropping like a stone.

The man who had brought the polythene was still in the room, but he'd immediately thrown his hands into the air when he saw the two armed police officers.

One of the officers moved towards the knife and kicked it away before picking it up. The other scanned the room, but could see no further threat.

"Room clear," he shouted.

"Hello Ann," detective sergeant Carter said as she entered. "I see you've single-handedly caused havoc to Manchester's criminal fraternity again. There'll be no work for us poor coppers to do at the rate you're going."

Ernie sunk to the floor as he smiled. "I think you'll find there's enough for all of us," he said. "You took your time. What kept you?"

"The anonymous phone calls were so specific we decided they were a hoax. Your guardian angels kept calling though, and kept insisting you were in trouble, so here we are. What we couldn't understand, and what I still don't understand, is how they knew you were here."

"Search me," said Ernie.

"I may just do that," she said. "Now then. What have we got here?"

Chapter Thirty-Three

Detective Sergeant Sarah Carter often worked late into the evening, but didn't often work nights. The last time had been over a month ago, and that was only because she was a few hours short of what she should have worked that month.

Tonight her night-shift served a different purpose. In a blazing row with her partner that morning he had complained about the long hours she worked. He did have a point, but that was the nature of her job and he would just have to get used to it if the relationship was to last. She told him things could be a lot worse, and to prove her point she had worked late. When she worked late into the evening, she usually left around midnight, but tonight she intended to stay an extra hour or so to teach him a lesson. Her boss sometimes dictated what hours she worked when they were involved in a big case, but tonight she worked alone and could do whatever hours she wanted.

Experienced at multi-tasking, she typed up various reports whilst keeping her eye on any emergencies being dealt by those around her and as she listened to the general chit-chat on the radio. She eventually called it a night and stood up to leave just as the first anonymous phone call came in. Someone was being held prisoner at Phimister's Financial Services in Levenshulme, so she hung around as a squad car was sent to check the building.

"I've checked the front and rear," said the

officer. "It seems to be all locked up. No lights on as far as I can tell. No sign of a break in. No sign of anyone on the premises."

"Roger that," said the dispatcher. "I'll log it as a malicious call. Just drive past periodically and keep your eye on it just in case. If you see anything unusual, let me know."

"Roger," replied the officer. He could think of no reason why anyone would be held prisoner at a financial services office, and he agreed it was probably a hoax.

Sarah also believed it more likely to be a hoax, but she made herself another coffee and hung around a while longer on the off chance.

By the time the police got the second call, many other things were happening. Domestics, drunks, breaches of the peace, and several other things resulting in no car being immediately available to deal with what they thought of as a second hoax call. Nothing required the attendance of a detective, and Sarah again prepared to leave. It was then the third call came through.

The first two phone calls insisted someone was being held captive at Phimister's office. The third call repeated the same information, but added they were being held captive at gunpoint. To reinforce the fact, they left an identical message on the Manchester Police Facebook page accompanied by an image, purporting to be the same location, showing a well-known villain holding a gun.

The immediate consensus was still in favour of a hoax, albeit a more sophisticated one, but they couldn't afford to take the chance. They called in the Tactical Firearms Team, and Sarah followed them in. The Tactical Firearms Team may have been the first in, but they have better things to do than interview suspects, so it had been Sarah who made the arrests once they secured the building.

Sarah assumed the kidnap victims were the two people in handcuffs and shackles, and the villains were the two without the shackles, but she insisted they were all taken back to the station for questioning. She still remembered Ann Perkins' aversion to making statements, and she now had even more reservations about her.

The forensic team entered once everyone else had left apart from a uniformed presence at the door, and it was not long before they found a wealth of evidence to further strengthen the case against those arrested. The mother-lode proved to be the computer from Phimister's office. It contained all the financial details of Alf Sidebotham's past activities and its examination led to several further arrests. They arrested Frank Wade and his companion at the scene, and they arrested both Phimister's at their homes around six o'clock the same morning. There were more arrests in various areas of Manchester later in the morning, and those led to still further arrests as evidence mounted from interviews and additional searches.

Maud, the receptionist, arrived for work as usual to find the office swarming with people in white suites, and was very quickly taken away to be interviewed. A relatively small fish, she nevertheless had the passwords for various encrypted files and databases and was encouraged to disclose these for the promise of a lesser charge to the conspiracy she was originally threatened with.

Despite being mid-morning, Sid's family were all still in bed when the police disturbed them by knocking on the door. He was already in a bad mood when he saw Sarah standing in front of two uniformed officers. "What the hell do you want," he shouted. "My kids have done nothing. This is bloody harassment." He shouted up the stairs. "Kids, come down here. Tell these bastards you haven't done anything, then we can all get back to sleep."

"Actually sir," said Sarah. "It's you we've come to see." One of the officers got hold of him as she continued. "I'm arresting you for conspiracy to rob, for theft, and for handling stolen goods."

By the time the other members of the household had come downstairs, Sid was already being escorted to one of the cars in handcuffs.

Alf Sidebotham was oblivious to it all and continued to consider his good fortune as he relaxed beside his pool on the Costa del Sol. He considered his retirement had turned out to be a blessing. He knew he wouldn't have voluntarily chosen to retire so early without Frank forcing him into it, but now he had retired he was enjoying life to the full.

Life in Manchester had been very stressful towards the end, but he'd left all that behind and was now enjoying a completely stress free life. Looking back, it surprised him how well things had worked out, and he complimented himself on the fantastic life he now enjoyed. He was no longer worrying about usurpers taking over his business, no longer stressed about having to maintain his position as leader of the gang, and no longer anxious about when the right time would be to retire. It was all behind him. He'd made his pile, was well out of it, and no longer had a care in the world. What happened in England could stay in England, and life was good.

He had arranged to play a round of golf that evening and thought it was a neighbour when the doorbell rang. Unconcerned when he opened the door, sight of the Spanish police officers immediately brought back all his old fears, and these were confirmed when they immediately arrested him with no formalities except to check his name. Later, he became even more concerned when they extradited him to Britain, and replaced his palatial home in the sun with less salubrious retirement accommodation in a far colder climate.

Ernie left the police station in Manchester about the same time Alf Sidebotham was being arrested by the Spanish Police. There was nothing wrong with Ernie's statement as far as it went, but Sarah Carter still suspected it didn't go far enough. This was the third major crime scene Ann Perkins had been at, and Sarah's incredulity was being stretched to the limit. She had questioned Perkins at length about how she had known Armstrong was in the building, about how she got into the building, about how the anonymous caller knew she was in trouble, and about where the CCTV image sent to the force Facebook page had been sent from.

Ernie feigned ignorance on almost all of those points whilst finding explanations for the others.

"Armstrong's mother commissioned me to find her son," he said. "I asked around and, like you, I received an anonymous message to say he was being held in Phimister's office. When I went there, someone must have forgotten to lock the front door, so I had a look around. That's when they found me, but how anyone else knew I was in there, I've no idea, just as I've no idea how anyone got hold of an image of what was happening inside."

Ernie's answers hadn't convinced her. Sarah Carter was even more sure Ann Perkins was holding something back, but she still didn't know what. She felt she should charge Perkins with something, but could find no evidence she'd committed any crime. Perkins was a witness not a suspect, and Sarah reluctantly allowed her to make a written statement and then leave.

As soon as Sarah released him, Ernie made his way home and took a shower before re-dressing as Ann Perkins to visit the Hinchcliffe's. He had just finished getting his makeup on when Colin knocked on the door.

"These are for you, Ann," he said, as he held out a bunch of flowers. "I saw you come in so I went out and bought them. Hope you like them. I've not seen you coming or going for a while, so I've still not had the chance to take you for that coffee I promised you."

"Thanks," Ernie said. "Come in. Let me put them in water." He led the way into the flat and left Colin in the living room whilst he went to the kitchen and found a vase. After filling it with water and putting the flowers in, he returned to his living room and placed the vase in the centre of his coffee table. "They'll look nice on there."

Colin had mistaken the invitation to come in, and as Ernie put the vase down Colin stood behind him, put his arms around his waist, and kissed him on the back of the neck. "I'm glad you like them," he said. "I've been longing to get you alone ever since I first saw you."

Ernie suddenly felt in almost as much danger as when he had been a prisoner at Phimister's. A different type of danger and not so painful but he felt almost as uncomfortable. He had already told everyone he was a widow and wondered if that had been a mistake.

One of the many ways in which Ernie had changed over the past weeks and months, was that he had become a much more accomplished liar. "I'm flattered," he said, "but we can only be friends. My husband's death was so recent that I'm not ready for a new relationship yet. I do hope you understand."

Colin immediately let go of her waist. "Sorry," he said. "Say no more, but when you're ready, I just want you to know I'll be waiting. I find you a very attractive and special lady."

More special than you will ever know, thought Ernie. "Thank you," he said.

Three narrow escapes within hours, Ernie thought. One from Phimister's office, one from detective sergeant Carter, and one from Colin.

A short while later he arrived at Hinchcliffe's home to talk over what had happened.

"I never want to go through that again," he told them. "I wasn't sure anyone was coming, or whether they'd get to me in time. I've never been as frightened as when he tried to kill me."

"Sorry it took so long," Bob said. "We thought the place was empty apart from Tim Armstrong. We watched as you entered the room, and then the screen turned black. That'd be when you dropped your phone I suppose. We'd seen the image of Armstrong on your phone before it dropped, so we assumed he was being kept a prisoner, but we still didn't think anyone else was there. We weren't worried at first, and just assumed you'd put the phone down whilst you tried to remove Armstrong's handcuffs."

"So, when did you first realise I was in trouble?"

"When I saw Phimister arrive," said Emma. "I picked him up on the outside camera, and followed him as he walked down the corridor and into the room you and Armstrong were in. We still weren't sure you were in trouble though, not till Phimister and Wade both came out together and went to Phimister's office. That was the first we knew about Wade being already there, but as soon as we saw him, we realised there were problems, and phoned the police."

"I phoned," said Bob. "Told them about two people being held prisoner at Hinchcliffe's office. We watched a police car arrive a few minutes later, but he only checked the front door and rear gate before driving away again. I phoned again when it became clear he wasn't coming back, but nothing happened. After Phimister left, I could see Wade with a gun and I watched him load it. That's when I got really scared for you, and I phoned for a third time and told them he had a gun."

"It was my idea to send an image of Wade," said Emma. "I put it on their Facebook page, and straight away someone identified him. I'd added the time and date to the image so it had obviously just been taken, and when others on Facebook kept asking what the police were doing about it, they couldn't ignore it."

"Well, I'm glad you did," said Ernie. "The picture seems to have done the trick. They turned up mob handed, and only just in the nick of time. Another few seconds and I wouldn't have been alive to see them arrive."

Chapter Thirty-Four

Some days later, Jessica Smythe and her son returned to the Agency office.

"I can't thank you enough for finding my son," she said. "Timothy is only here today because of your resourcefulness."

"It was nothing," Ernie replied. "All part of the service."

"It was not nothing," said Tim. "I'd have been a goner if you hadn't turned up. Put yourself in a lot of danger too, but I still don't understand how you knew I was there."

Bob put a tray of coffee and biscuits in front of them. "Just a trick of the trade," he said.

"Have you met my assistant, Bob?" said Ernie.

"No. Hello Bob," she said. "Did you play a part in Tim's rescue too?"

"Not me," he said. "I work purely on the administration side of things and I leave all the cloak and dagger stuff to Mrs Perkins."

"That's why we're here," she said. "I need to settle up. I owe you half the fee, and some expenses."

"I'll print the invoice off," Bob said. "That's if I can understand this accounting system."

"What are you using?" Tim asked.

"It's some system the guy at reception recommended," said Bob. "I've never kept books before and I'm not sure what I'm doing. I mentioned it to him and he recommended this double entry accounting software. I'm sure the software's fine for anyone who understands those things, but I've no idea what double entry accounting even is. To be honest, it's got me more confused than ever, and it's really complicated."

"I can help you there," said Tim. "Did you forget I'm a chartered accountant?"

"Not forgotten," said Bob, "but Mrs Perkins has only just begun the agency, so there's no way she can afford an accountant."

"You're right there," said Ernie. "It'll be a while before we can afford an accountant, but I'm as baffled about the bookwork as Bob is. I know we have to keep receipts for what we've spent and issue receipts for any money that comes in, but I don't know what to do with all the receipts once I've got them and I certainly don't understand what records we need to keep for the Inland Revenue. Tax records are like a foreign language to me."

"Who mentioned payment?" Tim said. "I wouldn't even be here if it hadn't been for you. The least I can do is look after your books and keep everything straight. Consider it done. There's no fee. There never will be, and if you like I'll pop in once a week and check everything over. A company your size will take me no time at all. It would be my way of saying thank you for everything you've done."

"You'd do that?" said Ernie.

"I'd be glad to."

"That'd be fantastic," said Ernie. "That's a load off my mind."

"And mine," said Bob. "I'm supposed to be the administrator, but I've no idea about tax and national insurance. I know the company has to pay it, but I've no idea how to work it out. They told me the accountancy programme was easy, and it may be for them, but I don't understand it at all."

"Leave that to me," said Tim.

"And I'll leave this with you," said his mother. "I don't know what your expenses were, but this will more than cover them. A small token of our gratitude. Just think of it as a bonus. Tim will sort out the paperwork and give me a receipt in due course."

She handed over a large wad of notes far larger than Ernie had expected, and once they finished their tea, they prepared to leave.

"I'll pop in tomorrow," Tim said. "Then I'll come back once a week to check over the accounts."

"That's brilliant," said Ernie and Bob together.

As Tim's mother left the building both Ernie and Bob contemplated how much their lives had changed. Bob had gainful employment instead of being incarcerated for years in one of her majesty's penal institutions, and Ernie was the managing director and only shareholder of his newly formed business.

Ernie had set out to steal a million pounds from the bank because he could see no purpose for his life, but such thoughts seemed strange to him now. He remembered being depressed as short a time ago as when he'd been to the cemetery, but he wasn't depressed at the moment and the future seemed a lot brighter. He'd thought money would cure all his ills, but he now realised money on its own would never have been enough to restore his self-esteem. He did have enough money to live on now, but he knew the real change had come through his life having a purpose again. He had made new friends who shared that common purpose, and his mind had stopped telling him he was worthless.

During the past year he had experienced many things for the first time, but the most recent experience had been the best. His knowledge the Ann Perkins Detective Agency had solved its first case was an experience like no other. The gratitude on Jessica Smythe's face at the return of her son had warmed his heart. As little as a few days ago his life had depressed him, but all that was now behind him, banished by the gratefulness of his client.

Apart from Tim Armstrong, who had more money than the rest of them combined, the restaurant was much posher than the restaurants they usually frequented. Most of them took one look at the prices on the menu, looked sheepishly at one another before gulping, and were thankful Ann was paying for everything. The whole evening's celebration was only possible because of the large bonus Tim's mum had paid, and Ernie was using the unexpected windfall to reward those who'd helped make it all possible.

The waiter poured the champaign before leaving. Champaign was something most of them were not used to drinking outside of wedding venues, but they knew enough to hold their glasses out and clink them together.

"Cheers," they said in unison before taking a drink.

"To Ann," said Bob.

They raised their glasses again. "To Ann," they

repeated.

Once they'd put their glasses down, they all looked expectantly at Ann. Most of them didn't know what to expect. Ann had invited them all there and told them she would pay for everything, but those that didn't know the real reason for the meal still had an inkling there was to be an announcement of some sort. Bob thought she may be announcing the closure of the agency. She'd nearly got herself killed on her first case, so he wouldn't blame her if she did, but it would still leave him out of a job and unlikely to get another.

"I'm delighted you could all come," Ernie said. "I wanted to thank you for all the help you've given the Ann Perkins Detective Agency. I've successfully completed my first case, and I couldn't have done it without all of you. Thank you."

"I'm sure you could have done it without me," Tim said. He was acutely aware he was the odd person out. A saved victim rather than a rescuer. "I did nothing to help. It was you who rescued me, remember?"

"I'm not likely to forget it," said Ernie. "It's not every day I nearly get killed." He laughed. "Actually, I have been nearly killed on a few days recently. Far more days than I'd have liked. It's true you started off as a victim, Tim, but you're one of the team now, and I'm grateful to you. Our books would be in a real mess by the end of the financial year without your help. God only knows what the tax man would have thought about our book-keeping efforts if Bob and I had been the only ones doing them. I'd have just put all the invoices in a box and somebody else would have had to sort them out. Besides, I'm also grateful for the extra work you've done for us over the past few days."

"I didn't think he'd been in this week." His community service had finally finished, and Bob had been in the office every day, but he'd only seen Tim the once.

"We were keeping it under our hats," said Ernie, "and he's been working from home for me."

Bob was intrigued. "Doing what?" he asked.

"I intended keeping it until after the meal," Ernie said, "but I'm bursting to tell you so now is as good a time as any. This meal is my way of saying thank you, but it isn't the only way I want to express my appreciation. The Ann Perkins Detective Agency is a limited company and I'm the only shareholder and the only director. My first case has taught me I can't work on my own. I needed your help in the first case, and I'll undoubtedly need your help again on future cases. I think it only fair that if you share the work, you share the rewards, so I'm making you all shareholders."

Emma had been miles away. Physically, she was there for the meal, but mentally she was looking forward to her forthcoming graduation. The graduation was still several months off, but she was already more excited than usual by Baz having confirmed he could attend. Despite their rather intimate friendship, they had never met. She had seen his picture, face timed him, and seen him on some videos, but they had never met in person. At the start of her degree course she had decided she could do without being distracted by the opposite sex, and she'd stopped dating. The relationship with Baz had always been different. They shared an academic interest and had always conversed at a distance, but had now agreed to meet outside their shared safe space. She was excited about him attending her graduation, but worried too. She wondered if seeing one another would spoil things, and whether their relationship would survive a face-to-face meeting.

Ann's words had jolted her out of her daydream and she suddenly took notice of what was going on around her. Did Ann say she was making her a shareholder?

They all began talking over one another. Tim had helped Ernie set everything up, so he knew what Ann was about to say, but Bob and Emma knew nothing. Neither of them had ever held shares, and neither of them ever thought they would.

Ernie held his hands out to stop them talking. "At the moment," he said, "I hold one hundred percent of the shares, but if you agree to accept them, I intend giving some of those shares to each of you."

Ernie looked around the table.

"Bob, you've been doing all the basic administration, not to mention keeping me supplied with teas and coffees, so I'd like to make you a fifteen percent shareholder."

That wasn't what Bob was expecting. All he could do is smile and nod his head. "Thank you," he said.

"Emma, you stuck your neck out for me, and if they'd caught you, they would have kicked you off your course. I'm extremely grateful, so I'd like to make you a fifteen percent shareholder too. Who knows, I may also need your skills again in the future."

He continued before she could say anything.

"Tim, you're aware of this already. You're keeping our books straight, and you've agreed to take a further fifteen percent."

Tim spoke to the others. "I've been working on this all week. Trying to keep it a secret until we all got together tonight."

Ernie had asked Tim to keep other secrets too. He was eager to keep everything legal, and had explained to Tim that despite appearances, Ann Perkins was not currently a director or shareholder of the Ann Perkins Detective Agency. Her name may be in the name of the agency, but Ernie was the only director and only shareholder.

"That still leaves fifty-five percent of the shares for me, but I'll be splitting my shares with my brother. Some of you know I have a twin brother named Ernie, and he'll be doing some investigative work for me. Some places it'll pay to have a man under cover rather than a woman, so we're going to split the work between us depending on which of us it's best suited for. Unfortunately, he couldn't be here tonight, but you'll get to meet him in due course."

They were all talking over one another now. All raising their glasses to toast their new share holdings and drinking to the successful future of the Ann Perkins Detective Agency.

Their raucousness was such that several other diners stopped what they were doing and looked in their direction. Among them, several tables away, was Sarah Carter and her boyfriend. She was having a celebration of her own and toasting her part in the arrest of several members of Manchester's criminal fraternity. She looked to see where the noise was coming from, and immediately recognised Ann Perkins, Timothy Armstrong, and Bob Hinchcliffe. She didn't recognise the younger woman but assumed they were all celebrating Ann's success too. She wondered what part each of them had played in Ann Perkins' first case.

Looking at Ann Perkins, Sarah still had suspicions about her. It was undoubtedly true she was making a success of her detective agency, and that her first case had given Sarah's own career a boost, but Sarah still thought it too much of a coincidence that Ann turned up in the most unlikely places. Still, she thought, she seems to have smartened herself up. She thought back to the first time she had seen her outside the jeweller's and what an unusual-looking woman she seemed to be. The contrast was striking, and over time she had become far more ladylike.

Ann saw Sarah staring at her, and they both simultaneously smiled at one another and raised their glasses.

"Cheers," they mouthed in unison.

Message From The Author

Thanks for reading my book. I hope you've enjoyed reading it as much as I enjoyed writing it.

When I first got the idea for the story, I had just finished checking my lottery ticket in anticipation of becoming a millionaire. Needless to say, I hadn't won the lottery, but it got me thinking about how else I could become a millionaire, and that in turn got me thinking about robbing a bank.

I never actually robbed a bank, but I would have made a hopeless bank robber. I've no criminal contacts (as far as I know) so I've no idea where to buy a gun, which bank would be best to rob, or how I'd disguise myself. What I do know is, with my luck, everything would have gone wrong.

The book grew from those simple thoughts, and the character of Ernie Wright / Ann Perkins developed a mind of their own and told me the story you've read. Not only that, but they told me how the second book in the series started too. You can read part of the second book in the series on the following page.

Thanks for reading my book. I hope to see you again soon.

Richard

http://richard-underwood.com

The Next Book in the Series

Accused
Book Two in the Ann Perkins Detective Agency series (2022)

Two men are accused of murders they didn't commit. Can Ann Perkins bring the real killer to justice?

(Excerpt)

Ernie Wright was a man in a hurry. A potential client had asked to meet at a city centre cafe and he was already late. The parked van barely registered as he passed it, and he only became aware of the two men as they grabbed hold of him.

"What the …?" He struggled as hard as he could, but his arms were pinned each side as they propelled him forwards.

He had no idea who the men were or what they wanted, but the way they were forcing him towards the van door left him in no doubt he was in trouble.

Other Books by Richard Underwood

A Brief History of Life: From the Origin of Life to the End of the Universe (2021)

A Brief History of Life: From the Origin of Life to the End of the Universe is a popular science book exploring the harmony between science and religion, and the scientific basis for believing life continues when the body dies.

Subjects include how the universe began, how life first began, the purpose of life, how life ends, and how the universe will end.

Life affirming answers to the most fundamental questions comprehensively indexed and referenced, and with many notes containing the latest scientific research.

(Excerpt)

Life is something we all understand. We feel it physically and emotionally. We have examined our own life internally and externally. We have examined other people's lives externally. Many of us have experienced the joy a new life brings, and the heartache the death of a loved one brings.

All adults have lived longer than it takes to complete a PhD, so when it comes to the subject of life, we should all be experts. Unfortunately, despite the accumulated years of study, 'life' is a subject which has few experts, and what experts there are disagree about almost every facet of the subject.

What is life? Take your pick. There are thousands of definitions, often within single scientific disciplines. Is there life after death? That depends upon your definition of death, which depends on which definition of life you have chosen. How did the first life begin? There are several theories. Any of them may be right. All of them may be wrong. Is there life on other planets? Possibly, but before you can find life on other planets, you first need to find a definition of life everyone on Earth can agree on. Can we create artificial life? We've not managed it yet.

My own years of study have led me to believe we have been too close to the subject. We are so familiar with seeing life all around us; we have lost the ability to view it objectively. Life is too complex for us to put it into boxes labelled biology, chemistry, physics, etc. Life incorporates all those disciplines, and many more.

Let me give you an example from history. Everyone knew the world was flat. The world was so obviously flat that nobody questioned it. They had all the evidence they needed. Whenever they opened their eyes, they could see the flat earth all around them and they never doubted what they already knew. Then along came someone who looked at things differently. They looked up at the distant sky instead of down to the ground, and the change of view changed everything.

This book is an attempt to do for life what the ancient astronomers did for the Earth. It looks at life from two different perspectives, the large and the small. What does astrophysics teach us about life when viewed from the largest level imaginable? What does quantum physics teach us about life at the smallest level imaginable? The result will surprise you, inspire you, and change your views about life forever.